A SHADOW AMONG THE STARS

COURTNEY DAVIS

5 PRINCE PUBLISHING
5PRINCEBOOKS.COM

Published by 5 PRINCE PUBLISHING & BOOKS, LLC

PO Box 865, Arvada, CO 80001

www.5PrinceBooks.com

ISBN digital: 978-1-63112-383-2

ISBN print: 978-1-63112-469-3

Cover Credit: Marianne Nowicki

F110324

To my wonderful husband and family who support this dream of mine and listen to me talk about story ideas with enthusiasm.

ACKNOWLEDGMENTS

Thank you to the team at 5 Prince Publishing for continuing to believe in my writing and especially my wonderful editor Cate Byers, I couldn't put out a story this good without you.

ACKNOWLEDGMENTS

ALSO BY COURTNEY DAVIS

A SHADOW AMONG THE STARS

CHAPTER ONE

Prit couldn't believe her bad luck. It should have been a routine snag and run, nothing she couldn't handle. She was known by many she worked for as The Shadow, because she did this sort of thing so well and so often. The target this time was a necklace belonging to the only princess of the ruling family on the planet Sabit, and she was supposed to be wearing it at the party celebrating her little brother's twelfth birthday. It wasn't the first time Prit had relieved a wealthy debutante of a piece of jewelry while they were still wearing it, so she wasn't worried about the circumstances surrounding the job. Her sleight of hand was legendary and for the last few years she'd entered many reinforced castles, spaceships and even one underground bunker, and left with a new shiny object in her pocket.

From one planet to the next it was all the same, the wealthy didn't appreciate what they had enough to really defend it, or they were far too confident in their untouchability and they couldn't conceive of her as a real risk.

Even in the opulent Sabit ballroom it was more about looks than safety. An open ceiling to show off the dark sky and passing planets, but nothing to stop an attack from above. The front doors had been unguarded allowing her to walk through with a crowd, no one so much as checking a list of invited attendees, just a few Tradjulians acting as security against obvious threats.

Tradjulians were a low tech but very strong alien race from the planet Trad that were often hired by the rich and pompous to keep the riff raff off their ships and out of their homes. Tonight they were also acting as servers for the prince's birthday party, handing out drinks to toast the preteen, and most didn't seem to be armed.

It was almost too easy. Or at least it had been until her fingers had touched the clasp of the necklace.

Tonight's mishap wasn't Prit's fault, she had followed a routine that had worked a hundred times. There was no reason to expect that the damn thing would have an alarm system. One so advanced not even her bionic eye had picked up on it, though if she'd been able to get a clear enough look at the thing in the crowd she might have been able to get a better assessment. She'd been so sure it was going to be as easy as every other time. One second she'd had her fingers on the prize as she passed behind the woman—silent as a shadow—the next everyone was covering their ears and cowering from the high-pitched squeal that seemed to be emanating from everywhere. And that's when she'd tried to run, but even she couldn't slip past the number of guards who seemed to emerge from the walls to surround the princess and anyone close enough to have touched her.

Prit could have tried to fight her way out, but she didn't want any innocents to get harmed in the process and she was confident of being able to escape any cell they put her in anyway.

Which is where she was heading now without argument.

"You know, I could probably double your yearly to let me

just... slip away," she said to the guard who was prodding her from behind with a charged stick. It was the usual method of controlling a prisoner within the Settled Space Alliance, SSA. It alleviated the need for handcuffs, which didn't work on every species, some lacking hands in a traditional humanoid sense. She was definitely not anxious to risk a zap from that thing, she'd be pissing herself and drooling for a day at least.

He was a Tradjulian of course but despite their difference in species, she knew he understood her, she spoke the official universal language of settled space. No modern alien grew up without it as a second language and many planets had made it their official language in an effort to increase their standing in the SSA. Those that held on to their old traditions were seen as barbaric and many weren't included in trade and commerce routes or agreements.

"Thieves don't have that much money, or they wouldn't be thieving," he said in a slow, deep drawl.

Prit rolled her eyes, he wasn't wrong. "How do you know I'm a thief by trade? Maybe I just like shiny things and I'm actually a very wealthy lady."

"If you don't want anyone to know you're a thief, you should wear gloves," he snorted.

Prit looked down at her right wrist where a *T* had been burned into her skin. A mark of love from the New Earth Commander. The one time he'd managed to get her in a cage for a day because she'd made a stupid mistake, she'd known better than to take a job somewhere that she had history and she'd paid for it. It was true she didn't take great pains to hide the mark, why bother? It proved she'd been caught and got out; it was a mark of power and pride among most of the people she dealt with.

"So what, you going to stick me away and call the New

Earth magistrate?" she tried to keep the worry from her tone. She surely wouldn't make it out of that again.

"No."

Relief made her shoulders slump, and she dared a glance back at him. Her bionic eye turned and focused and analyzed him.

Species: Tradjulian

Sex: Tradjulians have no sex they reproduce asexually every hundred years.

Age: Thirty-five

Danger: High, weapon detected

Wow he was a young one, she was willing to bet he wasn't the one in charge, just a security runner. Tradjulians were all tall, this one likely hit six-five. She was a perfect five-five herself and didn't let a little thing like height ever stop her from kicking ass when necessary. Tradjulian skin tones ranged from a deep burnt orange to pale yellow and this guy was somewhere in between, making her think of puke. His head was shaped like a rounded triangle with his chin jutting down low, and black horns curved out on the sides of his head surrounded by a greyish sort of fuzz that could barely pass for hair. His eyes were two tiny black marbles and his small mouth looked like it was missing its lips. He wasn't nice to look at, that's for sure. Maybe that's why their species had developed the asexual breeding thing. Who would want to get with that? His body was wide and bony, fingers like claws, and only three on each hand. He was wearing a sash with the Sabitarion crest on it, a sort of star but with far too many points, and in the middle, a bubbling spring. Sabit was a desert planet, so of course they would value water above all else. He was wearing a kilt-like skirt and his two strong legs were mostly bare, no shoes, but his feet were big and rough and likely it would take a bullet to pass through that skin so he hadn't bothered with shoes.

Overall, Tradjulians were not her favorite race of beings.

He had prodded her along down below ground and they were currently walking through some stone tunnels that no doubt led to a dungeon prison. It smelled musty, like there was water running somewhere not far away; whatever fed the spring that flourished in the middle of the castle courtyard, she assumed. Hot and fresh enough air that she knew there had to be a way out besides the way they'd come in, wafted by and she smiled, already planning her escape. She was taking note of the footsteps, calculating how far and in which direction he was taking her. This wasn't her first time in a situation like this and it probably wouldn't be her last. Every time she took on a job it was with calculated risk, but that was the life she'd found when she was desperate, and it turned out she was damn good at it.

"So what are you going to do with me?" She was pretty nonchalant now, she knew she could get out of any cell he put her in and she would be free and clear, aside from not collecting on the necklace. Barius was going to be pissed and she was going to have to placate him somehow.

The Tradjulian laughed, "What we do with all the females. Though I admit you're the first half human we've tried."

She was surprised by his accurate assumption that she was only half human, she wondered if it was because of the bionics, humans couldn't heal from the types of surgeries it had taken to give her the bionic eye and leg.

"Roast them on a spit?" she asked with a smirk and wondered if he had pinpointed what her other half was. She doubted it, no one did.

"The king likes to keep his favorite gladiator content, so we throw him a female when we can. If you survive, you'll have a hundred days hard labor to pay off trespassing and touching the princess."

Prit clenched her teeth, a hundred days! That was absolutely barbaric, she didn't have time to take a hundred-day vacation and even if she did, she wouldn't choose a dry as fuck planet like this.

He stopped outside of a solid looking door, Prit immediately assessed it as strong, but not impossible. It was made of metal and the hinges were starting to rust, probably an indication of water running through the rocks around here. The rock around the door would likely be a bit porous to allow for water flow and that would be a weak point.

She couldn't help smirking as the guard opened the door and shoved her into a dark room. "Play nice," he whispered, then shouted. "Brought you a fresh treat, Saluk."

The door closed behind her, and her bionic eye immediately adjusted to the new darkness and took it all in, assessing for danger, escape, and anything else of importance.

Thick stone walls.
   Twenty square feet of space.
   One lifeform detected with elevated pulse indicating distress.
   Danger: Moderate.

A large figure loomed against the back wall, but she didn't react, letting her robotic eye gave her all the details she couldn't see.

Species: Haladian
   Sex: Male

Age: Forty

Danger: High, no weapons detected but capable of hand-to-hand combat.

He was a gladiator, he could likely kill with his hands, and had, but she was also a trained assassin and he'd have a hard time getting a chance to throw those fists around if he wanted to try. She doubted he'd be coming after her for death though. If he approached, he'd likely be trying to take her to bed, another thing he'd find surprisingly difficult with her if he approached.

She went on assessing the cell but kept track of any movements from the gladiator. Her original assessment from the hallway tunnel was right, the best way out was through the door she'd come in.

She turned to the door and started feeling around it.

"I'm not going to hurt you," Saluk growled from the corner, he hadn't moved, she noticed.

"I know," she laughed, not because she didn't think he might try, but because she had every reason to believe he wouldn't succeed.

"What the hell do you mean, woman? I am a terrifying warrior. I have won every battle for the last twenty years, taken down every monster I've been put in the ring with. I—"

Prit gave a dramatic sigh and turned around, one hand on her jutted-out hip and slid her bionic leg forward through the slit in the black gown she was wearing. "Yeah, well, are you going to rape me?"

He moved closer. "No!" He sounded truly horrified by the question which surprised her.

"Well then, why the fuck do I care how tough you are? This isn't the gladiator arena."

She stared at him with one raised eyebrow. She could see

him clearly now, he was tall and broad, everything she'd come to expect from the Haladian race. He was dressed in a leather kilt and his chest was bare, covered in so many scarred-over wounds it made her cringe. He'd been through hell. The right half of his hair was long brown locks falling past his shoulder. The other half was shaved, revealing claw marks that ran from his scalp down the side of his face, eye, and mouth. She was surprised to see his eye was okay aside from the slight distortion from the scar, but his mouth was half mangled, she'd noticed the slight lisp to his speech. The marks continued down the front of his throat and ended at his collar bone. If she had to guess, she'd say it was likely one of the saber tigers that had been reanimated for use in gladiator-style battle rounds that had done that work. He was lucky to be alive.

He watched her silently appraise him, and stiffened visibly when she met his gold eyes, as if he expected her to scream in terror or cringe in disgust.

"Wanna give me a hand with this?" she asked with a smirk. She wasn't put off or intimidated by his scars. If anything, she was impressed. She'd seen men and women die from far less than the damage those scars indicated. He earned her respect for surviving that.

His eyes widened in surprise and she almost laughed. She did love putting tough men off their expectations.

"With what?" he asked in a gruff voice.

"I am pretty sure I can get the door off. We just have to break out the rock around the rusty hinges a bit."

"No way."

"No way it won't break, or no way you won't help me?" she asked with a little sass and a challenging raise of her eyebrow.

"Both, there's no way to escape even if we did get out of this room. Only punishment waits if we try," he said darkly, making her think he'd already tried more than once.

"Wanna bet?" she asked, holding out her hand to shake.

He looked skeptical but took her hand in his, his palm was as big as her entire hand, and she felt dainty as his warm, calloused palm embraced hers.

She met his gold gaze without fear and stated her terms. "You help me get out, I'll give you a ride off Sabit, I've got a ship waiting just outside of the castle."

"And if we don't?" he asked, his voice dripping with doubt.

"If it doesn't work, then I'll climb you like a tree, big boy, rock your world. It'll make the hundred days of hard labor pass quicker for both of us." She gave him a wink with her real blue eye.

He laughed heartily and pumped their clasped hands in agreement. "I won't hold you to that."

She shrugged, "Your loss, my ship is pretty nice." She heard him huff at her apparent assumption that he'd meant the ride and not the climbing. Truth be told, she never backed out of a deal, and she would rock his world if she lost. She may be a thief, but she abided by a personal code of ethics that included her word meaning more than gold.

But she wasn't going to fail so it didn't really matter.

Prit turned back to the door; the shocked expression on Saluk's face made her bite back a giggle. She'd surprised the big lug, she liked that a lot. Footsteps sounded out in the hallway, and she froze, motioning for him to be quiet, too.

"You two getting along in there?" the guard called and banged on the door.

"Oh yeah! Give it to me harder, big boy," Prit called with her best sexy imitation.

Saluk gave a choked sound from behind her and she threw a grin over her shoulder at him.

"Just like that, yeah!" She added and winked at Saluk who just stared at her with wide, panicked eyes.

The guard laughed and his footsteps continued on past.

"Help me with this, who knows when he'll come to check again," she ordered and pulled a piece of metal from a hidden compartment in her bionic leg. He gasped in surprise, but she ignored it. She was used to her extra parts surprising others.

The eye and the leg were souvenirs from her time as a proud member of the New Earth military. Thanks to her father's nonhuman genetics, she'd been able to survive the wounds and heal to the bionic implants without much issue at all. The only thing she was grateful to be half Eludian for.

Sometimes she covered her leg when she was on a stealth mission, it was all shiny silver metal and blue glowing fibers, not exactly subtle. Tonight she'd forgone that added bit of camouflage and worn a gown that would help her blend with the crowd and gave her easy access to the hidden weapons and tools. Her eye on the other hand was harder to notice so she didn't worry about hiding it. If you didn't look closely you'd miss the lights and moving parts within the lens and the subtle shine of metal around it could easily be mistaken for makeup or jewelry.

She crouched and started to dig at the rock around the bottom hinge of the door. After a moment a chunk of rock broke free and Saluk gasped.

"Told ya," she said.

He stared down at the chunk with wide eyes and what she thought might be a touch of fearful hope. He stepped closer and started pounding his large fists against the rock around the top hinge.

Fifteen minutes later they'd loosened the hinges enough that Saluk could yank on the door and the whole thing came off.

"Nice work," Prit said, putting the metal piece back into her leg. He watched her curiously but didn't comment. "Follow me, I smelled fresh air so I'm guessing if we continue this way, we'll find an exit." She pointed the opposite way that she'd come with the guard.

"Yes, follow me," he grunted and pushed in front of her, then took off down the way she'd indicated.

"Men," she grumbled, but followed, hoping he did actually know how to get out.

CHAPTER TWO

Prit wondered how many prisoners were being kept behind the doors they passed and if they were all stolen to be gladiators like Saluk. She didn't have time to investigate any as she followed Saluk through a seeming maze of underground tunnels.

Thankfully they didn't run into anyone, though she was prepared to kill in order to escape. She'd also push Saluk down and use him as a distraction if necessary. Not very honorable, but she wasn't spending a hundred days in this hell hole.

She started to wonder if he was taking the long way on purpose as they rounded another corner and she saw a long hallway in front of them. She knew how far she'd walked from the front door until she'd been put in his cell, and they should have made it that far twice over by now. She hoped he was being smart and they were avoiding any possible guards on this escape route.

There were no doors and no people in their current hallway, so she shifted her focus to the man walking at a quick pace in front of her. She appreciated the sight of his strong legs. He was wearing thick leather boots that laced up his calves. The Sabitarion king really liked to embrace ancient Roman styles from Old Earth apparently. Her gaze traveled up to his bare back and she cringed at the sight there. It was crisscrossed in scars that she'd guess came from a sword and one that definitely looked like a deep electrical prod wound. He hadn't always been as docile and accepting as he'd seemed to be of his fate when she'd entered his cell. That was a hopeful sign, she needed him as determined as herself to get out of here alive.

She continued her uninhibited perusal of him as they went. His shoulders were so wide she thought they were likely double her own, and his arms flexed as he moved, showing thick, bulging muscle under his scarred skin. He was surprisingly lithe and quiet for such a big guy; it likely made him a great warrior. She was suddenly quite curious about him, more than just as a means of getting out. She wondered why he was here and how long he had been living in the accommodations provided by the Sabitarion king.

"Here," he grunted and turned a corner.

"Thank fuck," she said as they came out of the dark tunnel. Then frowned when she realized they were in the arena hold, this is where the warriors waited before a battle. "This isn't out, Saluk," she said with a hiss of aggression. Silently taking back every nice thought she'd had about him.

Had this been a trick, or was he just an idiot?

"Trust me, I have to get something first."

"What? That's not the deal. I'm not interested in a hundred-day sentence for trespassing. I need to get on my ship, now."

Saluk turned on her, fast. He pushed her until she was up against the wall and his face was inches from hers as she strained her neck to look up at him. His arms on either side of her body blocked her in easily and his breath hit her face. His hair shifted and brushed against her cheek and shoulder making her shudder. Intense gold eyes stared down at her and for the first time since walking into his cell, she felt like he was a real threat. Her hand went to her thigh where a knife was embedded into her leg.

"I said, I need to get something. Do *not* leave without me, thief."

"How—ugh my name is Prit, and I am not going to leave you if you hurry."

"Prit," he breathed the word like a prayer and his eyes dipped to her mouth.

She sucked in a breath as her body suddenly wasn't sure if he was threatening her or coming on to her. "Be quick," she whispered, her voice not showing any of the turmoil he'd flared in her body with that one look.

He grunted and stepped back. "Keep that knife in hand until I'm back. If one of the guards comes out, slit his throat, don't try to negotiate."

She scowled at his back as he slunk away, she didn't like that he had sensed the knife, she prided herself on stealth, it was the only way to survive in her business.

She did as he said though because he was her best shot at making it out of this place without having to go back the way she'd come. She stood in shadow against the wall and looked around the battle arena. It was set up like many throughout settled space, made to mimic the Roman coliseums of Old Earth except that many of the surrounding seating areas were floating above the ground on cushioned air pockets allowing them to easily move in and out of the action for viewing pleasure. And of course, the sky was different than the one above Old Earth, she knew from pictures she'd seen. Prit looked up at a sky that was unfamiliar for her as well. There were very few stars here, but two large planets close enough to be mistaken for moons. The Three Sisters, they were called. She was currently trying to get off of Sabit. The other two were Pelliot and Stranlion. Pelliot was a lush green planet, much different from this shit hole dust planet but its air was thick, hard for lung breathers like humans and Sabitarions. Stranlion was similar to Old Earth with a little of everything, which had made it very popular with the humans originally, but they had soon found out that it was inhabited by very violent locals, and most had fled to discover New Earth in a neighboring solar system. She avoided that planet at all costs herself, no need to test her fighting skills against those vicious natives.

Saluk came back a few minutes later with a bundle under his arm. "Follow me and keep your head down."

"What is that?"

"Something I hid in the arena in case I ever got a chance to get out."

She was more curious than an Earth cat, but she didn't ask any more questions as he took off quickly again. She didn't want to risk being left behind.

They hurried through a back entrance to the arena and then they were out in the open, and the castle was in front of them in all its partying glory. The display of wealth made her sick, especially since she knew how poor the locals on this planet were. If they didn't work for the royal family, they were mining dirt and getting paid shit for it.

She really wished she could have stuck it to them a little by taking the necklace, but she knew when to say no to a job. Unfortunately, she usually did that before accepting it. She was in for some trouble after this failure.

"I'm over there," she said and darted in the direction of her camouflaged ship. They had a lot of ground to cross and no trees to offer cover, so crouching and running, Prit led the way.

"Ho, who's there?" a voice called out, halting her mere feet from safety.

Prit spun, knife out and ready to fight, but Saluk was faster.

He had snapped the guard's neck before Prit's eye could even register the species.

"Wow, I'm impressed," Prit said, a little breathless from the excitement.

"Good, now move before more come around. Where the hell is your ship?"

She mumbled about demanding assholes and rolled her eyes, but she obeyed his command because she really didn't want to stay on this planet any longer. His in-charge attitude would change when they were on her ship; that was her domain and she ruled it.

"Here," she said darting forward a few more feet.

When they were close it was easy to pick out the ship in the darkness despite its natural camouflage. It wasn't invisible, just tended to take on the shade of its surroundings, which worked especially well at night and away from lights. It was a decommissioned New Earth military small transport ship. It had mostly been used to take troops from New Earth to its moon where most of the training exercises had gone on. But when Prit had taken it, she'd amped up the engines and thrown out most of the guts, making it faster and more inhabitable for herself.

The hatch popped open and a small staircase descended. She scurried up and hopped into the pilot's seat to start throwing switches.

"Welcome to my home," she said when Saluk was inside and the hatch was pulling closed. "Now sit your ass down, we have to move fast."

That was the only warning she was going to give him. He wanted off this planet and so did she. The ship took a leap straight up and then she shifted it forward and they were flying out of Sabit's atmosphere.

Saluk went tumbling and slid to the back of the tiny ship. He scrambled for purchase as the ship moved at an insane speed and jerked around like it was being driven by a toddler. Was she trying to kill him now that she'd saved him?

He cursed and scrambled after the package. The little twit changed direction again and the wrapping unrolled sending the canister flying forward up against her robotic foot. She reached down and grabbed it without taking her eyes off the screens that were in place of a windshield and held it up.

"Secure your shit, Sal."

He swiped it out of her hand and plopped into the only other seat on the ship. It just happened to be the toilet and he tried not to blush when she looked at him and winked.

What the hell was her deal? He was terrifying. He knew he was terrifying. A woman hadn't come to him willingly since he'd left his planet, which meant he had been celibate for a long damn time. They screamed, they ran, they quivered, and he had no interest in any of that shit no matter how many the guards had thrown into his cell hoping to please him.

He let his eyes roam over Prit while she was distracted. Human, he thought. The robotic leg was high end, and she moved with it as if it were her natural leg. It was made of titanium, with blue light fiber that acted as tendons; moving and pulling when needed. He would bet she had five completely flexible toes under the thin leather slipper she wore, a thief's shoes. She was dressed like a woman who belonged at the castle. A tight black bustier top that hugged her small body and was cut low in the back. The skirt hugged her wide hips and flowed down to her feet with a slit in it to access the tools and weapons in her leg.

She was tiny everywhere except her bottom; below average

height for the human race and her body was slender, her chest a handful he decided, and her ass at least three. He shook his head and pried his thoughts off of her body and how it might feel under his large, calloused hands. She had saved his life; she didn't deserve to be ogled.

He wondered what her mechanical eye could do. It looked far too complicated to just give her regular vision and he'd bet it sent data straight to her brain. What had it told her about him? It had glowed slightly in the dark with a blue light, much like her leg, which took away from her ability to blend in, but it must be worth the risk because she didn't cover it. Her good eye was a pale blue and it lifted slightly at the corner as if she found everything amusing.

She smiled a lot, maybe she did find life amusing.

He did not.

His gaze traveled up to her hair. It was jet black and short but when she moved, he spied bright blue locks tucked up underneath.

She was unreal. He remembered his mother telling him stories when he was a young child about little magical beings that lived in the rocks and came out to make mischief. They flitted around on silvery wings and were no bigger than a thumb. Prit reminded him of them, if only she had wings to go with her tiny body and sparkling spirit. He remembered the way she'd acted out moans of pleasure when the guard was outside his door, and he had to adjust his legs. *Fake*, he reminded himself, she was trying to save her own life at the time, no matter how willing she pretended to be if she had lost the bet, he would never hold her to such a thing. Women didn't look upon his scarred face with pleasure and if she knew what he'd done, how many lives he had taken in the arena, she wouldn't want to be near him.

"Hold on," she gritted, bringing him back to the now and the possibility that although they'd made it off Sabit, that didn't mean they were safe. "We have company."

An explosion rocked the ship, and he nearly lost his seat as she maneuvered and dipped the ship. He felt as if his skin was trying to pull off his bones a split second before his body was lifted into the air and his brain decided it couldn't handle whatever insanity she was putting them through. A bright light lit up the interior of the ship just as his eyes blacked out and his mind froze.

CHAPTER THREE

When Saluk regained consciousness, he was lying on the floor of the ship, his canister was not in his hands, although thankfully they'd landed. He sat up carefully and rubbed his head where a large lump had formed. He hated space travel. Granted, this was only his second experience with it, but both times had been unpleasant. His head pounded as he looked around for Prit or his canister.

"Prit," he hissed as he stood on wobbly legs. "Where the hell are we, and where the hell are you?" It was easy to see she wasn't in the one room spaceship, so he walked to the front and looked out the windshield which was now a clear glass rather than the opaque screen-covered space that it had become during flight. He didn't recognize the place, but he didn't like the look of it. It was night on this planet, everything shrouded in a grey sort of darkness that looked wet. The few lights that were bright on the other ships parked around and the dull glow coming out of the windows of the one-story shack showed that the terrain was rocky with sparse vegetation.

A space stop for fuel, he assumed, since there didn't seem to be any other buildings lit up nearby. He'd heard of such places from other gladiators during trainings. A man had told him that he'd nearly escaped at one of these after being taken from his home planet of Ydlan because the crew had gotten drunk and passed out near his cell on the ship. The prisoner had managed to get the key from the pocket of a guard and even made it outside of the ship. He'd gone into the establishment for help and found it full of thieves. Instead of getting help he'd been tied up and sold back to the Sabitarions once they'd sobered up.

"Thieves have no honor," he hissed and with a bit of panic turned from the windshield and searched until he found his possession wedged under a small counter. She hadn't taken it. Not that it was of any value in these circles, but he doubted she realized what it was. He decided to leave it tucked where it wouldn't roll around with her crazy driving, then went back to staring out the window, waiting to see her walk out of the place. Hopefully alone. If she had anyone trailing behind her out of that place, he'd take his stuff and run. He'd rather find his way home from this planet himself than be sold back to King Lenkin of Sabit.

He'd do anything to not go back there.

The rowdy sounds of drunks coming and going from the place affirmed his idea of what kind of place they were parked at, and it certainly wasn't appropriate for a woman by herself. He watched nervously as patrons walked in and out of the place and he thought about how small she was in comparison to most of them. With every passing minute he imagined any number of horrifying things happening to her and he debated on going in himself. His thoughts shifted back and forth from her possible betrayal of him, to her in danger, and it filled him with a protective instinct he didn't know he had. He was moments away from rushing in there when a new thought occurred to him. What if she wasn't in there, what if she was somewhere else and he left the ship, then she returned and thought he'd run off. What if she left him here?

After twenty minutes, he decided he had no choice but to go in after her. She had probably found herself in some kind of trouble and needed saving, and unless she'd already betrayed what he was, there was no risk to him going in because no one would even know that he was valuable to sell. He looked down at himself and frowned. He would draw a lot of attention like this though, dressed in his gladiator clothes that King Lenkin forced him to wear. For the last twenty years, he'd been allowed nothing else. He craved the traditional loose, breathable fabrics of the Haladian people. He itched to have his sword strapped to his side, too.

He ached for home.

A noise brought his attention to a cabinet along the wall of the ship. The whole interior was smooth and contained, as a ship needed to be, he supposed. Anything left unattached would wander and possibly break, like his own goddamn head. Especially the way she drove.

The noise came again, a sort of snuffle, and he moved cautiously to the cabinet. A touch and it popped open revealing a small animal, a pet? Saluk was not impressed. The thing looked at him with big black eyes, it's wrinkled unsettlingly humanoid face curious as it chewed on some kind of pelleted food. It was about twelve inches long and round like a grub, it had tiny feet nearly hidden under its massive purple chub all covered in a downy pink fur. It had pointed ears atop its round head and short whiskers twitching beside its nose.

"She has a pet, good thing she didn't have to serve her sentence in the dungeon," he grumbled as the thing went back to eating, not giving two shits about the stranger glaring at it.

"That's Jet. He's a grub-cat."

Prit's voice behind him made him jump, ready to attack but

mostly filling him with mortification that she'd managed to sneak up on him. His head must still be addled from the injury she'd caused, and he glared at her for it.

She didn't seem intimidated. "He's my companion, loves it in there," she said and tossed Saluk a bag that smelled so good his stomach immediately started to rumble.

"Where the hell are we?" he asked as his eyes ran over her, looking for signs that she'd had to fight her way out of that place. Any sign of assault would send him into a rage, he could feel it under his skin, a fire of outrage ready to avenge her.

She was standing with one eyebrow raised and a smirk on her lips. She looked to be unharmed but he was having a hard time just accepting that.

She'd also changed her clothes while he was passed out and the realization that she'd been naked, at least partially, while he'd been in the same room with her made him thankful for the loose kilt he wore. She was now wearing a black one-piece suit that was skintight and left the entirety of her robotic leg open. It had no sleeves and was cut low in the front giving him a hint at the small mounds he'd appreciated earlier. His gaze traveled down to her wrist and the obvious mark of a thief there that she made no effort to hide.

His face heated and he tore his gaze away. Of course she was fine, she was a thief, this is where she was comfortable, he had no doubt.

He needed a distraction, he ripped the bag open, shoving the food in his mouth with a groan. "Fuck, what is this? It tastes like heaven." It was hot and greasy and salty. It filled his senses with an overwhelming desire to eat more and more. It was nothing like the gladiator diet he'd been on that was mostly protein and vegetables. Nor was it anything like the spicy and sweet traditional foods of Halador that were heavy in fresh game and fruits and nuts that were easily foraged.

She laughed and sat in the pilot's seat, then turned to face him with her own bag open and food in hand. "Cheeseburger. Space stop food isn't known for its health benefits but it sure as fuck hits the spot, doesn't it? There are fries in the bag too, try those. One thing the humans from Old Earth brought with them that everyone in the known galaxies seems to appreciate is their penchant for food that clogs up the body's systems and soothes the soul."

He grunted, his mouth full. "Where?" he demanded again, pulling out what she'd called fries and stuffing them in his mouth. Behind him, Jet had moved, he was sniffing as if he were more interested in Saluk's food than his own dry pellets now.

Saluk shooed him off, but the damn thing was insistent, one tiny paw reaching out uselessly, it couldn't touch anything even as far out as its own face with those pudgy legs.

"He wants a fry," Prit said with a laugh and walked over with one held out for the thing. Saluk didn't move so when she got close to give the fry to the pet her body brushed against his.

The light touch sent a jolt through him, a lightning shock of awareness up and down his spine. He disguised his sharp intake of breath with more chewing and turned away as she smiled slyly and slipped back to her seat.

"You'll make him fat," he said.

"Too late, he's already fat and happy," she said with a laugh. "What can I say, I like them big." Her gaze raked from his face all the way down his body and back up.

He nearly choked on the insinuation he was sure she'd made on purpose and pretended to be interested in the rest of the ship to get his body and mind back under control. Then he faced her once again as he crumpled up the now empty bag. Wishing there was about three times as much food.

"Want this?" she asked, motioning to her lap and his eyes widened, his heart skipped, and his mouth dropped open. His mind spiraled until he realized she meant the bag of fries in her lap and not her irritatingly delectable body.

He grunted affirmatively and she threw the bag at him. He caught it in one hand and forced himself to eat slower this time.

"You still haven't answered my question."

"True, but before I divulge all my secrets, tell me. Why were you down there?"

"A mistake."

She nodded and took a bite of her cheeseburger, chewing slowly, her eyes narrowed, and assessed him. "You're Haladian. You are obviously a gladiator now, probably were a warrior before being taken to Sabit. Which means you must have been spoils of war. Am I getting close?" she asked with a smug smile.

"No. Where are we?"

She rolled her eyes and set the cheeseburger down. She crossed her arms and met his gaze without blinking. Not an ounce of fear in her face and it seriously pissed him off. She should be afraid; he was ugly and scary, and he was a fucking fearsome gladiator.

"Tit for tat, Sal. I saved your ass," she said with a sly smile.

"I showed you the way out," he countered. "And I helped open the door. That's two for me one for you."

She bit her lip, but it didn't hide the smirk there. "I fed you."

"So we're even," he grumbled.

She smiled. "Alright, I'm not unreasonable. We had to take a wormhole at light speed when we were followed, sorry about that, it can be rough, but it worked; they didn't follow."

He grunted, of course they didn't follow, it had obviously been a dangerous maneuver.

"We are now on one of Jesit's moons."

"I have heard of Jesit," he said with a frown, trying to place the planet in his limited knowledge of the Settled Space Alliance. Halador wasn't technically part of the SSA, the united system of planets that collaborated and fought and tried to run the known universe. Halador lay outside the boundary that the SSA claimed and was uninterested in the supposed benefits of joining. It also didn't hold anything the others were trying to get, something he'd always been grateful for.

"Jesit is a small but well inhabited planet under Eludian control, this is a moon with a space stop, not much more," Prit explained.

"Shit," he said, his gaze shooting back outside to scan for danger. "Why the fuck are we in Eludian territory?" This was bad, she was more than crazy, she was a fucking psychopath with not an ounce of self-preservation in her. The Haladian people were not well-traveled or even that well-versed in the politics of the settled universe, however he'd listened and learned a lot while in captivity and everything he'd ever heard about the Eludians was that they were to be avoided. A barbaric but advanced civilization that patrolled its territory with militant fervor. As a warrior he respected it, as a lone warrior in their territory, he wanted out and he wanted her as far from this place as possible.

Prit leaned back in her seat and raised an eyebrow. "Scared, big guy?"

"The fact that you aren't, has me worried about who I threw myself in with," he said honestly.

"Well, Sal," she said standing up and putting her hands on her hips. "You just so happen to be in the presence of a real Eludian Princess. Does *that* scare you?"

"You're human," he gasped, running his eyes up and down her again. "You're short and you have no tail," he added shaking his head.

She turned and slapped her own ass, her head flipped around to look directly at him as she did and her blue eyes were half lidded but full of mirth. "Thanks to my human mother, I missed that bit, and the height thing." She laughed and handed him the rest of her burger. "Big boys need to eat. I'm going to fill the tank, then we can head out again. If you're scared of the locals, don't leave the ship," she said with a shrug. "If you're scared of me... well I guess you'll have to decide if you'd be better off without me, huh?"

Saluk watched her leave with shock running through his system. *She* was an Eludian princess! How the hell did she go from princess to thief, and how was it that she had a human mother? Was it a prisoner the king had impregnated? That wouldn't make her a princess necessarily. He didn't know how Elude ran things, but most bastard children weren't recognized with titles. This he knew from the many bastards that King Lenkin sired, and the guards talked about. It would explain why she had turned to thievery, and she was likely only calling herself princess to get a rise out of him. It seemed she liked to do that, and it confused him. She didn't treat him the way he had come to expect females to.

Nothing about her was what he expected, including the draw he felt for her. *You'll have to decide if you'd be better off without me.* He didn't think he'd ever be the same after meeting her, and he was undecided if he was better off or not.

He pushed those thoughts away and went back to trying to remember everything he had ever heard about Elude and the Eludian people. He'd met one, not in battle though, just in the training yard. The male had a long whiplike tail, he was tall and thinly muscled. She was short but she definitely had the thin muscles that could be attributed to her father's kind.

The man had bragged about the ferocity of their king, Dofsh. Anyone who crossed Dofsh would be tortured mercilessly and with relish, he was even known to keep hearts he'd personally torn out of bodies in jars in his bedroom. The gladiator had been convinced that the Eludian army would come save him, but he'd perished in his second arena battle and no one had ever come looking as far as Saluk knew.

Saluk finished off Prit's burger and opened cabinets until he found one with water, drinking three bottles before wondering if the ship was equipped with enough supplies to last their journey. Maybe he should have been more careful. He had no idea how long their journey was going to be. After he'd been taken from Halador, the ship that held him had traveled for months, picking up others before returning to Sabit. A direct route to Halador from Sabit might be much shorter, not that they were still technically near Sabit after that wormhole maneuver. What little knowledge he had of the SSA oriented him a bit. He knew that his own little planet was on the other side of the Blue Galaxy which held Elude and other planets in its controlled territory, and Sabit had been far from Elude in the Red Galaxy. So maybe their journey would actually be short, seeing as they were at least a galaxy closer to where he wanted to be.

A spike of hope mixed with anxiety shot through him at the thought of returning home after all this time. What would his people think of him? Would his parents still be alive? How was he going to tell them how badly he'd failed twenty years ago?

CHAPTER FOUR

By the time Prit was back in the ship and closing up the door, apparently having fueled up, Saluk was settled into the pilot's seat ready to demand a timeline from her.

"Do you like beer?" she asked, holding up two bottles and nearly derailing his determination.

He did like beer, had been given it as a reward after battle and the soft dulling of his senses was always welcome. Right now though, he didn't want to forget what he was after. "I like information," he said as he grabbed the bottle from her.

She hit a button and a seat appeared out of a portion of the ship's wall. He glared at it. That would have been mighty convenient when she was zipping through space earlier, it had a seat belt and everything. He shifted his glare to her as he opened the bottle and took a long swig.

She didn't even flinch, and he was reminded that she might be as big a monster as he projected himself to be, all wrapped in a tiny, cute package.

She sipped at her beer and looked thoughtful. "I want to hire you for a job."

"You're a thief. I have a feeling you are the one who usually gets hired," he countered. He couldn't imagine being helpful in any sort of sneaky theft, maybe if she needed something broken into; he was good with throwing his fists around.

She waved a hand dismissively. "I need muscle because sometimes that's all that matters to a man—what the picture is—you know. I can slit a throat faster than anyone, but I look like I would faint at the sight of a large cock, so I need a bodyguard."

He nearly spit at her idea of a good comparison. What the hell kind of woman was she?

He settled for addressing the concern of being her muscle. "I'm no mercenary," he said. "I'm not interested in stealing and I won't hurt innocent people."

"I would guess that's not completely true, and I said bodyguard. There should be no need for killing or stealing and if there is, I'll be doing it. I just need you to stand there and look tough, arm candy of sorts."

He frowned at her confusing human idioms. "What do I get out of the deal?"

"I don't leave you here among these hardened criminals you are so afraid of," she said with a grin and took a long gulp of her beer.

"You're backing out of our deal already?" he snarled.

She didn't even flinch at his harsh tone. "New deal," she said with a grin. "I got you off of Sabit, I did what I promised, now we are in negotiations again."

Tricky little thief, he mused, but he couldn't deny she was right, she had done what she said she would; he was off that hellhole planet. "I'll play bodyguard and you'll take me to Halador after," he said. His eyes darted to the canister still stuffed under a cabinet.

She followed his gaze. "Sure. What's in that thing? Is it valuable?"

"No," he said and stood up out of the pilot's seat. "Now let's get on with it."

She finished her beer and threw the bottle in a garbage compartment she opened on the wall, tucked Jet in safely, then nodded at the seat she'd vacated. "You might want to strap in properly this time."

"Are we going through another wormhole?" he asked, trying to keep the nerves down. His stomach might not handle another one of those so soon after eating.

"Nah, we aren't that far from where I need to go."

"Which is where?"

"Don't you like surprises?" she asked with a smirk.

"No," he said firmly, and she laughed.

Prit turned away from Saluk's scowling face and smiled, he was proving to be a fun companion, though she wasn't sure he was having as good a time as she was.

She drove the ship away from the fueling station and took off, smiling as Saluk grunted with the jerking movements. She was used to it, she hadn't learned to fly smoothly, she'd learned to fly fast and tight, to maneuver around the enemy and as close to targets as possible. And maybe she was enjoying his grunts of displeasure a little bit.

Once in the air and out of the traffic of the fuel stop, she set the coordinates for their next destination and hit the autopilot. When she unstrapped and stood up with a sigh and a stretch, Saluk was still gripping his seat and had his eyes slammed shut. She took a moment to study him closer. Out of the darkness of his cell she could more clearly see how deep the scar on his face was, the cut into his flesh must have been terribly painful. She respected him for living through such horror. She could certainly relate to surviving with the scars of battle.

"We're up, we're good to go, should be smooth space all the way in," she said and turned away from him as his eyes opened and his shoulders relaxed. "It will take a couple hours though and I'm beat." She hit the button that would bring a small cot down from the ceiling.

"What the hell are you doing?" he asked with a hint of panic in his voice that made her smirk.

He was a jumpy thing for a gladiator. Was he worried she was about to ask him to service her, or did he think she'd left the flying up to him?

She climbed onto the cot with a deep sigh. "Napping. I've been up for a good twenty hours and that's about my limit so if anything shakes the ship, feel free to wake me up." She rolled over, giving him her back and closed her eyes then hit a button that dimmed all the lights to a dull glow and immediately started to drift off. Her time in the New Earth military had taught her to take sleep when and where she could but also to always be aware of what was happening around her. She doubted she'd get deep sleep, but her body would have a chance to rest a bit, that would have to be good enough.

She heard him move around the small space; he went to the front by the sounds of his steps.

"Don't fucking touch anything, you'll likely crash us into an asteroid," she said.

"I'm not an idiot," he snapped.

"Remains to be seen," she shot back with a laugh, then settled into the pillow, one hand slipping under to grip a small blade she kept there. She wasn't an idiot either. Although he hadn't given her any indication that he would try something violent with her, she didn't plan on trusting him completely.

. . .

Prit woke a while later to a loud beeping and Saluk yelling. "What the fuck is wrong with you people?"

Prit was a trained military woman; she went from sleep to battle awareness in a split second so she was out of the cot and shoving Saluk out of the way before she even fully processed the thought to move.

She strapped in and snarled at him. "What did you touch?"

"Nothing, but I'm pretty sure those guys are shooting at us," he hissed and pointed at a blip on the screen.

Nothing showed on the large front screen, but he was right; they were being shot at by that little blip on the radar screen. It was a Bularian ship too, damnit. She could tell by the unique shape it made on the radar. Super tall and skinny with wide wings. It was probably one of Barius'. How had he figured out so quickly that she'd been unsuccessful with the take?

"Shit. Hold on," she said and banked a hard left, then slammed the ship forward. Saluk yelled as he slid and rolled to the back of the small space.

She quickly assessed their location and realized she'd actually slept for over an hour, pretty deeply too. She wasn't sure if she should be annoyed by the fact that she'd let her guard down, or impressed that Saluk emanated such non-violence that she'd trusted him.

Another beep was followed by a blast. Her ship rocked to the side and an angry red light came on to tell her the shot had connected with something semi vital.

"Fuck you," she hissed and hit a button that swapped the engines and dropped the ship like a stone in water. They went down so fast the only thing that kept her from hitting her head on the ceiling was her seatbelt.

Saluk wasn't as lucky. She heard a thump and a curse.

Before the Bularian ship could register where they went, Prit spun them around, jetting out in the opposite direction fast. There was a moon nearby they'd be able to hide on and assess the damage done to her ship. If Barius wanted to be an asshole, she wasn't going to be in any hurry to make a new deal with him and she knew he wouldn't follow where she was headed.

Even she didn't want to go where she was headed.

The ship was steady as they blasted forward, the pressure and gravity inside balancing out enough for Saluk to make his way forward looking like he wanted to throttle her.

"You are trying to kill me," he snarled.

"Oh come on, my driving isn't that bad. Besides, look," she pointed to the screen showing no nearby ships, "we got away. Those big Bularian battle ships can't maneuver worth a shit, but they have great guns." She was a little jealous of the guns, something this ship didn't have and she usually didn't need. Battling wasn't her thing anymore, she just wanted to sneak in and out of places and make herself some money.

Saluk grunted and went to strap himself into the extra seat. She turned back to the screens with a shrug, he'd have to get over it, she was his ride home. She readjusted their course for Zenzi.

Zenzi was one of three moons that circled Elude. It was the farthest from the planet but the largest and supported life well. It had a variety of animals and a few outposts for trade as well as a New Earth military base that they'd have to avoid. It was the only SSA associated military post allowed in Eludian territory and it was only allowed there because her father wanted to keep an eye on them for political reasons. According to Dofsh, he was stringing them along to make them think that one day, he might make a deal with the SSA.

She doubted he ever really would, he didn't think much of anyone who wasn't an Eludian.

His decision to impregnate a human, Prit's mother, had been a strategy for gaining an unofficial in with the humans, and it hadn't gone well. Although the relationship had been consensual, her mother had run when she'd become pregnant and had refused to return to Elude and act as some kind of ambassador. Prit always thought her mother's feelings had been hurt in the ordeal, she'd thought herself in love with Dofsh but he'd really only wanted the half human child. The allowance of the outpost on Zenzi was in part, a peace offering to Prit. He'd only done it after Prit had grown and joined the New Earth military but still refused to claim her place as a part of his royal house.

She frowned at her screens and pulled her thoughts away from her father. She didn't like the warnings she was still getting from her ship and she slowed down a touch as they continued to not detect anyone else in their vicinity. They might be limping in at this point.

CHAPTER FIVE

"Identify." A voice came over the radio about thirty minutes later when they got within range of the moon.

"This is Pritalia Dofsh of Elude and New Earth. My girl is injured and requesting a landing for repairs."

"Oh hey babe, bring her in," the now happy voice responded.

"Thanks, Josh, any military about?" she asked.

"Nope, clear as day out there right now, but make it fast," he replied.

She didn't reply, just flew into the atmosphere with her eyes on the screens for any indication that a military plane was doing sweep overs. She'd rather rush back out into space and take her chances with Barius than the Commander.

Lush green rushed up toward them and then a landing pad and she set her girl down with a light plop in the relative safety of the familiar jungle.

"So you do know how to drive this thing smooth," Saluk grumbled.

"Yeah, but where's the fun in that?" she said, throwing him a wink. She flipped some switches and killed the engine, then stood and stretched, rubbing at her upper right thigh. No matter how good the parts were grafted together, she still got sore there where her flesh met metal.

Saluk's eyes were narrowed on her as she moved. She hit a button to retract the cot then opened the hatch, letting the stairs down. A rush of hot, humid air wafted in and she inhaled deeply. She loved the smells of this place, the sweet flowers that bloomed everywhere all year round and even the grasses that had a sweet scent. She could have been happy living here, in another life maybe.

Saluk stood but made no other move. Looking unsure, his eyes darted from her to the canister.

"Your shit is safe here; Josh is an old friend."

"And what about the old friends who just tried to shoot us out of the sky?"

"They didn't follow us here, and they aren't friends, they are business associates," she said simply and started down the stairs.

"Josh," she called as the man hurried across the field to greet her. He was a full human, an ex-military like her and they were forever bonded because they'd shared some of their worst experiences, including the bar fight where she'd lost her eye.

Josh had short black hair, bright blue eyes, and an easy smile. He was dressed like a tourist on some tropical planet with khaki cargo shorts, hiking boots, and a flowered button up shirt left open to reveal an expanse of tan chest. Zenzi got a lot of sun.

"Babe," he replied and embraced her. "It's been a while." He squeezed her tighter. "I was starting to worry," he whispered.

"Yeah, sorry," she said, pulling back and rolling her eyes at his worry. They both knew the deal; she couldn't stay anywhere long. But he always harassed her about not visiting more often and she always appreciated the knowledge that she was loved.

"You look amazing as always—" his words cut off, and his

hands stilled on her arms as his eyes caught on Saluk who was finally making his way down the steps out of the ship. "Boyfriend?" he asked, removing his hands and taking a step back.

"Bodyguard," she said and turned around.

Saluk's face was set in a scowl she imagined he wore every time he entered the gladiator arena, and he had that damn canister gripped under one arm. Whatever it was, he didn't trust it out of his sight, and she was very curious. Her penchant for stealing and selling things of value was prickling.

"A princess needs a bodyguard," Josh said with a laugh. "Does he have a name?"

"Saluk. Haladian."

"Haladian? Wow," Josh said. "Though he's dressed like a gladiator so I'm guessing you didn't just pick him up on Halador." Josh threw an arm around Prit and led her into the building, dismissing Saluk as any kind of threat or particular interest, at least for the time being. "So, what is wrong with your girl? Piss someone off?"

"As usual. I took a hit from a Bularian ship."

"Why the hell are they mad at you? What did you take from Barius?"

"Nothing! Well, except for a job offer and I was unable to complete it," she grumbled.

"Prit, babe, you should *not* have taken a job from Barius if you didn't know you could handle it. Even a shadow has its limitations."

Prit sighed; she knew he was right. It had been a big risk, obviously, because she hadn't pulled it off. But it would have been a huge payout if she'd succeeded.

As they entered the small building that was used as the station control post and Josh's home, a boy ran forward with a huge smile. He was young, sixteen New Earth years, but he was already tall and broad like his dad, so much more grown than the last time she'd been here. It made her heart ache a bit, she'd been gone too long this time. His black hair was shoulder length and his eyes brown like his mother's had been. Prit knew those eyes so well.

"Aunt Prit," he called and embraced her. "Dad's been complaining about you not visiting us."

She laughed back the tears that wanted to leak out and hugged the kid fiercely. "Hey, Frankie, yeah, well, a thief's got to make a living."

"And stay alive," Frankie said. "Want me to look at your girl out there? I heard your incoming."

Frankie was young but he had a talent for repairing ships so she nodded and he rushed out, pushing past Saluk who was lurking in the doorway.

Saluk looked annoyed that the boy ignored him as he rushed by, which made Prit grin wide.

Frankie had grown up here on Zenzi and he had very little idea about the dangers that lurked out in space. It was the way his mother had wanted it and after she died, Josh kept it up. There was something wonderful about his innocence, thinking every creature that came through was just as happy and docile as him.

"Want a beer? Or are you on the other side of the day?" Josh asked.

Space travel made life weird. You sort of set your day and night where you wanted it and ate or slept accordingly. It didn't always match the planet you were on, and people didn't much care.

"I just had a nap so I suppose it's morning, got any coffee?"

"Sure thing, babe," he said and disappeared into a back room. The main room of the building held a desk with radio equipment, a table, and chairs. The walls were decorated with pictures of a very young Frankie with his mom and dad, making her heart ache a little for the happy family they'd once been.

Saluk slunk in fully and started to prowl, taking in the pictures. He stopped by one that made Prit cringe. It was her at fifteen standing next to Josh who had been about eighteen at the time. They were cadets, proud and ready to defend New Earth and all its claimed territory. She had an innocent smile and long blonde hair back then, both eyes and legs too.

It felt like a different life.

She'd been able to enlist so young because she wasn't fully human and that meant she could go off the age of adulthood for her father's species, which was fifteen. Her mother had already passed away from cancer and Prit had been desperate to find a way to survive that didn't include selling her body or begging her father for help. Her sister, Tiffany, just a couple years older and fully human, was working as a waitress to support herself and couldn't afford to take care of Prit too.

Little did Prit know at the time that once enlisted in the New Earth military, they owned her body and their only goal was to turn her into a weapon.

The one good thing that had come of her time there had been introducing Josh to Tiffany and getting to see them have a few years of happiness before Tiffany, too, died of cancer leaving behind a husband, a young child, and a very lonely sister.

"Coffee," Josh declared as he came back with three cups on a tray. "I know you take yours black as space, Prit, what about you, big guy?"

Prit grunted a laugh at Josh's use of the term she, herself, had been in favor of using for Saluk.

Josh set the tray down on the table with a grin. His back was to Saluk but Prit knew he was aware of every move Saluk was making. Their type of training didn't just go away. "I have a sweetener and a creamer. Neither real, neither good for you," Josh added with a laugh.

Saluk walked over to the table and pulled a chair back so he wasn't quite part of the group but watchful with a cup of black coffee.

"Thank you," Saluk said.

Josh nodded acknowledgment.

Prit smiled behind her cup.

"Your coffee reminds me of being young and dumb," she said as she took a sip. It was strong and harsh and brought back memories of their military days. They weren't all bad memories, he'd been a bright spot in her young life, taken her under his wing and helped her realize quickly that not everyone had her best interests in mind even if they wore the same uniform. They'd been each other's safe space through a lot of shit, she still felt like she wasn't as safe anywhere else as she was with him, she just hated that her being with him put Frankie in danger. The Commander would love to put Josh behind bars for aiding a criminal like her and that would leave Frankie alone in this world that ate up sweet kids like him. It was why she avoided coming here too often, even if she wanted to spend as much time with her nephew as possible.

"So where have you been that you picked up a Haladian dressed up like a gladiator?" Josh asked with a quizzical tilt to his lips and brow, then held up a hand. "Wait, let me guess." His gaze swept over Saluk with an assessing eye. Josh had always been a good one for extracting information, he knew at least ten languages and could identify over a hundred different alien species on sight giving their weaknesses strengths and allegiances. "Halador is relatively close to here but judging by the dust on his boots that's not where you're coming from. He isn't dressed in his traditional clothes, so he was fancied up for someone's enjoyment." Josh looked thoughtful then snapped his fingers, his eyes lighting up. "You're one of the Sabitarion gladiators, aren't you?" He turned his knowing eyes on Prit. "How the hell did you manage that?"

Saluk grunted in surprise, his eyes widening slightly.

Prit smiled. "I was after something for Barius and got caught," she shrugged. "They threw me in the big guy's cell thinking I'd make a tasty snack." She winked at Josh to let him know she was fine. He might be all bubbly and bright, but he was deadly, and he protected her like a big brother. "We found our way out and I gave him a ride. It's not as if he was there as a willing participant."

"None of them are," Saluk clarified.

Josh nodded. They all knew that Sabit was playing under the law but the bastards had something that a lot of powerful people in the SSA wanted, entertainment, so authorities looked past the forced violence and imprisonment.

"And you've convinced him to be your bodyguard?"

"Yeah, I figure going to Barius with him at my back will make a more convincing argument."

Josh gave her a hard look. "And beg for another chance? You shouldn't be taking jobs from that guy."

"Like I have a choice?" she snapped back, it was an old argument.

Frankie ran back in then, breaking their glaring contest. "Took a good hit but nothing disastrous, I think we can fix her up with spare parts we have right here."

"Great," Prit said and stood to take a look for herself. The sooner she could get the ship fixed; the sooner she could be away from Josh's accusing concerned gaze. It wasn't that she relished the idea of risking her life, she just couldn't really get free without Barius' money.

Saluk stood to follow Prit, not sure what the hell she was about to do, but he didn't trust her enough not to leave him here.

"Hey, big guy," the human, Josh, said, stopping him from walking out the door.

Saluk turned with a glare, he didn't like how much the man had ascertained about him, didn't like the way he argued with Prit. Really didn't like how fucking familiar they were with each other. Saluk didn't say anything, just glowered and waited for the man to talk.

"I know she's a bit much," he laughed. "But she's a good girl, tougher than she needs to be and smart." He had walked closer as he talked until he was close enough to whisper. "If you harm her, or let any harm come to her, I will hunt you down, skin you alive and hang your fucking head on a pike."

He stepped back and laughed then slapped Saluk's shoulder and walked out of the office.

Saluk scowled after him, his instincts were to kill anything that even vaguely threatened him. But he had a feeling Prit wouldn't appreciate him killing her friend and then she probably *would* abandon him here.

Saluk stepped out into the damp air and sighed a little. It felt more like home here than anywhere he'd been in a long fucking time. He'd hated being on that desert planet for more reasons than just his captivity. Halador was a lush garden planet, green and full of life. He missed it. His hands tightened around the canister and he whispered, "I'm taking you home, just like I promised."

Booming overhead had him searching the sky for danger, but all he saw were dark clouds rolling in and he relaxed. It wasn't an attack, just a storm. When was the last time he'd stood under dark clouds and felt the pebbling of raindrops on his skin? Long enough that he looked forward to the clouds opening up overhead and dousing him, but he wouldn't be able to enjoy it unless he was certain they were safe here.

He quickly assessed the surroundings. It had seemed pretty secure when they first arrived. A small station in the middle of a jungle area. The small landing pad was just big enough for transport ships like Prit's, nothing passenger-related. The office they'd been in was in a bit of disrepair but did the job he supposed, and he assumed it continued on back into housing for the two humans since no other buildings were visible around.

A drop of rain hit him and he turned his gaze to Prit and the others who were assessing damage on the ship. They were already removing pieces of it that were damaged and laughing together while they did it. She lifted her face to the sky and for a moment her bionic eye glowed brighter.

"It's going to really give it to us," she called out. "We probably need to wait it out somewhere dry."

All three of them hurried his way as the clouds opened up and let loose with a loud thundering and an increasing downpour. Saluk looked toward the safety and relative comfort of the ship, but Prit obviously wasn't thinking the same thing as him, she was going along with Josh and Frankie to the shop. He followed them, but took it a little slower, wanting to feel the rain hit his bare skin. The reminder that he was no longer in a prison cell, no longer on a desert planet, was exhilarating. He had given up all but the slightest bit of hope a long time ago.

Prit was laughing when he walked in the door not far behind her. She ran her hands through her short black hair, and he was entranced momentarily by the peek of blue underneath, it was such a bright shock of color and seeing it as she laughed and squeezed the water from her hair felt like an intimate moment. Josh said something that had her laughing again and Saluk resented that he wasn't the only one seeing her like this.

He wrung out his own long locks with a grunt, chastising

himself for the inappropriate and likely unwelcome thoughts he was having about Prit.

She shook out her bionic leg. "Well, looks like we're here for the next few hours. Got anything to eat, Josh? My big guy is a hungry one." She gave Saluk a wink and he glowered back at her.

He could go days without food and still be in top fighting form, why the hell was she trying to make him look weak to Josh?

"I'll cook up some steaks, it's dinner time for us," Josh said and headed into a back room.

"Tell me what you've swiped lately," Frankie said, his eyes wide with admiration as he looked at Prit who had settled into a chair with her bionic leg up on the table.

"Toss me a rag, will ya," she said, and the boy hurried to comply.

Once she had the rag, she began to meticulously wipe down her leg. She ran the soft cloth over the metal and blue tendon-like strands on the top of her leg slowly, her fingers dipped into crevices and left no piece untouched down to the top of her foot.

Saluk couldn't take his eyes off of her as she moved the rag up the back of her thigh next. So close to her actual skin that he saw peeking out right where the line of her outfit ended. It had to be right to her panties, she'd lost the whole damn thing. She moved the rag to the outer side where the metal went up to her hip bone. He was amazed at the extensive loss she'd suffered. She wiped along the seamless transition from metal to smooth pale skin and it made his mouth suddenly dry. Then she swept the rag back down and she ran it slowly between each delicate toe, they all moved independently, giving her amazing dexterity. When she did one more swipe up her inner thigh, he couldn't hold back a groan.

Mortified to realize how he'd been staring at her, his gaze shot to her face and found her giving him a knowing smile.

He scowled and looked away, meeting the big smile of Frankie who had apparently watched the exchange with amusement. A chuckle from the back doorway caught Saluk's attention and he met the knowing eyes of Josh.

Saluk slammed his chair back and walked out into the rain. He turned his face up to the sky and let the warm water soak into his skin. Let it cool his racing blood. She was dangerous, in more ways than one and he didn't understand her. Why was she teasing him? He knew she didn't want him to act on the desires she stirred to life with the performance, no woman did. He was a scarred-up killer. On Halador his scars wouldn't make him less attractive, they would be proof of what he could survive. But he knew someone like her wouldn't see that in his face. He touched the claw marks that ran down his features and marred his lips. No, she would never want to press her lips to that, she was just messing with him.

Angry, he stalked into the nearby jungle.

CHAPTER SIX

"You are a cruel woman," Josh said.

Prit laughed and threw the rag at him. "If he didn't like it, he could have turned away."

Josh rolled his eyes. "How long has the man been locked up? And you think he's going to turn away from a display like that?"

Prit just shrugged; she felt no remorse. She met Frankie's eyes and winked. The boy was more attracted to Saluk than he was to her, so she hadn't felt bad about flaunting herself in front of him either.

She watched through the window as Saluk stalked off into the jungle and noticed he'd left in such a hurry that he'd forgotten his canister on the table. She was curious about it, but she wouldn't risk pissing him off by touching it. It was a cylinder, about eighteen inches tall and eight inches across, made of brass. There was no noticeable lid but she'd held it once, she knew it wasn't a solid piece of metal.

"Seems important to him," Josh commented, noticing where her attention had fallen.

"Seems to be."

"Must kill you not to know what's in it, could be extremely valuable," Josh teased.

He wasn't wrong of course, she'd been chasing money for years, looking for that one big payout that could keep her for the rest of her life. What Josh didn't know was that she planned to take that payout and get out of the SSA completely. She dreamed of a life where she wasn't running. She'd be alone, but that wasn't anything new, she reminded herself sternly. Aside from Jet, she hadn't spent more than a couple days with anyone since she left the military, and it was better that way.

"Need help with the steak?" she asked, changing the subject and pushing down her emotions. She wasn't sure how she'd cope with never seeing these two again, but if she knew she was keeping them safe, she'd stay away.

Josh didn't miss the sadness in her eyes, he saw through her like no one else ever had. They knew each other too well. "Yeah, come on and make sure I don't overcook it."

She followed Josh to a covered porch out back and watched while he cooked. He didn't really want her help and she didn't really want to give it.

"Have you heard from the Commander?" she asked, breaking the silence and asking the question that plagued her every minute she was with them.

"He was through last week."

"Asking about me?" she asked with a wide grin to hide her worry.

"Always."

She took a drink and stared off into the jungle. "He comes through often?"

"Once a month, yeah."

They were a fair distance from the military base the New Earth military inhabited here, but it was a risk. If the

Commander knew, he'd be here in a second with guns drawn and a nice cell waiting for her.

"You shouldn't have slept with his wife," Josh said.

Prit rolled her eyes. "She shouldn't have confessed to our little tryst," Prit pointed out. Yeah, she'd been dumb, but the woman had pursued *her*, not the other way around and Prit had given her what she wanted happily. Eileen Paul was a gorgeous human woman with long blonde hair and bright green eyes. When her husband had found out about the relationship, he'd made it his mission in life to destroy Prit, and it would be all too easy seeing as he was in charge of the entire New Earth military in three solar systems. Prit had been left with no choice other than to duck out on her contract, stealing a ship and a few weapons as she went. Luckily all the things she'd learned as a spy in the military had given her the tools to keep herself hidden and able to make money with odd recovery or theft jobs. It had only taken three New Earth years for her to earn her reputation.

Of course, she could have gone back to her father. The New Earth military had no rights on Elude, but that would mean she'd have to live the life her father wanted for her.

Princess Pritalia, married off, attending events and basically being a pretty pet for everyone to look at and then taking care of her father in his old age. She would rather risk death at the hands of the men she'd once worked beside. Because it would be death, she'd fight until they had to kill her. She'd never go willingly into a jail cell for the rest of her life.

Four hours later the rain was done and the ship was repaired. Prit was too tired to think about going anywhere so she crawled into the semi safety of her ship, pulled Jet out of his cage, and settled on the cot.

Saluk said he was going for a walk and she drifted off.

A grunt and the sound of the door closing woke her enough to turn her head but one look at Saluk's sour, scarred face had her turning back. She wasn't afraid he was about to murder or arrest her.

"Take a nap," she told him.

"Where?" he snapped.

She managed an eye roll even with her eyes closed and scooted as close to the wall as she could, pushing Jet off to the floor where he scrambled to find a new spot to rest.

The stillness in the ship surrounded her for a full minute before Saluk finally made a decision. He laid down next to her carefully. His back pressed against hers on the small cot, but she didn't mind. She couldn't remember the last time she'd actually tried to sleep next to someone else. Usually she had her fun and sent them on their way, or went on hers. She didn't trust anyone enough to be around when she was sleeping, and she didn't want to share such an intimate and vulnerable thing as sleep with another.

Her hand remained on her dagger under her pillow as she fell back to sleep quickly.

She startled awake when her entire body started to vibrate.

She bolted out of the cot, dagger in hand and rushed to the cockpit.

"What is it?" Saluk roared, standing behind her.

"We were rocked, what the hell? Are we under attack?" She checked her screens and waited for it to happen again.

Nothing.

She shook her head, confused. "Maybe it was a dream," she mumbled, not that she'd ever dreamt an attack before. She was certain she'd felt her whole body moving, it had brought her out of sleep. She turned to look at Saluk and realized he had a sharpened stick in his hands. "Is that what you were doing on your walk? Making a weapon?"

"Yes," he said with a tilt of his chin. "I can defend you with my hands, but a weapon makes things easier."

"Great, can you defend me from dreams of the ship shaking?" she laughed.

His eyes darted away nervously and he lowered the weapon. His head shifted down and his hair swept forward on one side to half cover his face.

"What?" she demanded; he was hiding something. She held her knife out, threatening.

"It's a Haladian thing," he said carefully, sweeping a hand through the long locks on the right side of his head.

"*What's* a Haladian thing?" she demanded, lowering her weapon but not keeping the accusation from her face.

He let out a long breath. "In sleep, our bodies vibrate."

"What?" she asked, certain she'd never heard of any such thing and not able to hold the laughter from her tone now that she knew he hadn't been trying to kill her in her sleep.

His cheeks tinted red. "It's meant to soothe our mates and our children in sleep. To take them to a deeper rest."

She lifted an eyebrow, if she wasn't so tired she'd take advantage of his embarrassment and poke a bit of fun at the big guy. "Okay ... well can you not?"

"No," he said, his face turning a brighter red and making his scars stand out starkly white. "But I can rest in the pilot's seat so that I don't disturb you."

She instantly didn't like that idea, but she refused to think about why. "Don't be an idiot. If I know you're not trying to kill me, and the ship isn't about to explode, I'm sure I can sleep through it."

He still looked uncomfortable so she pushed past him and crawled back up on the cot and against the wall. "Do what you want, I need my beauty sleep before facing Barius."

She heard him settling into the pilot's seat and ignored the disappointment it sent through her. Before she'd woken, she was pretty sure she'd been sleeping better than she had in a long time. Something about having a big body between her and possible danger helped her relax, it made sense. Maybe she should get a big animal for protection when Saluk was gone.

She listened to him moving, grunting, and huffing as he tried to get comfortable in the small seat. It was meant for a pilot her size, maybe a little larger, human though for sure. He was way too big for it and sleeping in it would prove impossible, she was certain.

Finally he gave up and crawled back in beside her. Once again she felt the hard press of his back against hers and she started to drift to sleep. Jet jumped up on the cot and laid across her feet, adding to her feeling of comfort and safety.

When his body started a low vibration she smiled, she could understand how comforting this would be, especially for a child. How funny that such a large intimidating species would have such a gentle adaptation as this. Something so family oriented. Sleep overcame her quickly after that.

Saluk closed his eyes as the vibrations in his body started again. It was an odd feeling, one he hadn't experienced in so long he'd almost forgotten how wonderful it was. It reminded him of home, family, and friends. The Haladian people were fierce warriors, but they were dedicated to their families and clan. The vibrations only came out when they were resting beside another being who they wanted to care for as family or friend and since he'd been captured by the Sabitarions he hadn't felt another body willingly next to his, let alone wanted to care for anyone.

Prit was an unexpected thing to walk into his life. So happy and energetic, she didn't seem to take anything seriously, and her energy threatened to seep into his cold soul. He found himself wanting to be near her, to see what she was going to do next, everything about her surprised him.

She grunted and threw her body in her sleep, cuddling her front against his back and mumbling incoherently. His body stiffened and his vibrations stopped as he waited for her to wake up and push him away in disgust. Humans liked things pretty and perfect, Eludians were even worse. He lifted a finger and touched his lip where the scar ran so deep he'd been shocked it had healed together at all. He couldn't imagine her pressing her own perfect lips to this scar with anything other than disgust behind her eye. He moved his hand up along the scar lines. His left eye had barely been missed. His fingers traced higher to where the scars ran over his scalp. He'd decided to keep this half of his head shaved so that the scars would be more visible, a warning to his opponents that he could endure, and he had already survived more than most men could.

He thought about her own injuries, obviously she too could endure horrible wounds. He wondered if she would ever tell him what had happened to her leg and her eye. He didn't dare ask, knew she'd return the favor and ask about his wounds and some of them were far too personal to share.

Her wounds didn't detract from her beauty however. He didn't see her leg as a scar, he didn't view the mechanics deep in her left eye as a weakness, in fact, he had a feeling both gave her an advantage. She was stronger for her wounds, just like a Haladian who survived was viewed to be.

Warm pride he had no business in feeling swirled through his chest and he pushed it away. He had no right to feel anything for her other than a thankfulness that she'd saved him, and a duty to protect her on her journey as repayment. He was her hired bodyguard, nothing more and to wish for more would only lead to disappointment and frustration.

When she didn't wake after a few minutes, and her body continued to be soft and sagging against his back, he relaxed and his vibrations continued.

This is what it would feel like to have his wife in bed with him, perhaps a small child tucked to his front as well. They'd sleep soundly with his vibrations to soothe away the violence and hardships of their days as hunters and farmers.

An ache he hadn't felt since his capture welled up inside him and he pushed it down as Jet crawled from where he'd been curled around her feet to lay against his legs, apparently enjoying his vibrations as well.

Saluk clamped his eyes shut and ignored the feeling of family that threatened to overwhelm him. This wasn't his family, he wasn't home, and she'd drop him on Halador without a second glance and be out of his life as soon as she didn't need him.

Halador ... what waited for him there? Would his clan even still be around and thriving? It was always possible his clan would be attacked by clans from around the planet to take their fertile land and close proximity to such great hunting grounds. What would he do if he returned to a burned out and abandoned village?

It was a fear for the future, and it was out of his control, so he swept it from his mind. He couldn't fight a battle against thoughts, so he closed his eyes and concentrated on the vibrations of his body, and the steady breathing of Prit against his back. For this moment, he wasn't alone, and that feeling was so overwhelming he felt a prickle of it behind his eyes.

When he succumbed to sleep his dreams were full of her.

CHAPTER SEVEN

Prit woke up slowly, her mind groggy. She must have slept deeply because her body was stiff, and her mind was trying to catch up. She stretched and groaned.

"Good morning," Saluk grunted from where he stood staring out the front windshield. His body looked tight, and she wondered how long he'd been standing there and if he thought he was guarding her with his sharp stick gripped in his hand.

"Morning sunshine," she said with a smile. "Want some coffee?"

"No," he said and turned from the window. His expression was unreadable, and it made her want to poke and tease him until he snapped and revealed what he was really thinking.

"Your loss, it's god's gift to the universe, best thing next to sex in the morning," she said as she hopped off the cot and straightened the bedding, which had a new musky smell thanks to him that she wasn't used to but didn't hate. Then sent it away.

She opened a cabinet on the other side of her small living space and busied herself making coffee and feeding Jet before putting him in his cupboard with a kiss on the head and an order to *be good*. She grabbed some clean clothes, poured her coffee into a mug and turned to look at the now scowling man who had stood silently watching her every move.

She would give anything to know what was going on behind that shuttered look.

"I'm showering," she said in explanation and sipped her coffee. Her bionic eye alerted her to a spike in his pulse and rapid increase in his body temperature.

His face turned a delightful red and he quickly looked around in a panic.

She laughed. "Not in here, though it has a shower, it's not very pleasant. I'm heading in to use Josh's. You're welcome to as well and we can even get you some clean clothes maybe if you want something different to wear."

He looked down at himself and frowned. "I don't like these, but I am far bigger than Josh."

She rolled her eyes, men and their dick measuring. "Yeah well, a pair of stretchy sweats and a big t-shirt shouldn't be hard to find if you're interested. Shoes might be an issue I will admit." She didn't say that she'd miss seeing his thick thighs under his leather kilt and bare chest that she'd already spent far too much time memorizing every scar, mole, and hair on.

She opened the hatch to let the stairs down, she didn't care if he followed. She was desperate for a real shower while it was available. Her ship offered a light spray that was barely enough to get wet. It worked when necessary, but she avoided it when possible.

Saluk did follow and she couldn't help smiling behind her cup as Josh opened the door and greeted them brightly. "Hey you two, looking for some breakfast?"

"Shower," Prit said and swept past him. "Oh," she yelled before entering the bathroom. "Can you find something for the big guy to wear? He's worried his dick won't fit in your jeans so maybe some sweats?" she snickered when she heard Saluk's grunt of shock. She'd never get tired of teasing him.

Josh just laughed. "I think I can find something with room for the anaconda."

Prit took her time in the shower soaking in the hot water spray and washing every inch of skin before she stepped out and dried her leg thoroughly. It wouldn't rust and the water couldn't damage it, but she took special care of it anyway.

She dressed in a pair of black shorts and a button up floral shirt. No thief gear for a day of travel. Lastly, she hooked on a necklace, a silver chain with a simple letter S for her mother, Sarah. She touched the letter and closed her eyes, remembering the woman who'd raised her, taught her to embrace everything about herself and approach the world like it was meant to be enjoyed.

She'd never forgotten that. Even when she'd been in the thick of military life she'd found joy. Mostly it had been with Josh and her sister, damn she missed Tiffany even more than she missed her mother. As an older sister, Tiffany had been protective of Prit, and had even tried to take over parenting her after their mother passed, but Prit had rebelled against it. Now she'd give anything for her sister to try telling her what a bad idea it was to get involved with a Haladian she'd rescued from a gladiator prison.

She lifted the S and kissed it before tucking it under her shirt. She was almost certain her mother wouldn't tell her it was a bad idea to get involved with Saluk, the woman had had a wild affair with the King of Elude for fuck's sake. She was a woman who enjoyed life and embraced everything it had to offer.

Prit had always been a little more like her mother than her sister had been, which is exactly why she'd ended up in the bad graces of the New Earth Commander while her sister had been creating a family and settling down. Prit bit her lip and hung her head as thoughts of her sister filled her with sorrow. Would it ever get easier to know she was alone in the world? Would she ever stop feeling like the cancer that took out her mother and sister should have taken her instead?

Prit ran a finger over her bionic leg. She didn't have to worry about dying of the same thing, thanks to her father's genetics she healed faster than cancer could kill her.

When she left the bathroom, she found Saluk lurking outside the door with a bundle in his arms.

"Shower is all yours, big guy," she said and walked out to the office where Frankie was sitting behind the counter reading a book. "You got coffee back there?" She asked Frankie and held out her empty cup.

Frankie hopped off his stool and grabbed the pot. He poured her some with a grin. "He's grumpy in the morning," Frankie said motioning with his head to the bathroom.

Prit glanced back. "He's grumpy always," she laughed. "It's hard carrying that much manliness around, ya know?"

Frankie shrugged and laughed.

"Well, maybe you'll know someday," Prit added with a wink.

"How was your night?" Josh asked, coming in and giving her a look telling her he wanted to know if she'd seen the anaconda in question.

"Restful. Did you know Haladians vibrate in their sleep?"

"Really? Are you sure he was asleep and not," Josh made a jerking motion with his hand and Prit laughed, almost choking on her coffee.

"No, I'm certain I would have been aware of that. Apparently, it's supposed to soothe their mates and kids to sleep better."

"And did it soothe you to sleep, Prit? Were you playing the part of mate or child?" Josh asked with mirth.

"It did soothe, slept like the innocent," she said with a wink.

"Ha, innocent my ass," Josh said. "I found him some clothes but no shoes that will work."

"Thanks, Josh, I always appreciate your help."

His face turned serious. "You know I could help with the Commander, right. I could talk to the military magistrate, get them to negotiate and you'd probably only do a few years, or they might even take you back and let you finish out your term without any punishment. They all know how valuable you are to the military."

Prit sipped her coffee and frowned. He'd offered the same multiple times, and she figured he might be right. If she went crawling back and offered to spend the next ten years in service to New Earth they'd probably forgive her indiscretion with the Commander's wife and overlook her stealing of a military ship. But she didn't want that, didn't want to waste any more of her life doing what they told her, going where they told her.

She glanced down at the T that was permanently part of her body now. It was a mark against her soul according to many people in the SSA but what it symbolized to her was that she was a free woman, and she didn't want to trade that for the restraints, real or figurative, the Commander would put on her if he got the chance.

She had found freedom and she liked it.

Josh sat across from her with that serious look still on his face. "I worry about you."

"You shouldn't."

"You're flying around a ship that's barely holding up, you have Barius on your ass and you were captured during a job." He paused and shook his head. "Prit, that's not the signs of having your shit all together. That is a sign that you're risking way too much and honestly, I'm not sure what you're hoping to find." He reached across the table and laid a hand over hers.

"Let me do this for you, let me help you get back on the right side."

She shook her head. "It's too late, I'm never going to be on the right side." She smiled sadly. "I made my choice and I'm sticking with it. Barius will get over his disappointment and now I know I need to watch for alarmed jewelry in the future. What doesn't kill me and all that," she said with a wave of her hand.

"Barius is going to demand more than you can give, he doesn't forget disappointment."

She knew Josh was right so she didn't respond but started running her mind through what she might be able to placate Barius with. Maybe she shouldn't just approach him with excuses, even with Saluk at her back as bodyguard it was risky. But what did Barius want that she could offer?

When Saluk walked in, looking pissed as fuck in a pair of tight grey sweatpants that ended mid-calf and a shirt that hugged his muscled chest and showed a space of bare skin between it and the sweats, she laughed, hard. Frankie snickered too, which only made Saluk's face darken further with anger and embarrassment.

"This won't work," he snarled and tried to tug the shirt down, succeeding in ripping it.

"No, I don't suppose it will, big guy," she said wiping a happy tear from her eye. "Don't worry. We'll figure out something better. Let's get on our way."

"Breakfast!" Josh said and quickly ran out of the room, coming back with a bag in hand. "I knew you'd be anxious to hit it, so I made you something to take with you."

Prit took the bag and hugged her friend, kissing his cheek. "Don't worry about me," she whispered in his ear.

"I will always worry," he assured her and pulled away. "Stop back soon, let me know you made it away from Barius unscathed. You can be The Shadow to everyone else, Prit, but to me and Frankie, you're family."

Prit had to hold back the emotion his words triggered in her chest. "Yeah, yeah," she said but her voice didn't quite match the casualness of the words. She pulled Frankie in for a quick hug. "Take care of your dad, he needs to have more fun." She whispered in his ear. "Maybe find him a girlfriend?"

Frankie nodded and stepped back. Prit walked out of the office sad, she hated leaving those two, but they weren't her life, they were just a stopover on her search for life.

She checked on Jet before settling in the pilot's seat and flipping some switches, then she tossed the bag of breakfast sandwiches at Saluk where he was strapping himself into the seat at a near panicked pace. "Don't worry, we aren't leaving this place in a hurry, I won't go until you're safely tucked in there, darling."

He just grunted.

"It's like you don't trust my ability to get you there in one piece," she said with a smile and lifted the ship off the ground. He was strapped in, so she didn't hold back. She had a strong stomach after flying for so many years and craved the adrenaline a bit, she could admit. In the military she'd had to learn how to fly while avoiding being shot and outrunning enemies all while going through asteroid fields as well as populated, close to the ground areas. She was a damn expert, and Saluk just didn't appreciate it.

She got them out of the atmosphere fast and then set the course she wanted before unbuckling and walking back to where he sat clutching the bag with wide eyes.

"Did you squish my breakfast?" she asked, grabbing the bag from him.

"Did you have to do that?" he snarled back.

She just shrugged, grabbed out one wrapped biscuit and

tossed the bag back to his lap. "Why go slow when you can go fast?"

He narrowed his eyes. "Sounds like the words of a woman on the run," he said.

"We met in a prison cell; did you think I was a pretty princess in distress?" She grabbed out a couple bottles of water and tossed him one, then leaned against the side of the ship.

"I thought you were a poor soul trapped in my cage," he said quietly, staring down at his food. "But when you didn't run or scream, I thought perhaps your brain was damaged and you didn't realize what a monster like me could do to you." He lifted his head and looked at her. "I am still not sure you aren't brain damaged but at least you got me out of there."

Prit opened her mouth in shock, then laughed. "Sal, are you teasing me?" she gasped and took a bite of her breakfast.

His cheeks reddened slightly and he looked back down but not before she saw a slight smile lift the undamaged corner of his mouth. "Well, you have yet to prove yourself sane," he said.

"Don't hold your breath," she said. "There's a slight change of plans by the way. Before we head to Barius we are going to stop somewhere to get you something appropriate to wear. You won't intimidate anyone like that, and your gladiator clothes will give away your previous position which could cause problems."

CHAPTER EIGHT

They flew for hours, heading out of Eludian territory and landed on the planet Ione just outside the city of the same name, a market town that held the majority of the planet's population. It was a small planet that served as a crossing from a lot of places to a lot of other places which made Ione a great city to get lost or found in depending on what you were after. Prit had a couple goals in mind while there, first was appropriate clothing for Saluk, second was information. The problem was, she was coming in empty handed. The SSA had endorsed gold coins as a universal currency but bartering with whatever you had was still acceptable in most places. She had neither at the moment. She was supposed to have come away from the last job with a satchel of gold that would have taken her wherever she wanted to go. Now she was going to need to use more than her negotiation skills to get what they needed.

She wasn't sure how Saluk was going to respond to what she was willing to do here, but he'd have to get over it if he wanted to continue on this journey with her. She landed softly outside of the planet's main market between a thousand other ships, no one would spot hers as anything special unless they were determined to find her. She didn't think she had anything to worry about, the Sabitarions didn't know who she was, even if they knew she'd escaped with one of their gladiators they'd be unable to chase her down. Barius was mad, obviously, but he wasn't likely to come looking here, he was more the type that would wait for her to show up in his territory.

"I need to change," she said, standing up.

Saluk stood and looked uncomfortable.

His shyness was adorable and made her itch to push it. "Don't worry, I'll be discreet and quick." She pushed a button that shuttered the front window for privacy then opened a cabinet and pulled out what she was after. He watched her every move as if she were about to lash out at him with sharp teeth and it made her desire to tease him run rampant. With her back to him she dropped her shorts and pulled her shirt over her head.

He gasped behind her, and she smiled to herself. She was wearing underwear, he wasn't getting an eyeful of ass, just her back, and admittedly a lot of skin. She didn't bother with bras; her chest wasn't that glorious. She bent and slipped first her bionic leg through a hole and then her other leg into a pant, pulling the tight fabric up her body slower than necessary. Up and up until she was able to slip her arms through the long sleeves and she was covered in a matte spandex material that would blend with any shadow. Next, she bent forward, sticking out her spandex-clad ass and slipped on soft-soled leather shoes that were perfect for sneaking around soundlessly. She straightened and turned as she threw a black cape over her shoulders. It had a large hood and a few discreet pockets. It also hung to her feet and would provide necessary cover for her exposed bionic leg.

Saluk looked like he was about to explode, his eyes glued to the floor in front of him had her wondering how much of her show he'd actually seen. She'd be disappointed if he hadn't caught it all.

"I'm going to get what we need, you should probably wait here," she said as she adjusted the cape around her body. "You'll call too much attention to us."

His gaze shot to hers and a fire was burning there that made her catch her breath. Maybe he *had* seen her little display, she decided, and had a brief worry that she'd taken it too far, pushed him to a point that she shouldn't have.

"No," he hissed.

"No?" she questioned, raising an eyebrow and trying to remain casual even as her hand reached toward a blade she knew was tucked into one of the pockets of her cape. Her eye went to work assessing him for danger. It told her that his heart rate was elevated, his body heat was high, and his muscles were tense. It told her that he was highly likely to attack, and that he was aroused.

"I am your bodyguard," he added firmly.

She relaxed. "Yeah, and you look like you went from teen to adult overnight and are still wearing your jammies, so no, you can't follow me. I need to be unseen."

"Why, why do you need to be unseen?" he asked suspiciously.

She rolled her eyes. "Look, you know what I am. And obviously if I had enough money, I wouldn't be working for an asshole like Barius. So I have to go get you something to wear and I don't plan to pay for it. At least not with my own money."

"I can get my own things," he said with a frown.

"Oh yeah, big guy, how?"

His jaw clenched as she met his eyes with a challenge.

"Fine, but I *am* following you, I'll keep a distance, no one will know that we're together."

She knew it was still risky, but she could see he wasn't going to accept no.

"Fine, just stay back no matter what happens."

"Fine," he agreed.

Prit opened the hatch and paused as a new thought occurred to her. "What if some of your kind are here?" An emotion she didn't want to look at too deeply welled up. "You could catch yourself a direct flight home."

"They don't fly," he said as if it were obvious.

Relief spread through Prit as she descended into the frigid air of Ione.

It was a cold desert planet. Hardly any vegetation, even less rainfall and a weak star that lit up the sky for a mere eight hours a day during its summer. Right now it was twilight and the chill was intense. If she remembered right, this was their fall so it would get even colder very quickly, she was glad she had her cloak to huddle under. She flipped the hood up and felt bad for Saluk in his tiny shirt and sandals.

But he'd been the one to insist on joining her, so she didn't hesitate, just hurried forward in shadow, feeling his presence behind her. She avoided everyone as she made her way through the ship lot, but she wasn't going to be able to continue that as soon as she passed through the gates into the busy market city. She had to blink her eye off or she'd be so inundated with information about the many people she passed she would get a headache. Something she often did when she wasn't feeling in danger of any kind. She could turn it back on just as easily to assess who and what was around her.

She'd need to steal enough cash to buy him clothes, fuel for the ship and food for them both. Then she'd be seeking out information and she'd need to steal something to trade for that as well. If she could find out what Barius was interested in other than that damn necklace, she could offer it up as a consolation to her failure. The last thing she wanted to do was go back for the same take twice, that was something she'd learned long ago about being a thief. If you missed it on the first try, going back was insanity. She'd known others to make that mistake and spend the rest of their lives in various prisons—if not dead—for the mistake.

She had to wonder if she wasn't the first thief to go after the necklace, why else would they have it alarmed? Anger filled her at the realization that Barius had offered her such a high payment because he knew that it would be trickier, that he'd already sent people who had failed. If he'd warned her, maybe she would have been successful, would have approached more carefully.

She was an idiot for not being able to see past the promise of gold to the reality of the job he'd offered.

Prit slipped past the walls with a new determination to find out what she could about the necklace, why was Barius so determined to get it? What made it so special that the Sabitarions were protecting it so thoroughly?

As soon as she was within the walls of the city she let that line of thinking float to the back of her mind and focused on the task at hand. She disappeared into a crowd, letting herself become a part of it as it went along. This was a familiar technique, and she did it well because of her small stature. She would slip and slide around a large group picking easy pockets then disappear before anyone even knew what had happened.

This particular group was made up of New Earthers on vacation judging by their wide eyes and giggling comments. No doubt they were uber rich, and this was their idea of slumming it. They'd buy overpriced souvenirs and when they got home they'd brag about how they'd helped a poor family out.

In reality any shop that was on the main tourist shopping street was owned by one of five people, none of them poor and all of them with blood on their hands. Though they did have families, they were just rich and entitled. The people running the shops in this part of the city did well for themselves too, taking home a portion of the profits to keep their families living a good life, though there was always the overhanging threat from whatever family they worked under to pay a heavy tithe or be butchered and replaced.

Prit didn't resent their way of life, but she didn't shop on this street either. She just came here to make her own money.

Saluk shivered as he followed Prit, not used to a cold planet. He easily pushed his discomfort aside though and concentrated on her movements. She was like a shadow and more than once he briefly lost sight of her and almost panicked before he found her again. He didn't like this place, didn't understand what he was seeing around him. It was unlike anything he'd ever known. The sheer number of people was overwhelming but so were the noises and smells. It wasn't unpleasant, smelling of foods he was unfamiliar with, but it was strong. Everyone seemed to be talking around him as well, there was a feeling of joyous urgency to those walking in and out of shops and booths, as if they were in a rush to spend money.

He was impressed with Prit's skills but wasn't completely sure about her goal until one group that was already behind her and him started talking loudly about a lost bag of coins.

"You little thief," he whispered with a smile. Group after group she slid in and stayed with them past a shop or two then she was around and on to the next, never detected, never questioned. She was amazing. He kept a very close eye so he wouldn't lose her completely but kept a distance as promised, no one would assume they were together.

The darkness of night was creeping close, but the small street remained crowded and he was definitely drawing a lot of attention to himself, as she'd predicted he would. People eyed him with varying degrees of curiosity and pity, he looked ridiculous, he knew that. At least his fearsome face kept the looks from becoming stares or questions, he wasn't exactly approachable with the scowl on his scarred face.

There was a wide variety of species here he'd noticed right away, but he didn't hold out hope for any of his own kind. He'd told her that they didn't fly, and it was true. The Haladian people were content in their existence without technology. It helped that Halador was off beyond the edges of the settled expanse of space. It was considered a primitive planet by most and they had nothing to offer visitors, so none came.

He hadn't decided that was a bad thing in his twenty years off of the planet. Though in the last few days for the first time ever, he had found something outside of Halador that he thought was worth a damn.

And she was currently stealing gold from unsuspecting tourists. He almost laughed at the absurdity of the fact.

After a while Saluk became aware that Prit was being followed. The tall Silarian stayed far enough back that it didn't seem Prit noticed, but Saluk was even farther back and could clearly see the male's intentions as he watched her make her way through the crowds. Silarians were very similar to humans in appearance aside from their red skin, they could pass for New Earthers. Not Haladians, his people were far too tall and broad to be mistaken for humans. Silarians were short and thin, almost spindly in comparison. The Silarian following Prit was dressed as a traveler, much the same as half the others they passed. A simple suit of a muted color and a cape to work against the chill. His bright blue eyes darted around but always went back to her, making his focus obvious to Saluk.

When Prit took a sudden turn down an alley, the male was a step behind and Saluk panicked. He shoved through a group and rushed after the two, fearing for her life and not caring if he drew attention to her anymore.

He shouldn't have worried. By the time he got there she was standing back from the male's falling body.

Had she just killed someone?

"Hey, help me hide this body," she said with far too much calm.

"What happened?"

"I knocked him out for a while, so he won't keep following me. It's not a big deal, just a sign that we need to move off of the main street," she grumbled. "Linard doesn't appreciate me pickpocketing his customers and he owns everything north of here."

Saluk helped her move the man into a shadow behind a pile of refuse.

"How did he know?"

"They watch everything on their street."

"So they'll know you did this."

"Hopefully not before the guy wakes up," she said and grabbed Saluk's hand. "Come on, time to shop anyway, I think I got enough for what we need."

"But you just said—"

"I said we had to get off the main street market, we aren't tourists anyway, we don't buy from The Five."

"The Five?"

"The main market street is run by five families, each of them has a certain section. Each one takes more than their fair share of profit from the sales they make off of dumb tourists. We are going where the shops only charge what they should, and they keep most of the profit. There's still someone they are paying for protection against The Five, but from what I know, it's someone who plays fairer."

Saluk shook his head, overwhelmed by what she was saying and hating this place all the more. His time in the gladiator prison hadn't prepared him for what she described.

She pulled him until they came out into a brighter-lit street. This place was full of color and life, but nearly entirely made up of Ionites, the creatures native to this planet. They were a fur-covered race, not surprising for such a cold planet, their faces were flattened with whiskers jutting out from beside noses and sharp teeth held within large jaws, carnivores. They weren't known for being welcoming to strangers, which is probably why they kept off of the main tourist street. He'd fought a few of them as gladiators; they were fierce and he didn't like that they were surrounding him and Prit, but she didn't seem concerned at all, in fact she was more relaxed here than she had been on the main street.

Everyone they passed gave him a curious look and many gave Prit a wide berth making him wonder if they knew how sneaky a thief she was. She led him through a narrow alley and up another street to a small shop, just a tent really, with a wall held aside to show its contents. A woman stood there, about the height of Prit, covered in an orange shade of fur with big green eyes and a cautious set to her mouth as she watched them walk toward her shop. She crossed her arms over her front and stood wide-legged, blocking them from entering.

"Shalayla," Prit said perkily. "My big guy here needs some appropriate clothing."

"Barius sent me an update on you," Shalayla said quietly, still not moving to let them in.

Saluk darted his gaze around, making sure no one was listening to what he assumed was about to be a fight.

Prit looked down at her fingernails as if she didn't care in the least what Barius might have said. "Oh, he is a pissy thing, isn't he?"

"He's a dangerous fucking monster, Prit, what the hell is wrong with you?" The woman's voice broke with real concern, and she dropped her arms. "Prit, what have you gotten yourself into?"

"Let us in, let him shop and we can talk over a beer," Prit said, giving the woman a hug.

Saluk relaxed, realizing the anger this woman carried was out of concern and not hate. Though it was hard to tell with the inscrutable feline features.

The two women walked into the tent and Saluk followed, giving one last glance up and down the street but no one seemed to be paying them any attention.

Shalayla closed the curtain to give them privacy anyway and they headed further in. It was actually a very impressive little shop, going far back and stuffed full of all kinds of clothing.

"Find what you need, big guy," Prit said, slapping him on the back.

He didn't even know where to start.

CHAPTER NINE

Prit followed Shalayla to the back of the shop where they could talk privately but she stood where she could keep an eye on Saluk. She wasn't worried he'd do anything wrong or run off, but she *was* worried that he would get overwhelmed or confused in the overpacked shop. Shalayla had clothing from every species that visited Ione, it would be interesting to see what he picked.

The look that had been on his face when he came around the alley corner to find her with a passed-out enforcer had warmed her. He'd had death in his eyes and his hands were fisted, ready to start attacking anything necessary to save her. She hadn't needed any help, obviously, but it was endearing to know that he was willing to do violence for her. What more could a girl ask? To be honest it had made her kind of hot for him.

Her eyes traveled up and down his tall and thick form, the grey sweats he had borrowed from Josh did nothing to hide what he was working with, and she thought anaconda was a very apt description.

Shalayla jabbed her with an elbow. "Where did you pick up

the hottie?" she asked, obviously following Prit's gaze to Saluk browsing the shelves.

Prit took the beer she held out. "Broke him out of the Sabitarion gladiator prison."

Shalayla stopped mid-drink and gave her a raised eyebrow. "I thought The Shadow didn't trade in people."

"I didn't steal him, I saved him. They shoved me in his cell as a reward for him and punishment for me," she said with a laugh.

Shalayla gave her a look full of concern and a little envy.

"He's a gentle thing, didn't even try to touch me, and I managed to break us both out in record time."

"Of course you did. Still, he's scary as fuck with those scars all over the side of his face. Surviving that isn't gentle."

Prit nodded, "We all do what we have to in order to survive, don't we?"

"Indeed," Shalayla agreed and they both drank.

Prit had first met Shalayla right after she'd run from the New Earth military. This had been her first stop, thinking she might be able to find work. What she'd found was a lot of offers for her body and not much else. No one believed she could work hard or fly well, and she'd been too damn close to taking up someone on their offer for a bag of gold in trade for a night with her, which is what had forced her to discover her knack for thievery.

That's when she'd met Shalayla, desperate and at the end of her rope she'd picked a pocket right in front of Shalayla's store and the crafty woman had caught it. The unfortunate mark hadn't of course.

Shalayla had confronted her with a smile and a compliment, then bought her a beer. They'd become friends immediately and Shalayla offered her a place to stay for a few days to figure out her life. Shalayla had introduced her to some people who were interested in retrieving items she had the skills to get and that's how she'd become connected with the criminal underground of the SSA.

"I'm taking him home in exchange for acting as my bodyguard for a bit. I figure it can't hurt to have backup when I negotiate with Barius for my failure."

"Smart, Barius is pretty pissed from what I hear. His men came through looking for you this morning. What were you after on Sabit for him?"

"Just some stupid necklace, didn't look that valuable to me. The Sabitarion princess had it on at the celebration and it was alarmed," she added the last with a scowl.

"Alarmed necklace?" Shalayla said thoughtfully. "Why the hell would they bother?"

"I have no idea, but it looked like nothing special. A big pink diamond set in silver with pearls going around the neck. Looked like every piece of jewelry those types wear. Definitely worth a bag of gold, but not something to be so worked up about not getting."

Shalayla shook her head. "Doesn't make sense, there has to be more to it. Want me to ask around before you confront Barius?"

"Yeah, if there's something special about that necklace then I need to know." Maybe she could go to Barius with more than a hope of placation, if she knew why he wanted the damn thing.

"You two need a place to stay?"

"Nah, we'll be good on my ship, it's as good as any place to stay hidden out in the lot. I'll come back in the morning to check in before we take off though. What do I owe you?"

They both turned to see what Saluk had picked out. A pair of sturdy boots, leather leggings and a matching vest. He had a heavy cape held up for inspection as well.

"I need a weapon," he said throwing the cape over his arm.

"You *are* a weapon," Shalayla said with a laugh. "But I've got a few back here, come take a look."

Saluk picked out a sword and a dagger, then a belt to hold them and smiled with pure joy as he handled the steel weapons.

"Boys and their toys," Shalayla said as they watched him toss the dagger in the air and catch it then thrust forward at an invisible opponent.

Prit paid Shalayla, who did not give her a good deal just because they were friends, and they left the place with Saluk wearing more appropriate clothes and bearing weapons. He moved more comfortably and with more confidence, but his fierceness remained, and she noticed a lot of people they passed giving him a second wary glance. She felt herself relax a bit, knowing that she wasn't alone, that beside her walked a man who was more than capable of handling an attack, she couldn't remember the last time she'd walked down a street and not had every sense on high alert.

"We can eat up here and then head back to the ship for the night."

"Shalayla is going to find information about the necklace Barius wants?" Saluk asked.

"Yeah," she said, surprised he'd been able to hear their conversation, they'd been quiet, but they also hadn't been whispering, she just didn't think he was paying attention.

"Smart move."

"I'm a smart girl," she said with a wink and led him to a bar, *Intergalactic Scallywag*. It was decorated like an Old Earth version of a pirate ship complete with mermaid statues and a chest of fake gold. She activated her eye as they entered and did a quick scan of the place. It was mostly locals, Ionites, but there were a few others, all looking skulky and hunched over drinks and meals. No one came here to be seen which is why she chose it.

Prit sat at the bar and Saluk took a seat beside her, but didn't relax, his body clearly on the alert for danger.

The owner of the bar, a New Earther named Fallen walked over with a big smile. She was a tall woman with bleached blonde hair braided down her back and large brown eyes that made her look deceptively innocent, she was a skilled fighter and not afraid of getting in trouble for shooting anyone in her bar who caused a problem. Fallen was the adopted daughter of one of The Five and she ran a strict place, no violence inside, everyone got to eat and drink in peace, or she'd shoot them herself, no questions asked. Her version of walking the plank, Prit supposed.

"The Shadow is in town, I suppose that's why I heard so many tourists were finding lighter pockets today," Fallen said.

Prit shrugged, she knew Fallen wasn't judging but that didn't mean she'd admit to any wrongdoing. "Hey, Fallen, I'll take a beer and a burger, and the big guy will probably take three," she said with a laugh.

Fallen nodded, gave Saluk an appraising look, then raised an eyebrow at Prit. Prit gave a nod, indicating she'd keep him in line and Fallen walked off to get the beers.

"You can relax, no one here is going to try anything. This is a safe zone for everyone, no one wants to mess with that."

"You come here a lot," Saluk said, more a statement than a question.

"Are you hitting on me?" she asked with a laugh, trying to relax him before Fallen decided he was too much of a risk to allow in her place.

His face heated and he turned away to stare at Fallen pouring beers. "You know people here," he said.

"Yeah, I come here a lot, it's a safe place for people like me."

"Women on the run?" Saluk asked.

"Criminals and thieves," Fallen said as she set the beers down. "And I'm the captain."

"Yes, you are," Prit agreed with a wink and held up her beer in salute before taking a long sip.

As they drank their beer and waited for food, they sat in companionable silence until Prit couldn't help breaking it.

"Are you regretting your choice to be saved by a thief yet?"

He shook his head. "I regret a lot of choices I've made in my life; this is not one of them."

"Tell me one," she prompted impulsively.

"One thing I regret?"

"Yeah."

He looked thoughtful for a moment and finished his beer. Prit indicated for Fallen to pour him another. When Saluk had it in hand he turned to her with a serious look on his face.

"I was a confident young man, I thought I was invincible, thought I could overcome any obstacle. So when it was time for me to prove my manhood as is tradition on my planet, I chose something that was harder than it needed to be."

"That sounds intense."

"It was. I would be gone for a full moon cycle, I would climb to the top of the snowy mountain, kill a masat." He paused and looked at her. "That's a large creature with thick fur, big teeth and claws, a cave-dwelling beast that eats meat."

She nodded understanding.

"Once killed, I would prepare it there on the top of the mountain, I would fight the wind and snow and cold to smoke and prep the meat for my clan and the pelt for my mate."

Prit bristled at the mention of mate, did he have a wife? Children, perhaps, that she was keeping him from? She felt a prickle of guilt at the thought, and she downed the rest of her beer and asked for another.

"If I succeeded, I would return to the village with the meat carried on a sled I'd have made from the few trees that grew that high and wearing the pelt as a show of my victory."

He paused there, his eyes distant.

"Did you?" she asked quietly.

"My older brother was my watchman. There's always one who follows on the journey and makes sure that there is no cheating and to interfere only in case of imminent death. I found an old masat, a huge male with only one eye and patches of fur missing. Obviously he had fought and won many battles and I thought he would be a worthy opponent for me. I knew he would be my greatest victory and would prove my virility, my strength, and my right to take a mate and make a family."

Prit was riveted to the story and jumped when Fallen came over with their food. "Thank you."

"This smells amazing," Saluk said and began eating, his story apparently forgotten.

Prit wanted to beg him to finish the tale but the way he devoured the first burger told her he was hungrier than she'd realized. She was going to have to remember that a big guy like him needed a lot of food. She mulled over what he had said as she ate her burger. It didn't sound like he'd had a mate, or children. But he must have had someone in mind, someone he was trying to win with the effort he was putting in. Prit pictured a large and beautiful woman of his clan. She probably had huge breasts to go along with her height to match his. She was probably quite literally twice the woman Prit was.

But why did she care? It's not as if she was interested in the man beside her. Was she? She slid her peripheral gaze over to him. He was tall and strong, two things she appreciated in a male partner. He didn't intimidate her with those scars and scowls, but she liked how they intimidated others. His hair was shiny and clean, his eyes bright and watchful. Amazingly, he was kind and gentle under the hard exterior.

She could imagine doing all sorts of naughty things with him, especially after seeing him in those sweatpants, damn.

She shifted in her seat trying to get her heating body under control. Maybe she'd consider a little roll with him before she dropped him off, no reason not to if he wasn't mated and she was single as fuck.

Because that's what she wanted to be, she reminded herself, she'd always had plenty of offers, she just had never met a partner she was interested in for more than a night or two of fun.

Prit pondered the possibilities of Saluk being into it as they ate and drank in a comfortable silence that Prit usually didn't enjoy unless she was alone.

"Well, aren't you a pretty thing," a man said, coming up beside her with a lopsided grin, far too close and reeking of a substantial amount of alcohol. He was dressed in casual cotton pants and shirt, with short black hair peeking out from under an old cap.

Her eye assessed him quickly.

Species: New Earther
   Sex: Male
   Age: Forty-eight
   Danger: Minimal, inebriated, no weapons detected

"No," she said and turned away from him.

He reached out and touched her chin, not taking the hint. Her hand went directly to his crotch. She grabbed his junk so hard he squeaked and his face turned bright red, spittle forming at the corners of his mouth.

"I said no, and if you don't walk away now, Fallen is going to have a problem with you."

The guy's eyes darted to the woman in question. She was glaring at him down the barrel of a gun behind the bar. Fallen didn't allow any shit in her place, and that included men who couldn't take no for an answer. Next to her Saluk was growling but he didn't move to protect her, which she appreciated. She didn't need help with a worthless peon like this.

"S-sorry ma'am," the man whispered, and she let him go. He fell to the floor and a couple of his buddies were quickly there to help him stand, all mumbling apologies to her as well.

Fallen put the gun down and lifted a hand to indicate for her security to remove the man. He'd probably get a punch in the gut outside and banned from the place for a while. It was harsh but it kept the place from becoming another fight club like so many bars on Ione outside of the main strip tended to be.

Prit turned back to her meal and noticed Saluk sitting stiff by her side still.

"Chill," she whispered because Fallen was eyeing him too.

"I forgot to watch," he said quietly. "I forgot to be your bodyguard. I should have seen him approaching, I should have stopped him before he uttered one single word to you."

"No worries, we should be safe here, we shouldn't have to watch. That's why I come here."

He frowned, obviously not convinced but he went back to eating, just not as indulgently this time. They finished quickly after that, the peace ruined, and Prit paid Fallen.

No matter what she told Saluk, she was always watchful and so she noticed when a shadowed figure at the back of the bar stood right after them and started to make his way toward the door at the same time they did. She was already reaching for her weapon so she'd have it ready as soon as she stepped outside when Saluk grabbed her arm and pushed her forward out the door, then pulled her behind him and faced the door with his own dagger drawn.

Apparently, he had noticed their follower as well. She was just about to complain about him not letting her defend herself when the door opened and the man walked out.

Saluk grabbed him quick as lightning and held the dagger under his chin. "Why are you following her?"

"Ha, I am following you," the Tradjulian spat.

Prit moved from behind Saluk and let her eye assess the man.

Species: Tradjulian
Sex: Tradjulians have no sex they reproduce asexually every hundred years.
Age: Ninety
Danger: High, weapon detected

"What are you after him for?" Prit demanded.

"Bounty on his head. He is the escaped gladiator from Sabit, isn't he? Not likely two Haladians are wandering around off planet."

"Shit," Prit said just as the Tradjulian pulled a weapon from his back and jabbed Saluk in the stomach. The sound of the laser weapon was sharp and as Saluk jolted with its power, Prit lunged forward with her knife.

Saluk crumpled and Prit leaped to throw herself over him, her first instinct to protect him from further harm. Her knife was thrust out as she moved and it sliced the Tradjulian's thick neck as she went down on top of Saluk. Purple blood sprayed out of the gaping wound she'd inflicted, and his lipless mouth opened on a silent scream, his vocal cords having been severed.

She smiled; she knew how to kill quickly and quietly on a crowded city street.

He collapsed next to Saluk, and she searched the body for the bounty card. She found it stuffed into his shirt pocket, a thin white plastic card and when she pressed the corner an image of Saluk appeared and turned around showing his full body dressed much as she'd seen him when she'd entered his cell; leather kilt, lace up leather boots, and no shirt. But in this image he was obviously just out of battle, covered in sweat and blood, a look of deep anger on his face and a large axe in his hand. He was absolutely terrifying and not at all the image of the man she'd gotten to know.

She stuffed the card in her pocket, then turned back to Saluk, praying he was alive.

She pressed her hand to his chest and when she felt it rise with breath she wanted to cry in relief.

CHAPTER TEN

A crowd was gathering, drawn to the violence, and Prit looked around for a familiar face of any kind to help her. She'd never be able to move the huge man on her own.

"At least you waited until you were outside," Fallen said from the bar doorway. "Get out, all of you move on," she demanded, and the crowd dispersed, used to her authority. "Take the dead body out back," she ordered one of her guards and knelt beside Prit and Saluk. "Is he dead, too?"

"No, just stunned, they want him alive." Thankfully.

"You're in some kind of trouble, girl." It wasn't a question.

Prit looked into the older woman's face and grimaced. "What's new?"

Fallen shook her head. "Take him to the back room," she ordered another guard.

Prit followed along as two of Fallen's guards lifted Saluk and carried him around the side of the building and through a door, down a hall and into a small room. It had a bed and a sink, that was about it. They dropped him roughly on the bed and she scowled at them as they left.

Prit hurried to his side and ran a hand over his face, moving his hair out of his eyes and touching the scars that lined the left side of his face. "Don't even think about giving up now, that was just a little zap," she whispered to him as she traced the scars over his lips.

Being this close to him without his gaze on her gave her the freedom to investigate every slope and freckle on his skin. It was incredibly intimate and she forced herself to step back before she was tempted to do something ridiculous like press her lips to his and see if they were as soft as she thought they would be.

"You didn't have to try and save me, you big dumb brute," she said to distract herself. "But I owe you one now, I suppose." A few particularly sweaty and fun ways to repay the favor popped into her head and she pushed them back out with thoughts of his history.

She wanted to hear the rest of his story. Was this face scar from that quest he'd been on? Were the scars why he regretted the quest? Did he believe he was ruined somehow? She had come to appreciate the scars, they made him frightening in a delightful way and attractive on a primal level. Even if he hadn't just proven that he'd die to protect her, she would have believed him capable of anything, judging by what he'd obviously already been through.

Fallen walked into the room with a bowl and a rag. "How's the wound?"

"Shit," she hadn't even checked it. She moved from his face to his stomach and unbuttoned the vest. There was a shock mark there, a black indication of the volts he'd taken and a gash of ripped flesh from the impact.

"Wow, that looks bad, he's lucky to be alive," Fallen commented.

"He's tough," Prit said with a hint of pride in her voice that she really didn't deserve to have. He didn't belong to her in any way.

"Wash it and wait, those types of shocks take a while to wear off but if he's still breathing at this point, then he should be okay."

Hardly comforting, but Prit did as Fallen suggested. She took the damp rag and began to clean around the wound. Some of the skin sloughed right off—blackened and crackling—leaving behind a red and angry layer of skin that had to hurt like hell. But it needed to be done and best when he was unconscious.

The bigger issue was the gash, it was deep and still oozing blood even after she'd wiped it gently. She dabbed at it to try and get a better idea of its depth. His body jerked and her eyes shot up to his face.

Still unconscious.

She let her eye assess the wound now that it was clear.

Wound: minor laceration and burning
  Patient: pain induced sleep
  Treatment: clean, salve, and cover wound, rest body
  Prognosis: good, victim will recover full function with scarring

Prit gave a relieved sigh, no sign of damage to anything vital.

Fallen handed her a small pot of green goo. "This should work well on the burned skin as well as the wound."

"Thank you," Prit said, taking the jar and applying the goo generously to Saluk's skin. He was so muscled she couldn't imagine anything hurting him, but if he were invincible he wouldn't be unconscious right now, and that was a sobering thought. He was mortal too, no matter his immense size and history. And every moment he was with her, he was in more danger because King Lenkin had put out a bounty on him.

Hunters were searching for him and the only place he may be able to hide is his home planet.

Prit took a steadying breath and focused back on his body, she may have let her fingers linger a bit over his abs, trailing down farther than necessary to appreciate the feel of him while she had the chance.

Fallen cleared her throat behind Prit.

"What are you going to do? They put a hefty bounty on his head, I checked. He must be quite the gladiator for them to want him back so badly. No mention of you though, did they even get your name?" she laughed.

Prit smiled. "No, they didn't. They probably expected me to crumple with the threat of this big guy and tell them everything, didn't even attempt to question me before they threw me in his cell."

"Underestimating women is a common weak point across the known universe, Shadow or not," Fallen said then gave her a serious look. "He's not safe anywhere in the systems, you should take him straight back to Halador, it might be the best place for him to hide. Bounty hunters aren't likely to make a trip like that, even for the kind of gold the Sabits are promising."

Prit hated that Fallen was speaking the thoughts she'd just had. "Doesn't make for a very good bodyguard, does it," Prit admitted.

"I think he needs you more than you need him at this point."

Prit smiled down at the scarred face. Nothing new there.

"What are you doing with a bodyguard anyway?" Fallen demanded. "What are you running from? I know it isn't King Lenkin."

"Besides the usual?" Prit said with a grin. Fallen just arched a dark brow, not in the mood for Prit's personality. "I failed to get something for Barius."

"Barius. Pritalia, are you insane? Why the hell did you take a job from Barius?"

"Limited options," she said honestly. "But I swear, there's no reason for him to look for me here, he probably thinks I'm still hiding in the Eludian star system where my dad's threats of violence will protect me."

"Maybe you should be."

"My father's idea of protecting me involves marriage, you know that. I would rather take my chances with Barius."

"You are a woman of many enemies," Fallen said with a slight smile.

"Which is why you love me," Prit laughed. "Don't worry, as soon as he's awake we'll get out of your hair. You know I'd never bring trouble to your doorstep on purpose."

"I know that, Prit, and no rush, I can keep you both safe here until you're ready to leave. You know you could collect on the bounty."

"I don't deal in people," she said firmly.

Fallen nodded and left.

Prit took her time bandaging Saluk's wound, once again letting her hands roam a little and appreciate his firm body. When that was done, she sat beside him and stared at his face. It was so calm and almost soft in sleep. His usual look of annoyance and untrusting surprise was lifted. She almost missed it. She loved to shock and tease him, she wanted to keep pushing him as far as she could. In the short time she'd known the man, she'd become quite addicted to making him uneasy, wondering when he'll finally snap and what he might do with those big hands when he did.

Prit picked up one, stroking her fingers along his and biting her lip as she felt the callouses there, imagining them rubbing against sensitive parts of herself. These hands that had no doubt killed so many, could he use them gently to bring pleasure, would he be skilled with them in bringing her body to life?

She had a feeling he would, and she couldn't stop herself from bringing one hand up to her face and pressing her lips to his palm. "Maybe before I drop you off we can find out," she whispered and set his hand back down on the bed.

Unsure of how long he would be out, she decided to take advantage of the opportunity for a bit of rest herself and crawled up carefully next to him to sleep. She laid her head on his shoulder, careful to keep from touching his wounds, she slid one leg over his thigh and set a hand on his stomach. It thrilled her to be so intimate with him.

She closed her eyes as his body began to vibrate gently; even in his condition he was attuned to her presence, or at least the presence of someone who might need soothing too. Her last thought before sleep claimed her mind was that she hoped Jet was doing okay.

CHAPTER ELEVEN

Saluk woke slowly, his body hurt, and he tried to remember who he'd fought that had gotten such a good hit in. He came out of the coliseum beat up on a regular basis, though always the winner, and always with blood on his hands because he was forced to kill or be killed, and he hated every minute of it. Surviving only because he'd promised his brother he would, determined to keep his word somehow. Even at the expense of others forced into the same situation.

He started to feel his body, stretching gently to see how bad it was going to hurt to get up and pee like he desperately wanted to right now.

A moan beside him as he stretched had his eyes flying open, and when he saw the dark head resting on his shoulder he remembered where he was. No gladiator battle but an attack outside a bar is what had injured him and beside him lay his savior and possible angel of destruction. He stared up at the ceiling, unwilling to disturb her, she didn't get enough rest, he reasoned, but in truth he loved the feel of her small body pressed against him far too much to make it stop sooner than absolutely necessary.

She didn't see him as a monster whose only value was the death he could bring in the arena. Right from the start she'd assessed him as not a threat, she hadn't judged him by his appearance, she'd helped him. She had offered him a way home in exchange for nothing more than a little safety of her own. He'd nearly failed at that, *had* failed. She'd had to save him, it was unthinkable.

No one had ever saved him. And he'd never saved anyone else.

His mind drifted to his brother and the last thing he needed to do for him.

"What are you thinking about that has your face twisted up so much?"

Prit's voice startled him and he moved to give her space now that she was awake. He groaned at the harsh stab of pain in his stomach and she jumped to her knees, pushing his chest down and looking at the wound.

"Careful, dude, you got really hurt back there."

Her hands were soft and gentle as she pressed his chest, as if she could stop him from moving if he wanted to, she weighed nothing.

"I just moved a little too fast, I'm fine."

"You aren't fine, you took a major hit, and you were bleeding."

"Yes, I'd like to return the favor to the man who did it," he said with a frown.

"I killed him," she said without emotion.

It made him sad to know her life had been one of such harshness that killing didn't make her blink. It wasn't the life he would wish for anyone. He wanted to wrap her in his arms and protect her from the life she had been forced into. Wanted her to not need to do such things in order to survive.

But would she want that? She hadn't ever given him an

indication that she lived a life she didn't enjoy. Perhaps she was happy to steal and kill and wander. The life of a thief in space is what she'd chosen over the Princess of Elude hadn't she?

"He was a bounty hunter," she added. "He was after you and there will definitely be more looking, so we are going to need to be careful." She looked away from him and sighed. "I think I should take you to Halador straight away."

"But you need me," he said quickly. "You need a bodyguard to deal with Barius," he added.

She looked back at his face and frowned. "Not really, I mean I was happy to take along some extra muscle but really, I'll just figure out what made the necklace so special and then I'll negotiate out of it, like anything else. He isn't that big a threat to me, I can fight better than most," she said with a wink.

Saluk didn't like it, not at all. She was going to be in added danger just because she wanted to protect him first. He couldn't let her do that. "No, I will go with you. I will do what I bargained a ride for. This changes nothing."

She slipped off the bed and shook her head. "No worries, I made the bargain, and I am changing it. You get a ride home in exchange for your pleasant company, nothing else is necessary."

He frowned at her, no one had ever described his company as pleasant. Not even his brother.

"Yeah, that smile, makes it all worthwhile," she laughed. "I'm going to get us some food and see if Fallen has any information. We'll need to see Shalayla too before we head back to the ship."

Prit left the room in a hurry, and he slowly sat up, inspecting what lay under the bandages. The skin was red and sore but aside from the one rather deep wound, it was all minimal damage. The wound was oozing but healing already thanks to whatever Prit had put on it and he knew from experience that in a couple days a wound like that would be nothing more than a scar, added to the collection. Knowing her hands had taken care of him as he'd been passed out left him with an oddly warm feeling. She could have left him for dead on the street, cut her losses and left. Why hadn't she abandoned him? She owed him nothing.

He owed her everything.

There was no way he was letting her meet up with this Barius guy alone, no matter what she said.

He replaced the bandages with some clean ones he found by the sink and Prit came back quickly with a tray of sandwiches and coffee.

"Breakfast? how long was I out for?" Could it really be the next morning already?

"We slept for a good six hours. Sun will be up soon and the crowds will be good for us to travel, better to be unnoticed in a crowd if you can't guarantee darkness," she said with a grin.

His lips lifted in a half smile for his little thief's words of wisdom.

"You'll need to keep your head down, you have a wanted face now," she added.

"So we have time to eat, maybe use a bathroom?" he asked, a little uncomfortable.

"Yeah, through there to the right," she said, motioning to the door she'd come through. She sat and started in on a cup of coffee, closing her eyes and making sounds of delight that had him anxious for a whole different reason.

By the time he returned to the room she was done with her coffee and half a sandwich.

"Those two are yours, big guy. I know you have a good appetite."

He sat and grabbed one, watching her carefully, trying to decide how to approach what he wanted to say.

"I am honor-bound to help you because you saved me. First

from the prison of Sabit, and second here, on the street where a bounty hunter would have taken me back to Sabit. I will repay that the only way I can. I will see that you make it through your meeting and negotiations with Barius." He paused and gave her a serious look. "To do anything else would be shameful and I could not return to my clan with honor."

She gave him a look that clearly said she wanted to argue but she didn't.

"Fine, I wouldn't want to do anything to detract from your honor," she said with a wink. "When we walk out of here, you'll need to cover yourself and make yourself as small as possible, stay close to me." She laughed. "Try to blend in, big guy, be a shadow."

Satisfaction filled him. She wasn't going to refute his ability to watch her back. In that moment he realized how big the fear was that she would dismiss him from her life because he had failed her outside of the bar. He had been surprised by the strength of the attacker's weapon, overtaken, and injured. He had left her to the mercy of someone else and yet she still accepted him as bodyguard. He would take this chance to prove that he could save her too. He was a warrior of Halador, a gladiator of Sabit. He had defeated monsters twice his size, and this tiny woman had killed his attacker while he crumpled in the street.

He wanted to prove his worth to her more than he wanted to survive to carry out his promise to his brother and that realization made him stop and stare at her with a new realization.

Was she his?

His gaze swept over her body, slender and beautiful, it attracted him, as it would any male with a pulse he supposed, but was there more? In Halador when two people found each other attractive they happily came together for pleasure, but it wasn't until a bond stronger than family was formed that there was a true mating. They would each forsake their family, leave the home of their parents and siblings and truly become one with another, a forever and deep bonding of the two and they would create their own family. The female would change her name, Prit would become Prituk.

Prituk, the word slid through his mind leaving behind a burn of satisfaction.

He shook his head and went back to his food. No, it wasn't possible, he was merely following his honor, merely repaying her the deeds she'd done for him. It was nothing more. She certainly wasn't meant to be his. She was a wild and free female who would never choose a life that he had always imagined having on Halador with a wife and children in a small home, working the land as his father had done to help support the village. No, she was used to having everything at her fingertips and running from one adventure to the next, never settling down.

She wasn't for him.

"Let me check your wound before we go, I have a bit more salve from Fallen I can put on there and fresh bandages."

Saluk nodded and she approached.

"Lay back, let me see," she said then paused and frowned at his bandages. "You replaced the bandages already," she said surprised.

"Yes, I wanted to inspect the wound for myself, obviously. I am sure it could use more of that wonderful salve though; it is healing things faster than I've ever seen."

She nodded then gently removed the bandages and tsked at the exposed wound. Her mouth pursed and her mechanical eye brightened and turned. He wondered what it was telling her. She fetched a cloth and washed the wound. He flinched as it ran over the gash, but the burned skin around it was already mostly healed beyond sensitivity.

"I think you'll live," she said with a wink.

"Thanks to you," he whispered, his voice deep with emotion. Her fingers stilled on his skin and she looked into his eyes.

"I have only done what's decent," she said with her usual sass, but her words were thick with something that spoke of emotions.

"You have done more than necessary for a stranger you were put in a cell with, Prit. You are an honorable thief."

Her smile was huge and lit up her face in a delightful way. "I always heard there was no honor among thieves."

"Ah, but I am not a thief," Saluk pointed out.

"Does that make you the damsel in distress?" she teased.

"Distress, maybe, but I am not sure anyone would mistake this face for anything close to a damsel." He frowned and looked down at his body, scarred up as much as his face. He was a ruined piece of flesh and although it showed his power in battle, he wondered if it would ever be attractive to her.

She made a sound he couldn't interpret and began to gently apply the salve. Her touch was featherlight and slow. He looked back at her face and saw a wrinkle between her eyes that told of worry or concentration. He ached to lift a hand and touch it, to smooth away whatever thought was troubling her. She shouldn't worry about him; she shouldn't worry about anything. She should be taken care of, cherished, and loved. She should be treated like the princess she apparently was.

Had anyone in her life ever done that for her? Perhaps her mother. He knew her father's people were not the loving caring type, and she didn't seem to have anyone else. Even Josh and Frankie were held at a distance.

Jet, her pet might be the only thing she truly let herself care for and let care for her in its own way. What was she so afraid of, he wondered.

"All done," she announced and placed the last bandage carefully back over his wound.

"Thank you," he said as she cleaned up, not meeting his gaze.

CHAPTER TWELVE

Prit made her way to Shalayla's shop, Saluk on her ass and huddled over in his cloak as if he were a hunchbacked old man. He wasn't as stealthy as her, but the crowds were thick enough even in this part of the city that they went unnoticed. It helped that he kept his head down so no one realized how tall and broad he was. Not a lot of races were as large as Haladians.

She was confused and, admittedly a bit happy, about his insistence on helping her instead of going directly back to his planet. She knew she should insist on taking him straight back to Halador where he'd be safe, far from her and her insane life, but she also didn't want to lose his company. She *wanted* him around, and that was something she hadn't felt toward anyone, maybe ever. Aside from Jet of course. She couldn't even imagine living with Josh and Frankie long term without going completely insane, but something about Saluk was just easy. He didn't demand anything from her, not conversation or attention. They could sit silently together and be comfortable.

She had a feeling that finding that was a once in a lifetime sort of deal.

For so long her life had been one of self-imposed solitude.

After she'd lost her mother and joined the military there had been no room for attachments beyond a quick roll in the bed.

Was that what this was all about? Was she not thinking clearly because it had been too long since she'd had a good toss around? She could sleep with him and cut ties easier, she never had any interest in sleeping with someone more than once or twice, especially someone who was available. Clingy was definitely not her style.

She dared a glance back at him, his face peeking out of the darkness of his hood. His eyes were bright and assessing, showing his intelligence. Even hunched as he was, she could see he was all power and coiled energy. He was strong, and yet so kind with an edge of something she'd never run across and couldn't name. He wasn't like anyone else she'd met, and she wondered if it was that seeming novelty that was attracting her to him.

One thing she did know, she didn't want to lead him into danger. Which is exactly what she was doing, he'd already been hurt once with her. It was selfish to accept his help further.

She wasn't good at not being selfish.

They arrived at Shalayla's shop and found her helping a customer, a New Earth family on vacation. They were chatty and light, no worries even though they'd wandered far from the safety of the main strip. Prit hoped they would make it back safely.

The family bought enough to fill two bags and as they headed out, Shalayla motioned to a man across the street to follow. "Tortora will make sure they make it back where they are relatively safe again."

"Tourists *here?*" Prit asked, pushing her hood back from her face.

"Yeah, the New Earthers tend to be the least capable of

realizing they aren't safe somewhere and wander in every once in a while."

"No sense of self preservation, I'm lucky I got a more critical mind from my father," Prit said.

"And a penchant for violence," Shalayla added. "I hear you're leaving bodies in your wake," Shalayla chastised.

Prit rolled her eye. "Just one. Saluk was attacked, there's a bounty on him."

"I saw that too," Shalayla said, her eyes sweeping over Saluk who was skulking in a shadow still. "High price."

Prit put her hands on her hips so she was close to a weapon in case Shalayla decided to make a move against Saluk. Money was the ultimate motivator and often outweighed friendships. "Do you have any information on Barius?"

Shalayla slid her gaze back to Prit and showed her hands in a motion of peace, she wasn't going to try for Saluk and his bounty.

"I am told that the princess of Sabit was given an engagement present, a necklace that holds a stone of Earth."

"There are a thousand stones of Earth," Prit scoffed.

Shalayla shook her head, "Not New Earth, a stone of *Old* Earth, brought on the last exodus, a large pink stone shaped into a heart and made into a necklace with pearls from the oceans of Angstar. Her fiancé is the son of some high-profile New Earth politician. King Lenkin is trying to wrangle his way into a firmer standing with the New Earth organization, thinks he'll be able to use their military to squash recent uprisings in his mines. Apparently the locals are tired of being poor while his family lives in luxury."

"Sounds like the necklace Barius sent me after, but he didn't mention it was an Old Earth stone, or that it was a gift from a New Earther. That would explain why it was alarmed," she grumbled. That would have been good information to have had.

"It's worth way more than he offered you too, I have no doubt," Shalayla pointed out.

"Oh yes, he was trying to cheat me for sure," she scowled. "If he'd told me it was alarmed, I would have charged more, and knowing it's Old Earth, that would have tripled my price."

"What are you going to do?" Shalayla asked. "You can't exactly offer him something equal to it and he's pissed you didn't succeed."

"He probably can't get anyone else to go after it, if they have any idea what it is."

"Does that mean you were the only one stupid enough not to ask the right questions before taking the job?" Shalayla teased.

"Apparently," Prit laughed.

"It doesn't really explain why he attacked your ship," Saluk spoke up from the corner.

"No, it doesn't," Prit agreed. "Unless he thought I succeeded and was keeping the thing."

"Or he just wanted to convince you to go back in because not only are you the one stupid enough not to ask questions, you are also probably the only one skilled enough to succeed. You're a fucking shadow, Prit," Shalayla praised.

Prit smiled; it was true.

"I know that smile," Shalayla said.

Prit met her friend's gaze and nodded. "I am going to get the necklace, and then I am going to use it to get everything I want from Barius," she said.

"And what is it that you want?" Saluk asked.

She turned around, surprised to find that he was now standing very close behind her. His face was still shadowed by the hood of his cloak, but his eyes were intense.

Suddenly her mouth was a bit dry and her mind filled with images she didn't want to think about. Things like home and family. Things she could never have. She steeled herself against the wayward desires.

She swallowed and forced out a half truth. "Whatever I want."

"Which is what?" Saluk pressed, his eyes narrowing on her intensely and his voice pitched low.

Prit felt her body heat under his scrutiny, as if he wanted more than anything to hear the answer to that question, but she couldn't imagine why. "True freedom would be a start," Prit said. "If I could finally stop running and hiding, I'd be happy."

Saluk's eyes softened, and the unscarred side of his lips lifted slightly as if he were happy with her answer. She was about to scoff and ask why he cared but Shalayla interrupted and drew her attention back.

"You'll have to kill the Commander first, for that to happen," Shalayla said.

"True, so then maybe just a faster ship so I can keep outrunning him and his minions."

"You ever going to want to settle down?" Shalayla asked with a laugh.

"Not in this lifetime, but who wants to sit around and grow old anyway," Prit said with a shrug. Somehow that statement didn't feel as true as it usually did.

Behind her she heard Saluk grunt, and she had the weirdest feeling that she'd disappointed him. Not that it mattered what he thought of her life goals. So why did she want to turn around and justify them to him?

"I'll stop in again soon, hopefully with a shit ton of money," Prit said and hugged her friend.

"Stay safe," Shalayla said then looked at Saluk. "And you watch her back, big guy," she said sternly.

"Of course," Saluk said.

Prit rolled her eyes and they left the shop after that. They made their way back to the ship without anyone taking notice of them aside from the usual passing glances. There were always those who worked for The Five watching but they wouldn't bother her, especially as she made her way out of the city. Her only concern would be if they had caught wind of the hefty price on her companion's head.

And just when she thought they were free and clear, something prickled her senses. "Shit," she hissed as she tried to keep a casual pace weaving between parked ships outside the city walls.

"What is it?" Saluk demanded, moving next to her and darting his gaze around from under his hood.

"We are being followed. Someone must have heard about the bounty on your head and knows you were seen with me last night." Prit didn't stop her forward movement and to anyone watching, it wouldn't even seem like she had been alerted to anything. If she'd been alone, she would have slipped into the shadows and disappeared into a crowd or between ships unseen—it was her special talent—but she couldn't expect the same from Saluk, so she needed to think fast.

Her ship was too far away to get to before whoever was following decided to make themselves known. She grabbed Saluk's arm and changed direction, heading away from a group of tourists. If she was going to be forced into a confrontation, she didn't want to do it where innocent people could get hurt.

"What are you doing?" Saluk demanded.

"Veering away from innocents in case I have to kill someone."

"Oh," Saluk said with surprise.

Prit laughed, "Don't worry, I won't kill without cause."

Saluk grunted, and when they rounded the front of a parked ship he pushed her behind him. It was déjà vu, and Prit worried as she envisioned him getting another prod shock; there was no way he'd survive another one so soon.

She didn't bother arguing who should be in front of this confrontation; there wasn't time. She could hear the pad of footsteps coming quick now that they were out of sight.

Prit put her hands up on the back of Saluk's shoulders and quickly catapulted her body up and over him, landing in front of him just as their follower appeared. Prit had her dagger in hand and a sneer on her face. Her eye instantly assessed.

Species: *Gougran*
    Sex: *Female*
    Age: *Twenty*
    Danger: *High, spiked tentacles along body are poisonous*

The Gougran were taller even than the Haladian people, but slender, and although they had arms and legs like most species had developed, they had added tentacles on their bodies that made them highly dangerous to wrestle with. Prit stood her ground despite her momentary fear as she looked at the woman. Slick grey skin and large yellow eyes glared at her from under her hood. When she sneered, Prit saw her sharp teeth.

"Pritalia, I don't need to harm you, I just want the Haladian," she said.

"Yeah, that's not happening. Do you really want to die trying?" Prit spun the dagger in her hand and raised an eyebrow.

"For the price on his head, I would risk it," the Gougran said and lunged forward. Her cloak opened and her tentacles reached forward.

Prit knew she had one chance to stop the woman and it wasn't going to be fast enough to avoid some of those poisonous blows. She aimed her knife high, going for a throat slice but a flash of silver swept between them.

Saluk's sword cut through four of the Gougran's tentacles and the ear-piercing scream of pain that she let out had Prit slamming her knife into the woman's mouth just to stop it.

The Gougran's body jerked and shivered, her eyes grew even wider, and then she fell to the ground, sliding off of Prit's knife with a sickening wet sound, and leaving behind green, gooey blood.

Prit leaned down and wiped the blade on the dead Gougran's cloak then stood and faced Saluk with a smile. "You're fast."

He wasn't smiling. His face was hard and glaring, his chest heaving with heavy breaths despite the lack of physicality of the short battle. "Why the hell did you put yourself in front of me, I am supposed to be your bodyguard. I can't guard you from behind," he snarled.

"Well, actually you can, obviously," she said with a wink, "and I didn't feel like seeing you take another shock so soon after the last. As tough as I am, I probably wouldn't be able to drag you back to my ship on my own." She didn't add that the thought of him dying because of her was, surprisingly, a fear unlike anything she'd ever known.

Saluk just shook his head at her, still scowling. She put her dagger away and started walking toward the ship. There was no use worrying about the body, they were on their way off planet now anyway and someone would find it soon. It would be assumed to be just another criminal deal gone bad.

Saluk followed a little closer this time, and he didn't bother hunching or hiding his face, now that their cover was already blown.

Once safely on board, she checked on Jet, giving him a quick refill of food and water, then sat down and got them moving. "Buckle up, big guy," she said as she launched the ship straight up and then out of the atmosphere. Saluk grumbled but was quick enough securing his belt to keep his seat as she started to dodge a few incoming ships. She was sure she'd earned a few choice words from their captains; she wasn't much for following space etiquette, especially when she was in a hurry, which was most of the time.

Once up and away from the main traffic she hesitated to set a direction, and just stared at the screen with indecision.

CHAPTER THIRTEEN

Saluk touched her shoulder, making her startle. "I am sorry you had to kill that woman to protect me," his voice was low and gentle. "I can assure you I won't let it happen again. Twice now you have taken a life in defense of mine. I've never experienced that before."

Prit shook her head and looked up into his face, so full of concern for what he thought she was dealing with emotionally. Fuck, just another reminder that he was something soft and gentle and didn't at all deserve the life he'd been thrust into and was far too good for her. She needed to get him home safe before she got him killed.

"I have to go back to Sabit. I have to get that necklace."

Saluk nodded agreement.

"King Lenkin put out a bounty for your return, Saluk. I can't take you back there, it's far too dangerous. I would never ask you to risk becoming one of his imprisoned gladiators again."

"It is dangerous," he agreed.

Her heart clenched. "Okay, so I will drop you first on Halador." She ignored the feeling of loss already creeping into her stomach at the decision. It was the right thing to do.

"No," he said firmly and kneeled beside her so that he stared into the depths of her eye.

Prit swallowed, her throat dry and tight. "No?" she asked.

"No, Prit. I want to see you through this. I want to help you, and guard you, and be beside you as you go to Barius with the necklace. I will not abandon you after all you have done for me, that is not the way of Haladian men; we don't run from a fight, and we do not abandon those who need us."

Prit shook her head, a small smile on her lips. His damn sense of honor was going to get him killed. "But we are going back to Sabit. This is different than we discussed; this is too much of a risk for you."

"It changes nothing, I agreed to protect you through this mission, and the mission isn't complete."

"The mission has changed," Prit insisted.

"And you need help more than ever. Sabit has proven to be a more difficult job than you have known in the past, has it not?"

"True," she gritted, "but how the hell do you think you are going to help me? You aren't stealthy," she laughed, and he narrowed his eyes at her. "You're big, strong, and imposing. Great for a bodyguard, not so much a thief."

"I know how to get in," he challenged. "In my years there I have been through enough of the tunnels and arena rooms that I know where you need to go and where you should avoid. It will take out some of the guesswork for you. I think a smart thief would value the information I can give."

"You can give me the information without being there," she pointed out. "Why are you really insisting on going there again and risking recapture?"

"Perhaps I'm looking for a chance for a little bit of revenge," he said darkly.

Prit reached out and touched his face, her fingers sliding

along the deep scars. "For this?" she asked softly, her heart aching for the pain and anger he must be holding on to.

"No," he said quietly, surprising her. "That was done on Halador as I fought to save my brother from the beast that turned to take him down when he stepped in to save my life. That is the scar that I hold as proof that I went against a vicious beast and survived." Tears filled Saluk's eyes and Prit dropped her fingers from the scars. "These scars show the graveness of the injury that knocked me out and left my brother to fight the Sabitarions from the seeker ship alone and injured. It had come to capture warriors and it took us that day. He was able to fight back more than I was at the time, but it wasn't enough, their weapons were too strong. They threw us in a cell together and I couldn't save him. He would have survived the injuries from the beast alone, but not mixed with the weapons of the Sabitarions. My brother died in transport but I lived, I survived, and I promised his spirit I would return him to our home one day."

Saluk left her briefly to grab the canister.

"These are his ashes, I will return them to Halador to finally rest as promised, but first I will help the angel who saved me, and I will seek a piece of revenge against the king who enslaved me. Pritalia, I will stand at your side, and I will fight for what we both want most."

Prit's eyes widened and she wondered briefly if he had seen into her mind, had touched on the vision of them in a future with a family. "And what is that?" she asked, breathless. "What is it we both want most?"

"Freedom and peace to live as we desire," he said, but there was something more in his eyes.

Something he wasn't saying that made her breath hitch.

Saluk looked away from her and continued quietly. "It is what my brother would have demanded I do anyway, it is what my honor as a Haladian male would demand that I do, and it is what I *want* to do, so don't ask me to return to my planet in dishonor."

"Okay," she said because no matter what she knew she *should* do, she didn't *want* to tell him no. She wanted to extend their time together. "Strap in, big guy."

The journey back to Sabit wasn't going to be a straight shot, they had enemies— and more than just Barius—since word had spread that she'd been seen with the gladiator who had such a large bounty on his head, hunters would be looking for her ship too.

This meant they were going to be taking the scenic route back and stopping for supplies as far from the usual flow of space travel as possible. Prit pulled out a map to show Saluk when he asked the plan. It was weird for her to treat someone as a partner of any kind, she was so used to working alone. But if he was willing to risk his life and freedom to help her, the least she could do was involve him in the plan.

"See here," she said, pressing on a portion of the digital map. The map showed all the settled and unsettled but mapped parts of space. Saluk's eyes were wide as he stared at it. "Have you seen a map like this before?" she asked.

He shook his head. "Where is Halador?"

Prit pressed on a space of the map that showed the blue galaxy and suddenly they were looking at all the planets in and around the Eludian territory. It was a small galaxy on an outer edge of discovered space and then she swiped to move the map over. "Here, just outside of Eludian territory is Halador. I guess I'm not surprised that the Sabitarions came all that way to gather warriors since the wormhole on the other side of the Blue Galaxy leads straight to Sabit. They wouldn't have had to travel more than a month to get to Halador and it's probably one reason why your planet has remained unclaimed by the SSA, no one likes to go through Eludian territory, so you guys are kind of safe tucked up there next to that little star."

Saluk didn't say anything, just stared down at the map with a confused look on his face.

"Where is Sabit then?"

Prit zoomed the map back out to full then pressed on the red galaxy which was on the opposite end of discovered space. This was where Sabit was. Quite a large distance to travel without the aid of the wormhole, but there were a lot of little places between that were quite habitable which made it possible for ships unable to travel safely through wormholes able to get from one end of discovered space to the other. New Earth was on the upper end of the map near the red galaxy but in the green galaxy which was full of lush habitable planets that New Earthers now inhabited. It seemed their desire to take over other places was insatiable.

"And where are we now?" Saluk asked.

Prit zoomed out again. "Here," she said, pointing to where the market planet sat outside of Eludian territory.

"How the hell are we going to go all that way?" Saluk asked, drawing his finger across the map to Sabit.

"We can't take the Eludian wormhole and make it a quick trip, too risky with you such a wanted man, so we will stay out of the heaviest traveled areas and head through the Ice Stretch, here." She pointed to a line of light blue that indicated an outer space river of ice that no one chose to pass through. "It will be free of interference and then we can hop through this wormhole here, it's rarely used because it is so close to the Ice Stretch and spits you out in the red galaxy but not near Sabit which is their main hub."

Saluk shook his head. "I never would have been able to imagine something like this, it's beyond the comprehension of any Haladian," he admitted.

"You knew of space travel before you were captured though, right?"

"Yes, we had heard stories of visitors in the past and the danger that newcomers could present to our way of life. But in my lifetime, none had ever arrived near our village. When I was on the Sabitarion ship I saw and heard of people and things that were mind-blowing, but I never saw a map of what the known universe encompasses."

Prit wasn't sure what to say to that, she was almost jealous of the Haladian people and their ability to exist outside of all this, it must be what Old Earth felt like before they were first visited and then forced to abandon their planet because of the destruction they'd caused themselves there.

"Where is your home planet; where is New Earth?"

"In the green galaxy." Prit pressed the map and brought it up. "This is New Earth and I grew up there until I entered the military, then I was never stationed on-planet again, haven't been back either." She shrugged. "It never really felt like home once my mother died. It was just a place. I think that's what's wrong with knowing about the vastness of places." She zoomed the map out to full again and motioned to the edges. "They are still exploring and finding more you know. Every year a new map is made with updated planets and systems and wormholes to distant galaxies. So how can anyone find a home in all of that? How can you be sure that the place you were born is the place you were meant to be? I could have just as easily been raised by my father on Elude. Would that have made Elude feel like home? Having been raised there and a living parent still residing there?" she shook her head; it was something she'd always struggled with.

Where was home and how did one find it?

Saluk rested a hand on her shoulder and she looked up at him with a shaky smile. "So now that we know where we are going, we should probably stop for supplies," she said, breaking the moment. She moved back to the pilot's seat and put in the coordinates for a fuel stop nearby, hoping they'd make it in and out without incident.

Saluk settled into his seat and strapped in as Prit went back to pushing buttons and flipping switches, apparently setting their course. He couldn't stop thinking over what she'd said though, about home and the sad look on her face while she spoke of it as if it were a missing piece she'd forever be searching for.

What if he was facing the same thing? What if when he arrived back on Halador it didn't feel like home anymore. What if he was just as lost as she was?

Could you go back to a home that you'd been away from for so long and really belong there again, after going through so much? He'd always imagined, in his fantasies about escape, that he'd walk back into his village, be embraced by his family and friends, and pick up right where he left off as if he'd just walked down the mountain a victor. He'd claim his intended mate and start a family right away. It was what he'd always dreamed of doing when he didn't really think it would ever be possible.

Prit's words stuck with him. Was he being naive to think that home would feel anything like it once had? Was he chasing something impossible to find? Or was he looking in the wrong place for his future and his home? His gaze drifted to Prit. Her short black locks shined in the light of the ship, and he wanted to run his fingers through them, to see the peeks of blue as it drifted through his fingers. He knew what that hair smelled like up close. Sweet like nectar and floral too. It was a scent that reminded him of home.

Again he had a thought that made his heart lurch and his body heat.

Was she his?

CHAPTER FOURTEEN

Two days later they entered the Ice Stretch.

"Fuck it's cold out here," Prit said as she watched ice crystals start to form on the windshield of the ship. She shivered in the shorts and t-shirt she had put on for sleep and snuggled Jet closer to her chest as she whispered. "Good thing we have a big warm gladiator to keep us warm while we sleep, huh."

Prit carried Jet to the cot and settled in next to Saluk who was already laying down looking uncomfortable, which was basically his usual look. She hit the lights to dim and laid on her side facing his back. He was shirtless and his back was covered in so many wounds it made her stomach ache. He'd been through so much. His chest was healing fast, she could tell it still pained him though. Every once in a while, when he thought she wasn't looking, he'd grimace as he stretched. But it was healing, and she knew he'd be alright, just another battle wound.

She ran a finger down one particularly deep and jagged scar on his back.

Saluk shuddered and she pulled her hand back, knowing she was crossing a line to touch him like that. Especially when it made her want to follow her finger with tender kisses as he told her the story behind every scar.

The feelings were too real, too strong and she didn't know what to do with them. So she ignored them, and she held herself back. The last thing she wanted to do was ruin the peaceful existence they'd settled into in this small space.

"Goodnight, Saluk," she whispered and turned so her back was pressed to his and Jet was snuggled against her chest.

As soon as he started to vibrate she was lulled into a deep sleep feeling safe and warm.

They continued for the next three days companionably. They ate and slept and talked of nothing important most of the time. She noticed he paid careful attention whenever she did anything with the ship and even asked a question here and there. She wondered if he'd be interested in learning to fly it, but he didn't bring it up and she didn't offer. She liked that he was at her mercy out here in the middle of dark space.

Saluk described his home planet which sounded peaceful although primitive.

"I doubt my parents are still alive. They were old when I went on my journey."

"Do you have other relatives waiting for your return?" *Or a girlfriend*, she wanted to ask, but didn't.

"I have cousins and nephews who I imagine are still alive and well. They likely all assume I failed in a mortally dangerous way and my brother tried to intervene, tried to save me, and we both died. When I return, I will tell of his bravery. He died because the monsters that took us have weapons beyond our abilities to fight."

Prit could see the guilt in his face and it hurt her to know he blamed himself for being too injured to help fight the

Sabitarions. "You did the best you could, you survived," Prit said quietly. "If you hadn't been injured you wouldn't have been kidnapped, I'm sure of it. Even with their weapons you would have fought back hard and made them regret messing with the Haladian brothers. You would have returned to the village a hero, and mated, and had children." Prit's voice choked at the end.

He looked at her with a deep hurt in his eyes. "I wish I knew that was true," he whispered. "I wish I knew that the Sabitarions are what kept that life from me, but I don't. The ship coming in is what scared the beast away. I don't know what would have happened otherwise. I was injured and going to attack it and try to save my brother who was trying to save me." He paused and shook his head. "I hate that tradition. Let a man die trying to be a man. It wasn't his place to intervene like that. I want to honor him, let his son know he was a hero, I owe him that. He proved himself worthy on that trip more than I did."

"You are an honorable and worthy man, Saluk, fierce and strong in body and spirit. You have nothing to prove to anyone." Prit met his gaze across the small distance of the ship's cabin and took a deep breath, knowing she was about to do something that could be a huge mistake. But the last few days had been something she hadn't experienced in so long, comfort and quiet with another person. The last few days of getting to know Saluk had made her want to spend more time with him, it was unheard of for her. She didn't need people; she didn't want to need people. It was too dangerous, for both of them.

"Saluk," she said with a sigh. She stepped forward until she was close enough that her breath touched his face as she looked up at him. "Saluk, you would have survived, and you would have ruled Halador, I know it." She reached up and touched the scars on the side of his face. "You would have gone back to your village and married the prettiest girl there and had so many strong babies you'd have been overwhelmed with love. You would have achieved every one of your wildest dreams. It was ripped away from you when the Sabitarion ship took you. And you still survived, against all odds you killed, and you survived, you were treated like an animal, and you survived. You are the most amazing man I have ever met in my entire life, and you have nothing more to prove."

"I am a warrior and I have the scars to prove that I am capable of surviving anything," Saluk agreed gruffly, his body stiff. "A Haladian woman would agree that I am a worthy mate."

Prit ran a finger down the scar on his face. "This doesn't make you less attractive to any woman," she whispered.

"No female has looked at me in anything but fear since I left Halador. I know what I look like, Prit," he argued.

She bit her lip and smiled. "Obviously not," she said and then she was on him. She pressed her body against his, her lips to his, and she wasn't taking no for an answer. The idea that she wanted him wasn't new. She'd been attracted to him since they'd first met. He was big and strong and definitely her type, but it was getting to know him and his personality that had kept her from him. She had never found anyone attractive beyond physicality and the idea that his personality meshed so well with hers frightened her a bit. Now she didn't care, she wanted to show him that he was desired and she wanted to give herself a taste of what he offered.

He didn't respond at first, no doubt surprised by her attack, but as she ran her tongue between his lips his chest rumbled and his arms went around her, holding her tight against his hard body. His lips parted and his own tongue slid against hers eagerly.

His hands slid down to her ass and squeezed, pulling her against his hardening member.

"Big guy all over, I am not surprised," she teased and nipped at his lower lip and rolled her hips into him.

"Pritalia, I—"

Whatever he was about to say was cut off by an explosion and the ship rocking with the force of it.

Prit pushed Saluk away from her and jumped to the pilot's seat, her mind switching from sex to battle instantly. She flipped switches, assessed screens, and analyzed beeps.

It wasn't good.

"Fucking brace yourself, we're going down," she snarled as she zeroed in on the nearest planet and changed direction. Their only hope was that the hostiles that had attacked wouldn't follow them down.

"Is it Barius or bounty hunters?" Saluk asked as he frantically strapped himself in while the ship began its rapid descent.

"Worse," she grumbled as another hit shook the ship and more warning beeps filled the cabin.

"What could be worse?"

"New Earth military. No one else would patrol this far out, because there isn't shit out here anyone wants, it's too damn cold."

"So what are they doing out here?"

"Being assholes," she hissed and gave the engines one last thrust as they entered the atmosphere of the planet she'd aimed for. "And looking for me," she added as the ship rocked with another blow.

"Won't they just follow us down to the surface?"

"They can't," she said with a grin, knowing they were almost over the line into territory that the New Earth military was forbidden to enter.

"Why?"

"Because Elint is technically my father's territory."

"Shit," Saluk hissed.

"My sentiments exactly," she mumbled as they crossed that invisible line that would keep them safe from one sort of enemy and put them right in the hands of another.

Saluk didn't know what to expect when they crashed onto Elint. They were far from a useful star and just outside of the Ice Stretch which made the snow they landed into expected, but the rise of a pearlescent fortress in front of them was not something he would have expected.

"Princess Pritalia," a voice boomed out of the ships system eliciting a groan from Prit.

She lurched forward from where she'd been sitting dazed in the pilot's seat after the harsh landing. Saluk was already standing behind her and glared out at the scene in front of the ship.

"Hey, just thought I'd drop in and say hello to my favorite brother," Prit said.

"You're not alone, there is a rather large heat signature coming from inside your ship."

Prit looked up at Saluk and grinned. "That's my big strong bodyguard, Saluk."

"What is he?"

"Haladian."

"Fine, as long as he isn't a dirty New Earther."

"As if I would associate with such beings, so far beneath me," she scoffed and the man on the other end of the speaker laughed.

"We'll be out in a second," she said and flipped a switch, cutting off whatever her brother might have been about to say.

"You have a brother?"

"Half-brother, yes. Jattin runs this outpost for our father. We can stay with him until the ship's repaired." Prit got up and started throwing a few things into a bag, then tossed it to Saluk and pulled Jet out, wrapping him in a blanket. "Cold as fuck out there, put on your cloak," she said and wrapped one around herself and Jet.

Saluk didn't like the thought of going with her into her brother's fortress, especially considering the kiss they'd just shared.

Fuck, that had been a kiss unlike any he'd ever experienced. Just thinking about it now had his body reacting and he pulled the cloak around himself to help cover the fact.

He wanted to make her stay on the ship, wanted to discuss what had passed between them because his instincts were screaming at him to grab her and claim her before any other male could. It's what he'd have done if a Haladian woman had thrown herself at him like that and made his body react so strongly. But she wasn't Haladian and this was definitely not Halador.

Prit didn't seem at all concerned or distracted by the kiss, didn't seem to have an ounce of embarrassment or excitement that she wanted to talk about, and to him that could only mean she wasn't feeling the same thing he was. That it had been a moment of boredom perhaps, or worse, pity. And the last thing he wanted was to be a way she passed the time between death-defying adventures. She was obviously an adrenaline junkie, and he had no interest in being her next fix.

He *would* be her bodyguard though, no matter that they were about to walk into her brother's home.

Saluk held himself stiff and battle ready as he followed her out of the ship. The wind hit him hard and he shuddered. When he breathed in, it felt like his lungs iced over and he immediately started to cough.

"Oh yeah, breathe shallow," Prit threw over her shoulder. "Cold as fuck out here." She was trudging toward the high gates of the massive building, her feet breaking through the surface snow with each step and making her progress slow. He hurried behind her, despite not being able to breathe properly. He didn't bother lifting his feet above the snow, just plowed forward.

"This is bullshit," Prit said with chattering teeth.

The building seemed to blend with the surrounding snow. It was light blue and shined with what little sunlight did hit the planet, and illuminated the space around it like a beacon. As they slowly made progress forward, a black slit pierced the side of the building and a gate swung wide. An army of green fur-covered men mounted on riding animals emerged and headed toward them with seemingly no trouble despite the snow and cold.

"Oh great, the welcoming committee," Prit said. "Stay close and remember, you're just the bodyguard."

Saluk grunted, but he didn't argue. He had no interest in interacting with anyone here in any capacity other than keeping her safe.

"Throw us some god damn furs," Prit yelled as soon as the men were within shouting distance.

"Princess Pritalia, welcome to Elint, can I offer you a ride?" One of the men responded.

Saluk couldn't tell anything about him since he was head to toe covered in furs, but Saluk automatically didn't like the guy. Unless he was Prit's brother, he shouldn't be offering something as intimate as a shared ride with her.

Because it wasn't safe, he reasoned, it wasn't jealousy. If she was on the back of some stranger's mount then he wouldn't be able to properly protect her.

"Get me out of this fucking snow," Prit said and accepted the man's hand as soon as he was close.

Saluk gritted his teeth as the man hoisted her up on top of a small, fur-covered beast. The thing was barely taller than Saluk's waist, but it was sturdy and round and covered in the same green fur that made the cloaks of the men. Together they would appear to be one large intimidating beast from a distance, Saluk supposed it was a smart move. Its large flat feet helped it stay on top of the snow and move across the land with apparent ease.

The man opened the front of his cloak once she was sitting and wrapped it around her. "I've missed you," he said.

Saluk's body burned with rage and his muscles ached to tear her out of the man's grasp, but he didn't move, didn't speak, only waited to follow them. He was *just the bodyguard.*

"Allow my bodyguard to ride as well, he's not dressed to travel in this crap," Prit said with a shiver.

The man holding Prit laughed a deep chuckle that didn't quite ring genuine and motioned with his hand. Another guard hopped off his beast and led it to Saluk.

"Do you know how to ride, Haladian?"

Saluk nodded and easily mounted the beast. He wasn't given a warm cloak but he wasn't about to complain, he wouldn't show these men any more weakness than Prit already had in asking for someone to give him a ride. Saluk met Prit's eyes and he saw a thankfulness there. Was she glad that he was going along without complaint? As if he really had any other choice. If he was her bodyguard, he wouldn't question her orders, would he?

"Your brother is anxious to speak with you," the man who sat behind her said and turned his beast, the rest of the men followed and even Saluk's beast turned without any prompting at all, just going along with the rest of the herd.

"I'm sure he is," Prit said.

CHAPTER FIFTEEN

Prit wanted to snap and snarl at Beldar, but she knew it was better to get herself and Saluk safely into the warmth of Elint city as soon as possible. She'd give him a sharp elbow in the gut as soon as they were through the gate to remind him that his hot breath on her neck and roaming hands along her sides were more than unwelcome, they were repulsive. When she felt his tail slip around and touch her ankle she didn't hesitate, she pulled the knife from her leg and pressed it against the hand on her ribcage. He hissed and stiffened, then chuckled.

"Feisty as always," he mumbled but his unwanted touching stopped. Her brother would cut his hands off if he knew they were taking advantage of this situation. Her father had plans for her that didn't include marrying someone of Beldar's ilk.

The fortress on Elint was something of a marvel, made of mostly glass to mimic the fortress city of her father's on Elude. A bubble of glass that was so clear it was nearly invisible even up close surrounded the entire area and amplified what little heat there was coming from the sun. It also trapped the heat made by a few hot springs trapped within the boundary of the bubble and provided the inhabitants of the city with constant hot water.

The effect was a balmy heat that was welcome and Prit threw off Beldar and his fur cloak as soon as they were through the gate.

"Sleep with one eye open," she sneered as she hopped off the animal. The man just laughed.

"Sister!" came her brother's booming voice. Jattin strode out of the fortress dressed in a sleeveless light blue tunic and black pants. His tail whipped behind him and Prit wondered if it was in irritation or excitement. She never was sure when it came to her father's family how she would be received. She was the third oldest child, the first daughter which in Eludian tradition meant she should marry someone that her father picked to be worthy and spend her life at her father's side, having given him not only a new son through marriage, but also producing babies for him to enjoy grandfathering. She wasn't valued for anything beyond that by her father and siblings.

Her two younger sisters were off the hook for most of that, they could marry and leave the family home, they'd be absorbed into their husband's families; but her, she was supposed to stay with her father until he died. To serve him, her older brothers, and her own husband, to run the household in place of her father's wife, because he hadn't taken a new one since his last wife died birthing twins.

All the more reason for her to make her own money and live her life on her own terms. She'd never settle for serving anyone.

"Jattin," she said with a half-smile as her brother approached and embraced her. He was tall and thin with a long proud tail. He resembled her father quite a bit with his dark short hair and big black eyes. His chin was slightly pointed and his lips thin. The only thing that he'd seemed to have gotten from his own Eludian mother was his slender frame. Their father was fairly thick for an Eludian, of course that could have a lot to do with his sedentary and overindulgent lifestyle.

Saluk had hopped off his own ride as soon as she had and moved to stand close behind her. Jattin gave him an appraising look.

"This is my bodyguard, Saluk," Prit explained.

"I see. He looks quite capable though I've never pegged you for one who requires a bodyguard. Aren't you an assassin?" Jattin asked with a raised eyebrow.

"No, I am a thief, and that means many people want me dead," she said dryly, and her brother laughed. She liked to point out how unfit she was to be any part of the Eludian dynasty when her family was around. Not that it stopped them from pushing her to do as expected.

"I need my ship repaired; we took some damage just before crash landing. Can you have it dragged into the bubble so I don't freeze to death out there?"

"Of course, I'll get my men right on that." He motioned without even looking and men were rushing to do his bidding.

This was quite the little empire he was running, she realized, she would have to step carefully if everyone was so devoted to him. They were all Eludian, she assessed quickly as they walked toward the steps of the main entrance to the building, so of course they were loyal to him. Any sign of dissent and he'd have them executed, it was the same way their father ran Elude.

The main house was huge, it rose up into the sky with sharp spires and a glistening blue banner declaring the Kingdom of Elude as the settlers of this land.

She wondered what the locals thought of this place. They were mainly a small-statured, furry mammal that talked in a grumbling language. They had sharp teeth and claws, and they were not known to be welcoming to outsiders. Nothing on this planet was hospitable, and it offered nothing to draw in other species to try and make any kind of peace with the land or its inhabitants, especially with its location so close to the Ice Stretch.

No one except Elude that is, because Prit's father had discovered a secret about this place that no one else had.

There was a vein of rich soil underneath the frozen tundra that they mined out and took back to Elude, where they were able to make plots of land and grow crops above the watery surface of the planet.

Saluk was right behind her as she walked beside Jattin and she was thankful for his presence at her back even though she was fairly certain she was safe with Jattin because, unlike her younger siblings, she wasn't in the way of his inheritance. But she was never quite sure what to expect from any Eludian so she moved with caution always.

She was also thankful that Saluk was playing the bodyguard role perfectly, after that kiss on the ship she wasn't really sure what to expect from him. It was her own fault, confusing things like that, but she couldn't help it in that moment. She'd wanted him fiercely and she rarely denied herself anything, but she did wonder what he was thinking about it now. Was he sad it had ended, was he glad? Did he want to forget it ever happened or hope for more? She wasn't even sure herself, so she was thankful she wasn't faced with alone time with the man just yet.

"I should warn you, Mindal is here checking up on things for Father."

Prit's entire body went stiff at the mention of that man, and she heard Saluk growl behind her, alerted by her movement.

"Wonderful, you know you don't have to tell him *I'm* here."

"Too late. Try to be nice," Jattin said quietly as the man in question rounded a corner and approached them with a wide grin.

Mindal was an Eludian from an affluent family, and her father's top choice for marriage to her. He was tall, even for an Eludian, reaching seven feet or more and his large blue eyes stared out of a gaunt face. His body was typically built for an Eludian, lean-muscled, and with a long tail that was currently twitching with happiness as he smiled at her with full lips.

Prit's stomach tightened, she had no interest in him or any other Eludian, ever.

"Princess Pritalia, what a delightful fate that has brought us both to this frozen wasteland at the same time."

"Mindal," she said, giving him a tight smile.

He rushed forward and grabbed her hand, lifting it to his lips for a kiss that lingered until she jerked her hand away.

"My ship was attacked; we are here for repairs." She didn't hide the fact that she wiped her hand off on her cloak.

He straightened and scoffed. "Who would dare? Tell me who and I will bring you their heads as an engagement gift."

Saluk gasped but she didn't have time to deal with what he might be thinking, she just glared at Mindal. "I don't think you can take out the New Earth commander for me so just back off."

"Are you challenging my ability to care for you?"

"I can take care of myself."

"Obviously not, otherwise why would you have hired a bodyguard," his gaze flicked to Saluk and back to her. "A barbaric Haladian makes a good one though, I'll give you that. Where did you find him? I didn't think they left their planet."

"They don't, willingly," she said and waved a hand dismissively. "The point is, you don't need to do anything for me."

"Needs and wants are two different things," he said with a sly smile, his gaze raking up and down her body making her want to punch him in the mouth.

Prit gritted her teeth and was just about to let him have it when her brother interrupted.

"Okay, let me show you to a room. We just had lunch, are you two hungry? What schedule are you on?" Jattin asked.

"We can wait until dinner," Prit said, thankful for her brother's interruption, she didn't really want to get into a physical altercation with Mindal; he wasn't worth the energy, but damn, he was annoying.

Jattin continued on toward the house and Prit followed. They walked through a large foyer and down a hallway then up some stairs and to the wing of guest bedrooms. The whole place was decorated in a traditional Eludian style, lots of white with blues and greys as accents. Nothing overly comfortable, no chair overstuffed, no embellishments on drapery. All very austere and almost clinical. Prit didn't hate it, but it wasn't welcoming, and she wondered what Saluk thought of it.

Mindal didn't follow but she knew she'd have to see him again at dinner and that soured her mood. There was probably no way to avoid it, she couldn't get the ship fixed that fast, and even if she could, it would be far too rude to her brother to bail so quickly. She may not be close to her siblings, but she did want to have a decent relationship with most of them.

"You can have this room; it's got a sitting area and attached bedroom so your bodyguard can sleep on the couch there unless you want him down in the staff quarters."

"No," Prit said quickly and cleared her throat at her brother's questioning look. "No, I want him here so I don't have to worry about Mindal trying to sneak in," she added with a laugh.

"You know I would never let him take liberties with you, you aren't married yet," Jattin said.

Prit smiled warmly at her brother, appreciating his protectiveness. Although she didn't miss the unsaid implication that if they were married, he wouldn't stand between her and Mindal no matter what Prit's wishes were.

"Thank you, we'll be good here, and gone soon anyway."

"No need to rush, you're welcome as long as you need. I'll have some clothes sent for both of you and bathing attire as well in case you want to hit the springs later for a soak."

"I just might!" she said excitedly thinking of sinking into a pool of natural hot water. She hadn't had a real soak like that in years.

As soon as the door shut behind Jattin, Saluk stalked around the space including the bedroom and bathroom, apparently looking for hidden assassins. Prit sat on the couch with Jet and closed her eyes. She was exhausted. The kiss, the attack, the cold, and Mindal. She just wanted to sleep for a week.

"It's safe," Saluk said, coming back into the room.

"Sure, my father doesn't mess around with security. I'm safer here than anywhere in discovered space."

"What—" Saluk's words were cut off by a knock at the door. He moved to it and accepted a bundle of clothing from a maid who squealed at the sight of him and scurried away quickly. Likely to tell everyone about the horrible, ugly, large man staying with Princess Pritalia.

Prit frowned and wished she'd seen who it was so she could reprimand the woman later, Saluk didn't deserve that kind of reaction.

"We will be off this planet as soon as possible, Saluk, and until then, I'm glad you make a good bodyguard," she said with a smile and took the clothes from him. "I'm going to shower and change."

Prit had her back to Saluk and was about to shut the bathroom door when he spoke.

"Are you engaged to that man?"

"According to my father," she admitted, not turning around, a little afraid of what she might see on his face.

"You don't want him for a husband?"

Prit laughed and looked over her shoulder at Saluk. "No, I would never marry an Eludian, but sometimes it's more beneficial to let my father think I will come around to the idea sooner or later."

"Deception."

"Yes, I guess I'm just a thief with no morals."

Saluk stared around the room. He'd positioned himself in front of the door in case anyone tried to enter while Prit was showering. He didn't think she was in any real danger here, but he was supposed to be her bodyguard and he got the feeling that if he didn't play the part right it could mean trouble for both of them.

How would her father feel about his Princess sharing a room with a man who was just her ... what? What the hell was he really? Saluk supposed the bodyguard title was right, she'd basically hired him. As payment for getting him home, he was acting as her bodyguard.

Which made that kiss highly inappropriate.

He had to tear his mind away from that thought so he glanced around the room again. It was large. The couch he'd be sleeping on later wasn't big enough though, he had figured that out immediately, had even seen a glint of mischief in her brother's eyes when he'd mentioned the thing. Saluk could stretch out on the rug though, it was covering about a third of the room. It was a thick green woolly thing that had to have come from one of the beasts that the guards had been riding.

In a way, that rug reminded him of home. The obvious use of the land and its animals was something his people did a lot of. He thought laying down on an animal fur rug would actually feel quite nice, despite the hard floor underneath.

The large window at the end of the room looked out on the frozen land stretching to the horizon. This really was a terrible planet. Nothing about that frozen land going on forever reminded him of home. And Prit didn't like it either. He couldn't help wondering what she'd think of Halador. It wasn't civilized, wasn't technological or advanced, but it was warm, and it was beautiful.

She hadn't seemed to mind riding on the back of an animal so he could probably take her for a nice journey to some of his favorite spots on the back of a lemtar, a large thick-skinned beast that his people often used when traveling far. It didn't give nice furs when killed, but its furless hide was used for a lot of clothing and braided for rope that his people used for so many things. A truly useful beast.

Would she go with him on one? Or would she insist on riding her own? He fisted his hands as he remembered her riding in front of Beldar as if it were no big deal. He really didn't like the way the man had leered at her and had obviously enjoyed his time with her so close. Saluk had never wanted to kill anyone so much, until he met Mindal that is.

Was she really promised to the man? Would she eventually marry him and have his Eludian babies? It was what her father wanted, and he knew in his village that a young woman rarely went against the wishes of her father.

Why did he have any right to care? Sure, they'd shared a kiss, but it didn't mean anything. He was her bodyguard, and they had a deal. She wasn't looking to settle down with him, had never indicated anything even close to that. Just because it was the best kiss he'd ever experienced in his life didn't change the fact that they weren't a good match and could never be meant for each other.

He frowned at the opulence in the room. She was used to a level of luxury that he'd never be able to offer her on Halador.

He was just a big, scarred, primitive and he knew better than to expect someone like her to truly desire him. It hadn't been until days of no other interaction that she'd kissed him, days of endless black space had driven her bored enough to consider him a good time, nothing more.

This whole place was a show of wealth, and wealth was power throughout settled space. Prit deserved wealth and opulence, she deserved to have everything her pretty little heart desired. And he was here to keep her safe so she could get that one day.

A knock at the door brought him out of his grumbling thoughts. He turned and opened it with a blank face, his body blocking the room from whoever was there.

Mindal stood in the hallway with a grin that dropped when he saw it wasn't Prit answering the door. Saluk wanted to snap and snarl at the man, demand why he was knocking on Prit's private room, but he was afraid he knew the answer. So he stood stoic and stared at the man.

"Where's Princess Pritalia?" Mindal asked, trying to peer around Saluk's large form.

"Resting before dinner."

"Oh, well maybe I'll just go make sure she's comfortable," Mindal said and took a step forward.

Saluk didn't move and Mindal stopped just short of running into him.

"Excuse me, bodyguard, that's my intended in there."

"She's resting," Saluk growled. "And she asked not to be disturbed by *anyone*."

"Where the hell did she find you?" Mindal asked with a scowl.

"I picked him up on Sabit after they threw me in his cell to pleasure him as a reward for his winning streak. What the hell do you want, Mindal?" Prit said from behind Saluk.

Hot anger filled Mindal's eyes before he quickly shifted his expression to disbelief. "I just wanted to see if you'd join me for a walk before dinner. Your ship was dragged in and as you know, I'm quite talented with repairs of those old technology things."

"Sure, I want off this frozen wasteland as soon as possible," she said and shoved Jet at Saluk.

She'd showered, her hair was still damp, and she smelled like some kind of sweet flower he couldn't name. He wanted to grab her close and keep any of that sweet scent from entering Mindal's nostrils. She was dressed in her usual style of tight and black, stunning as always but the way that Mindal eyed her as she walked towards him made Saluk want to wrap her in as many thick layers as possible. The man's gaze was predatory and Saluk had to remind himself that she was capable of protecting herself and was never without a weapon.

But she'd be safer with him.

She grabbed her cloak and smiled at Saluk. "Stay here and take a shower, rest, whatever. I'll collect you for dinner and hopefully have good news about the ship."

Saluk didn't like the order at all, but he didn't have any choice other than to agree as she gave him a firm look. He was playing a part, and a bodyguard wouldn't argue with an order.

Mindal gave him a triumphant look before turning to follow Prit down the hall.

Saluk frowned down at Jet then shut the door. "What the hell are we supposed to do?"

CHAPTER SIXTEEN

Prit trod ahead of Mindal, not wanting to be friendly with the guy but at the same time, she knew that with his help she'd be off this planet faster. He really was a pretty good mechanic. He was in charge of the upkeep of all her father's personal ships and oversaw the team that took care of their army ships. He was an important man on Elude, which is why her father thought he'd make such a great son-in-law.

"You didn't really mean that," Mindal said as they crossed to the hangar that held the broken ship.

"Didn't mean what?" Prit said, really having no idea what he could be talking about, they'd been silent for the entire walk.

"That you were given to him as some kind of reward, that you were forced to..." he hesitated, anger filling his words and expression.

Prit looked him up and down and sneered. "You afraid I rode that big guy and liked it, too?" she whispered, stepping closer to Mindal. "You think it ruined me for anyone else?"

He shook his head, horror clear in his eyes. "No, I—"

"I can assure you; you have nothing to worry about," she said with a sly smile and ran a finger down his chest.

Mindal caught his breath and his eyes half closed, a groan rumbling his chest.

"Because I will never be anywhere near *your* bed, asshole."

Prit turned and walked into the hangar. She smiled as she waited for him to catch up, both in thought and body. Taking men down a peg was one of her favorite activities and Mindal had been begging for it since she arrived.

"Oh my poor baby," Prit groaned when she saw her ship. All thoughts of torturing Mindal gone as she immediately started to mentally catalog the damage and needs.

She got to work ordering around the men there and rolling up her own sleeves to dig in as well. There was no time to waste, she wanted away from here.

Five hours later Prit was walking back to her room, greasy but happy. The ship was flyable, and she'd given directions to the remaining men on what still needed to be done to get her in top form.

When she walked into the room Saluk jumped up from the couch, Jet cradled in his arms. His eyes swept up and down her body, assessing.

"You were gone a long time," Saluk accused.

"The ship took a lot of damage," she said with a shrug. "Sorry, I didn't mean to leave you alone so long. I hope you weren't too bored."

"Do you know when the last time I was alone in comfort was?" he said with a serious tone.

Prit shook her head.

"Not since I left for my journey on Halador."

"So long."

"I've been alone a lot, but never so comfortable as this."

"Of course," she said with a laugh. "I see you showered. I

need to again as well; it'll be dinner time soon and my brother will expect us dressed up and on time."

"They brought more clothes for both of us," Saluk confirmed.

Prit didn't miss the slight scowl on Saluk's face. "You didn't like what they chose?"

He shrugged "I didn't think it was necessary unless you wanted me to wear them."

"Honestly I don't care either, but in the interest of avoiding my brother's annoyance, let's put on what he sent up."

Prit showered and changed into a long dark blue tunic style dress with white loose pants underneath. There were even gold slippers for her feet. She didn't love playing dress up in her father's people's style, but she also knew she looked good and when she walked out of the bedroom she was feeling confident.

Saluk was dressed very similarly in a short blue tunic that matched hers and gold pants that were tighter than intended due to his gladiator physique.

"You look good," she said with a chuckle, "I hope your big dick can breathe in those pants."

"Hardly," he grunted.

"Well, it's just for dinner, then you can try to peel them off."

"I might need help," he said with a slight grin.

"Saluk! You tease," she said laughing and grabbed his arm, surprised and delighted by his light comment, she hadn't been sure he had a sense of humor.

She decided she didn't want to let go of him, so she didn't. She held his thick bicep as they walked down the hall but when they reached the top of the steps she let go; it wouldn't be fun to deal with the questions if she was hanging on her bodyguard like a girlfriend.

When they entered the dining room she was surprised to

see the number of people present and her eye immediately assessed them all for her.

Lives in the room: Fifteen

Species present: Three; Eludian, New Earth Human, Haladian.

Danger: Unknown, all present species dangerous, proceed cautiously.

Prit nearly snorted, her eye sometimes forgot what kind of weapon she was, and it certainly wasn't smart enough to realize that she was related to the one in charge in this room. Five of the people present were servants, and the Haladian was her bodyguard. There were just some things that technology couldn't assess accurately. Not that she wasn't going to be on guard throughout dinner, but more to the advances and marriage proposals of Mindal than anything else.

Prit walked to the long glass table where her brother was seated at the head in a thronelike white chair. The other chairs matched but were slightly smaller; enough to make sure everyone knew how important he was. To his right was a woman, the New Earther, with red hair and a lot of makeup.

Species: New Earther

Sex: Female

Age: Thirty

Danger: None, small muscled, no weapons detected

. . .

When the woman saw Prit, her eyes narrowed slightly as if she didn't like the competition, but when the woman's gaze went to Saluk her face showed horror immediately, making Prit's defensiveness rise.

"Sister!" Jattin said happily and the woman immediately turned to him and started batting her lashes.

To his left sat Mindal and beside him was an empty seat obviously meant to be for her. The problem was the seat next to that was filled with some Eludian she didn't care to try and remember the name of though his face was familiar. Prit just looked at the man and said, "Move."

The man sputtered a bit and looked at her brother who just nodded and the man scrambled to obey. Sometimes being Princess had its advantages.

"Sit," she told Saluk who glared at her briefly before sitting and she took the seat next to Mindal.

"I'm Jackie," the New Earth woman said once Prit was settled. She stuck out her hand across the table and Prit shook it. "I'm here with your brother. I didn't know his sister was on planet, and you're human, or, um, well you look human." Her cheeks turned red with embarrassment, and she darted glances at Jattin as if to make sure she hadn't offended him with her comment.

"I do," Prit said giving Jattin a sly look, she wondered if her father approved of this little houseguest. "I'm here, and ready to eat."

The woman looked disappointed at the short reply, but Prit wasn't here to try and impress some female her brother was passing time with briefly.

Jattin just shrugged and motioned for the servants to begin serving the food. The meal passed pleasantly enough. It was good food, and she enjoyed the meal, except that Mindal kept talking to her about how things were going on Elude. She feigned just enough interest to keep him going so she didn't have to try and make conversation with Jackie who kept looking at her like she wanted to become best friends.

Prit glanced over to Saluk every once in a while and saw him scowling at his plate as he ate, she wasn't sure what was bothering him so much until she realized that when the servants came to his place they were acting as if being near him was a horrifying situation.

Prit immediately saw red. "What the fuck is wrong with your staff, Jattin?" she snapped.

Every eye turned to Prit except Saluk who scowled harder at his meal.

"I'm sorry, did they do something to offend you?" Jattin asked with surprise.

"Not me," she gritted. "But they are treating Saluk like a fucking diseased peasant. What the fuck, haven't they ever seen a Haladian before?"

"Well, no, they certainly haven't," Jattin laughed.

"I think it's the scars, honey," Jackie whispered loudly as if she really thought Prit didn't realize. "They do tend to startle you to look at."

"Oh is it, Jackie?" Prit hissed. She felt a strong hand on her thigh, squeezing and she looked over at Saluk. He was looking at her with a blank face, body stiff, and just shook his head. She wanted to wrap him in her arms. Wanted to kiss his face and tell him that she didn't care what anyone else thought. Didn't care what these perfectionists were offended by. She thought he was perfect, and she thought he was amazing, and she thought ... well she thought things about him that she had no business thinking.

"I can assure you no offense was intended, Saluk," Jattin offered.

"None taken," Saluk said tightly, squeezing Prit's thigh.

"I think I've had enough for one night," Prit said, throwing her napkin on the table and scooting back. "Thank you for dinner, Jattin, and it was great to meet you, Jackie, I'm sure we'll be seeing each other again," she added with a smirk for her brother. There was no way this woman was going to last, none of them had in the past and this one seemed particularly clueless. Jattin was sleeping his way through settled space, one species at a time, it seemed.

Saluk stood to follow her and Mindal tried to as well, but she gave him a hard glare and for once he seemed to understand he wasn't wanted and cleared his throat as he readjusted in his seat.

"See you at breakfast," she said to Jattin and, ignoring everyone else, made her way out of the room. This was the kind of shit she hated about Eludians and humans. Perfectionists.

Saluk was lying awake on the soft fur rug, staring up at the ceiling. He couldn't sleep, and not because of the annoying fear he saw on every servant's face during dinner, he knew what he looked like. It wasn't because of the frustrating reminder that Prit would never really be attracted to him, not next to so many other options. He was too damaged.

No, it was because he was alone. A few nights with a family of sorts around him and he was ruined for this lonely existence. He craved the warmth of Prit and that stupid pet of hers. He ached to feel his purr being drawn out of him, recognizing the presence of someone to love and protect.

He never wanted to sleep without her again and that pissed him off because he knew that one way or another, they'd be going on their separate ways eventually. She'd leave him on

Halador to go back to his tribe and she'd be gone, off to make her way in the world. To thieve and adventure and put herself in danger over and over then eventually, she'd probably settle down with someone, Mindal perhaps or another worthy male like him.

It was best that he got used to sleeping alone again. He'd likely be doing it a lot; even if he rejoined his tribe he wasn't sure anyone would want to mate with him. He hadn't proven himself and he wasn't sure he would want any of the Haladian females anyway. None could compare to the tiny beauty sleeping on the other side of a wall.

After dinner she'd gone into that room with a simple goodnight, cradling Jet in her arms. No invitation, no hesitation, and that had said it all.

On the ship they had no other choice but to get close, but apparently if it wasn't necessary, she wasn't interested.

Saluk was deep into his wallowing of self-pity when a noise in the hallway had him up and moving, bodyguard duty back in the forefront of his mind. He crept to the door that led into the hallway and listened at it.

Another small noise.

He opened the door a crack and peered into the shadows, seeing nothing. He opened it a little further. A noise to his right brought his head around and then a sharp pain erupted right between his eyes.

He crumpled, his vision momentarily going dark. When it returned he was staring up at Mindal and unable to move. Whatever the man had hit him with packed a punch and might mean the end of him.

Mindal crouched and smiled down at him. "I hear you're wanted for escaping the Sabitarion king. No good there, we can't be harboring a dangerous criminal, and having you so close to the princess is a definite no-no." Mindal chuckled and stood, then three men stepped forward and grabbed at Saluk, lifting him and carrying him away from Prit.

He couldn't move or scream or fight and he wondered if Prit would even notice before morning that he was gone, and when she did notice, would she know that he hadn't left willingly? He would never willingly leave her; he knew that deep down in his soul.

More worrisome was what would become of her without his protection. Would Mindal trap her here, force her into marriage? His mind raged at the possibilities of harm that could come to her.

CHAPTER SEVENTEEN

Prit woke up in the night and immediately knew something was wrong. She didn't move, didn't want to give away that she was awake in case there was an intruder in the bedroom. After a moment she peeked around the room and her eye determined that there was no one there. She got up and crept to the living area which she found equally empty.

A terrible feeling of foreboding filled her gut, and she raced on silent feet to the hallway, whipping her head back and forth. No sign of anyone trying to get away from her room. She slipped into the hallway and hurried toward the main part of the house hoping she was wrong about the darkest thoughts pushing into her mind. A maid squealed when she came around a corner and saw Prit running in the dark.

"Ma'am?" the maid said.

"My bodyguard is missing," Prit snarled, and the poor girl trembled visibly.

"You mean that scarred man, the Haladian?"

"Yes," Prit hissed, the anger at this woman's judgement of Saluk had her clenching her fists.

"I think Mindal and his men took care of him, he was a

wanted criminal. You probably didn't realize, but he was an escaped prisoner from Sabit," the woman said with an attitude that made Prit want to punch her in her upturned nose. They never treated her like she belonged when her father or siblings weren't watching, they all thought she wasn't worthy of her title because her mother was a New Earther.

"Where was he taken?" Prit demanded.

"What the hell is going on out here?" her brother demanded, coming around the corner in a robe and pajama pants. The maid straightened and cast her eyes down, immediately going into a proper respectful pose.

Prit swung around and faced Jattin. "Mindal took my bodyguard."

Jattin addressed the maid. "Sersa, is this true? What do you know of it?"

The maid shot a glare at Prit before answering Jattin. "Mindal had a few men help him take the man away, he's a wanted criminal."

"Where the fuck did they take him?" Prit demanded again.

The woman pursed her lips as if she were going to refuse answering but Jattin's cleared throat had her meek again. "To Sabit, to collect a reward and return him to his prison, of course."

"Fuck!" Prit shouted, not caring if she woke the entire house at this point. She had let her guard down and Saluk was suffering for it, she should have known Mindal wouldn't have left things alone. She pushed past her brother to rush back to her room. She needed to get off this planet and catch them before Mindal did something seriously stupid.

"What's the real story, Pritalia?" Jattin demanded as he followed her.

"I saved him, he was being held prisoner on Sabit, yes. But he committed no crime, he was forced to be a gladiator for that bloodthirsty king. Lenkin has no right to demand Saluk back and Mindal is going to lose a few appendages if I ever see him again."

"Why do you care?" Jattin asked carefully. "What is this man to you?"

Prit froze in the middle of her bedroom, clothes in hand, she turned slowly to face her brother. "I care because I promised him safe passage. He helped me off of Sabit and I promised to take him back to Halador. I care because no one deserves to be held in a cage and forced to fight and kill."

"That's it? You aren't ... attached to the gladiator?"

Prit knew what her brother was driving at and also knew she had to tread carefully, whatever she told him would get back to their father and she didn't need any more pressure on her to marry Mindal.

"I keep my promises," she sneered and finished grabbing what she needed before pushing past Jattin again and out of the room with Jet in her arms. "And I don't like Mindal interfering in my business."

"Your ship won't make it fast enough, Mindal's is top of the line."

"Are you offering one of yours?" she asked hopefully.

"No, just telling you that you're wasting your time trying to save him because of some stupid deal. Some people are just meant to serve others. A scarred-up gladiator like him, he wasn't suffering there, they obviously fed him, provided women after he won. Not to mention the glory of battle with each death blow he struck. Whatever sob story he gave you was nothing more than a run at your bed, sister. I just hope you didn't fall for it," he said sternly.

"I guess I'm just too stupid to know when someone is tricking me, huh? I should let someone else decide who to be with," she sneered, knowing he thought she should settle with

Mindal, same as their father did. "I'm my own person, Jattin, always have been. I appreciate you giving me the place to fix my ship and hide from the New Earth military ships, but you aren't changing my mind now. I am going after Mindal and I *will* save my bodyguard again."

Jattin sighed heavily. "That's what I figured. Here take this." Jattin handed her a bag heavy with gold. "I know you need it."

Prit smiled and pulled him in for a quick hug. "Thank you, brother, I'll catch you again sometime, try not to freeze your tail off here."

He hugged her back and laughed. "Try not to get yourself killed out there, sister."

She left the house and ran across the yard. "I'm coming, Saluk, don't lose hope," she whispered as she pushed the doors of the ship hangar open.

Saluk could only hope that Prit didn't come for him as he was shoved back into a familiar cell. The door had been reinforced after they had broken out and there would be no easy escape this time. Not that he had any reason to escape if he couldn't get off the planet, if he couldn't get back to Halador, what was the point? He'd already lost his brother's remains, no hope now of carrying out the man's dying wish.

"Hope you're feeling well, gladiator," the guard sneered. "You'll be in the arena in two days and the crowd won't be rooting for a deserter."

Saluk didn't care, nothing mattered. He didn't have his brother's ashes, he didn't have Prit, and he didn't have his freedom. He laid down on the cold lonely cot and stared up at the rocky ceiling. Maybe he'd let them kill him in two days. Why fight when there was nothing worth living for anymore?

He'd had his one chance and he'd let his guard down, let himself be captured again. He didn't deserve another chance, if this was his manhood trial on Halador, he'd be called a failure destined to never take a mate or have children.

"I failed you brother, perhaps you'll find peace wherever Prit decides to leave you along her journey. I'm sorry I couldn't do better for you."

He closed his eyes against the pain those words caused, and images of Prit flitted through his mind. He knew he'd never really had a chance to possess her the way he desired, knew she wasn't really for him, but she was impossible to forget, and he knew that when he allowed the death blow to come in the arena, it would be the image of her face he'd hold on to. Her memory would be the last thing he knew before the end.

That decision gave him a bit of peace and he felt some of the anger leave his body.

His cell door opened and he turned his head but didn't move off the cot. Whatever was coming in he didn't care anymore.

"You ungrateful tripe," King Lenkin snarled as he waltzed into the cell flanked by two guards. The old man was too afraid of his precious gladiators to ever meet with them alone. Like all Sabitarions, he had a greenish hue to his skin and coarse black hair which he kept long and flowing around his shoulders, an obvious sign that he didn't engage in hard work or battle. Which his body also made obvious. He was quite fat for a Sabitarion, who were a fairly firmly-built race usually and although he was a decent height compared to many races, he still only came up to Saluk's chest. He wasn't a warrior king, but he pretended to be one when he sent his prisoners into the coliseum arena to fight for their lives.

Saluk sneered in the man's direction but he didn't say a thing, just went back to staring at the ceiling.

"You thought you could escape me? You thought some idiot girl could save you?" He laughed. "You are nothing, you were nothing when my men first took you off that godforsaken planet and brought you here. I made you into something and you owe me now not only for the glory you've received but also the high price I just paid to get you back. You *will* continue to pay that debt in blood and sweat and violence. I hope you enjoyed your freedom and the ass of that thief because you won't be seeing either ever again."

Saluk seethed at the way this man dared to speak of Prit, but he held himself silent and still, staring at the wall with hands and teeth clenched.

King Lenkin took a step closer, obviously feeling bold. "I hope her cunt was—" his words were cut off when Saluk flung himself up off the cot, hands stretched towards the king's neck.

He wasn't fast enough though, the guards pulled Lenkin back and thrust their prods toward Saluk. He crumpled to the floor as the volts passed through him, making his muscles spasm.

King Lenkin leaned over him with a grin on his face. "I think my gladiator is in love, how interesting. Too bad your ugly mug is unlovable; I am sure she's glad to be rid of you and your beastly form."

The king left and the guards each kicked him once before leaving as well, the door closing with a final thud behind them and the locks clicking into place.

When he was able, Saluk moved himself back to the cot and rolled to his side. His anger was white hot, but his sorrow was like a black hole swallowing him alive, because King Lenkin was right.

He had fallen in love with Prit, but she was likely happy he was out of her way.

CHAPTER EIGHTEEN

Prit hovered just outside of the atmosphere of Sabit, fairly certain that she was a couple days behind Mindal's ship. He would have gotten through the wormhole and to the planet in half the time as she had, which meant Saluk could have been down there suffering already for a day or two. She didn't have a plan, but she knew she wanted him out of there as soon as possible. Even if she had to get herself thrown in his cell again to do it.

What were the chances that they'd throw her into his cell as a reward again and not recognize her from last time and just execute her on sight?

Not good, she decided. She needed a different plan.

She glanced at Saluk's brother's ashes strapped into the extra seat. She'd taken to talking to the thing during her lonely trip to this planet and had even given the man a name since Saluk hadn't shared it. "We'll figure something out, don't worry, Ted."

Never had she felt such loneliness while on her ship as she had since leaving Elint. She'd always relished the silence of being on her own, the ability to do as she pleased, when she pleased. It had been freeing.

All of that was different now that she knew what it was like to share the small space with someone she actually enjoyed the company of. Someone who talked back and was a solid warm presence in her cot at night.

As much as she hated to admit it, because it felt like a weakness, she missed Saluk and wasn't sure she wanted to continue on like she had before she met him.

"I'm going to get him back, Ted," she said to the canister, then jetted through the atmosphere, careful to slip in far from the city before flying low and landing some distance from the coliseum and mansion.

You two stay here, she said to Jet and Ted as she pulled on a black suit that would cover her body and disguise her in the shadows. It even had a hood she could pull up and down low to conceal her face further. She was going in as The Shadow, and like a shadow she would move without sound or notice.

She'd never missed a mark before the last time she'd been here, and she would rather die than have the same result again. The mark was different, and the stakes were higher.

She was going in after Saluk and she was going to leave with him, or she was going to burn the fucking planet to the ground trying.

She left the ship and was immediately overwhelmed by the heat of the desert planet. Even with the sun not up yet she wanted to strip off all her clothing. She made her way as quickly as she could manage through the dark toward the coliseum, planning to enter where they'd escaped from, basically backtrack to the cells and find wherever they'd stashed him. If she'd broken out of one of those cells once, she had no doubt she could do it again.

Holding back near the shadow of a small grove of spindly

trees, she watched the entrance for a bit to determine where the guards might be. She timed them as one passed by and then another. Figuring they were both on loops, she was able to determine her best shot when the next passed at the expected interval.

It was almost too easy for a seasoned thief like herself. She went through the open and unguarded entrance to the coliseum, then found the tunnels where the gladiators must go from cell to arena. It wasn't until she'd made her second wrong turn within those tunnels and ended up going through a door that emerged into what looked like a hallway in the main house that she decided to change her plan of being lucky enough to stumble upon Saluk's cell. Her confidence in remembering the way she and Saluk had come from his cell was obviously misplaced. She hadn't even managed to find any of the gladiators' cells, just a few empty rooms that looked like they were meant for training and a storage closet of medical supplies.

By the looks of the sky outside a window in the hallway, she could tell the sun was just about to rise. Already she could hear servants moving about, starting to get ready for the day while the rich members of the household slumbered on. The risks, even for an experienced thief like herself, were too great to go traipsing through the house or tunnels in daylight. She needed a place to lay low until nightfall, and she wasn't sure the tunnels were her best bet. She imagined they were full of gladiators and guards during the day, training and whatnot. She couldn't be seen even by a prisoner who might unwittingly raise an alarm.

Unsure and wishing she could make it back to her ship, she stood frozen until a noise to the right had her bolting for the nearest door. She slipped inside as silently as she could.

The room was dark and she pressed herself against the wall as her bionic eye assessed the space.

. . .

Lives in the room: One, currently in a state of rest.
   Danger: Low

"Shit," she hissed quietly. She'd ended up in someone's bedroom. This was bad.

The noise out in the hall was getting closer though so she had no choice but to stay put and hope whoever was in that bed wasn't an early riser.

Steps in the hall stopped just outside the door and Prit threw herself to the floor then rolled behind a small couch just as the door opened and a maid walked in. Prit's eye immediately assessed the creature as dim light from the hallway flooded the room.

Race: New Earth Human
   Sex: Female
   Age: Twenty two
   Danger: Minimal, no weapons detected

Prit barely held back a gasp when the assessment scrolled across her eye, a New Earther servant, likely a slave who the Sabitarion king had bought on the black market. That would mean whoever's room this was, was an important member of the royal family. If it was King Lenkin she'd be tempted to kill the bastard here and now for all the suffering he'd heaped upon not only Saluk but countless others.

Prit bit her lip and looked around in the now dim light as the servant went about her duties, cracking the curtains and setting a tray near the large bed. The room was decorated in bright reds and golds, a vanity on one wall with trays of makeup and hair products. Not the King's room, this had to be a woman's room, either the queen or... could she be in the Sabitarion princess' room? Could she be within spitting distance of the necklace?

Prit's heart started to race at the thought of all her problems being solved. Right here in this room she could get what she needed. She could just wait here, hope to stay hidden, then she could find the necklace as soon as the princess left the room. She could leave and she could sell the cursed thing to Barius for twice what he'd intended, and she could have enough money to buy whatever she needed, whatever she wanted, for a very long time.

But how long before they knew it was missing, how long before they'd be looking for her? Could she rescue Saluk if she tipped them off by taking the necklace first? Or would she have to run as fast as possible once it was in hand, back to her ship. She was a smart thief; she knew better than to stick around after getting what she came for. Of course, she also knew better than to return to the scene of the crime, especially after being caught once already, and yet here she was.

Prit's gut twisted with indecision. She'd never turned down a risky move that would benefit her, but she'd also never had someone that she wanted to help. She'd never missed someone—who wasn't dead—the way she missed Saluk.

If she didn't prioritize saving him, would she be making a huge mistake?

If she left this room, this planet, without the necklace, would she be making a huge mistake?

"Morning Princess," the maid said quietly and poured something hot into a cup. "Your father is preparing for today's gladiator matches already and has requested that you make yourself presentable and be seen downstairs as soon as possible to greet important guests."

"Ugh, Daddy's favorite little monster is back and suddenly we have to rise at the crack of dawn to watch him kill someone. Does that really sound like something I want to do, Brittany?"

Prit's stomach clenched, knowing exactly who they were talking about. Every instinct in her screamed to save Saluk from having to go through the terror of killing in forced battle again.

"No ma'am, but it's his orders."

"His orders," the princess grumbled.

The servant snorted and left the room, closing the door behind her. The Sabitarion princess sat up and began sipping her tea while Prit's eye assessed her from the shadow of the couch she still laid in.

Species: Sabitarion
Sex: Female
Age: Nineteen
Danger: Minimal, no weapons detected but possible hand to hand combat ability.

But is she observant? Prit wondered as she remained in shadow throughout the princess' breakfast of some kind of tea and a bowl of fruit that was likely not native to this desert.

A banging on the door had the girl reluctantly leaving her bed. "I'm up, give me thirty minutes!"

Whoever had been banging was satisfied with that answer and apparently left. The princess shuffled across the room and into a door opposite the bed. As soon as Prit heard water running, she knew this was her chance to get out. She looked longingly at a large dresser that no doubt held a jewelry box but knew she'd already made her choice.

Saluk didn't deserve to have his freedom ripped away or to be forced back into the arena and she couldn't stand the thought of him having to risk his life for the entertainment of others.

He deserved so much more. He deserved to have everything he wanted for his life; a wife, children perhaps, all happy and together in a hut on Halador.

With a new determination and a half plan forming, she slipped into the hallway and back to the secret opening that led into the tunnels.

Saluk had a routine, and he slid into it despite his decision to lose the match that day; on the morning of a battle he meditated at dawn. Even though he couldn't see the sun, he could feel the change around him as the world outside his cell became bathed in sunlight. He sat cross-legged in the middle of the floor clearing his mind. He always saw his brother during these meditations. The familiar and comforting face would smile at him reassuringly, forgiving him for what he would have to do in order to survive.

But today it wasn't Tuk, today it was Pritalia who stepped out of the fog of his brain and smiled at him.

It's okay, I just need you to survive, Saluk. Whatever you do in there, it's not your fault and I won't hold it against you. We all do crazy things to survive. Stay alive for me.

"But I don't want you to come for me, I don't have anything to survive for any longer. I lost Tuk, I failed you, and I don't know why I'm holding on anymore."

You're holding on because you know I am a fierce warrior too, and I would never leave a man behind. I didn't leave you behind when you were injured, and I won't leave you behind now. Stay alive for me.

Saluk's eyes popped open and he took a shuddering breath in the dark empty room. He ran a hand over the freshly shaved side of his head settling himself back in reality. He knew that it wasn't real, that she wasn't here talking to him, but that didn't change the way he felt after hearing her voice in his head again.

He would do anything to see her, even survive years more of this gladiator life. If only he knew that she would be waiting for him at the end of the torture.

The door swung open and for a moment Saluk's heart stopped, his body tensed with dangerous hope. Was Prit here to save him?

A familiar and hated form filled the doorway. "You are back under my thumb," Gormar, the gladiator trainer said with a gruff laugh. He was a large Sabitarion, tall and broad, close to Saluk's size, but still smaller. He was large for his race, worked out constantly and ruled over the gladiators like a king.

Saluk glared at Gormar, knowing he was going to make Saluk's last moments hell if he could. Saluk wanted to tear the man apart, but he knew that a Tradjulian or two were standing just outside the door with weapons ready, and if he made even a slight move toward the man with malicious intent, they'd attack him with joy.

"I hope you're ready for the fight of your life because Lenkin is pissed and he wants to see you bleed," Gormar continued, leaning forward. "And if you win, you can expect to be thrown into match after match with the best I've got until Lenkin is satisfied with your punishment or you're dead, whichever comes first." After a moment of no response, Gormar chuckled then turned and left the room. "Get him to the armory and lace him up in proper gear, the king wants to see a good fight," he ordered the waiting guards.

Saluk stood, he knew the drill. The guards motioned him

out of the room and he walked in front of them toward the room where he would be readied for battle. Sometimes that meant nothing more than a loin cloth, other times he was given a weapon or armor depending on who and what his opponent was and what the king wished to see that day. If he was decked out in armor and given a weapon, Saluk knew to expect an opponent that was skilled, but if he went into the arena with nothing more than a cloth covering his cock, he knew that he was about to kill someone who could barely defend themselves and those were the kills that haunted him the most.

A scent drifted to him as they walked down the hall and he almost stumbled, his heart skipped, and he had to bite back a groan.

Pritalia, did her scent linger in these tunnels from their escape? Was it a trick of his mind trying to convince him to save himself? Or did he dare hope that she was here to rescue him?

If she was here, she likely was only here as planned for the necklace and her own freedom she could buy with it.

He hoped she got it and ran, he hoped she found everything she was looking for with the money.

Without him.

His heart nearly stopped, wanting to give up before he even entered the arena, just wanted to lay down and die at the thought that she could be so close and yet he wouldn't get to see her or touch her. Wouldn't get to hear her teasing laugh one more time. What was life anymore, what did any of this shit matter? But his body wouldn't let him die like that, he would die a warrior in a battle orchestrated by a bloodthirsty king. He would know peace today.

CHAPTER NINETEEN

Prit pressed herself firmly against a wall and prayed that the shadows would swallow her up as Saluk passed the tunnel she was hiding in followed by two Tradjulians with prodding weapons. She wished she could tell him she was here, but she knew she had to wait until there was a clear path to escape for them, and right now, the entire place was filling with guests ready to watch a battle to the death, starring Saluk.

She stood there unmoving, trying to decide what to do next. She needed to get to the coliseum, and she needed to remain unseen. Dressed as she was, she'd never go unnoticed in the crowd that she expected there.

Prit made her way back out of the tunnels and crept back to the princess' room. A quick listen at the door told her it was empty and she slipped in, going straight to the closet. Her eyes flicked to the vanity where makeup was laid out and a necklace of gold tossed aside as if the Princess had decided against wearing it. Prit's hands clenched and she bit her lip. Was it possible to just look? Find the necklace, assess for alarms and take it if it was free and clear and easy?

A shout in the hallway had her ducking behind the couch.

"I will see blood today!" a voice that she assumed to be King Lenkin shouted merrily and she was refocused to what she needed to do. She wouldn't risk Saluk's life for the necklace and she didn't have time to waste searching for the necklace that was likely in an alarmed box or locked vault anyway.

She went back to the closet. Lucky for her the traditional dress of the Sabitarions included veils to cover the face and it would provide enough distraction to hide her eye. She couldn't hide her black and blue hair, but the color wasn't something so unusual for many species that she should gather attention for it. She pulled a dress from far back in the closet, hoping it wasn't something that anyone would recognize as belonging to the princess. It was a floor length gold dress with long sleeves that she slipped easily over her black outfit. It was lightweight in deference to the heat of the planet and slightly big, allowing her to move easily in it. It wasn't fancy, no extra detail, no beading or jewels stuck to it for decoration. It seemed casual and she figured unless she ran into the princess herself, no one would question her for wearing it.

When she left the room this time, she avoided the tunnels and instead walked as if she belonged there in the house. The first servant she passed didn't give her a second glance and that gave her even more confidence. The next she passed looked at her strangely but went about his business as if whatever she might be doing was above his paygrade.

She emerged from the house and hurried toward a crowd that was moving in the direction of the coliseum entrance. There were so many different species present she knew she'd never draw attention as she was, but it helped that she had a talent, even dressed brightly, for moving along unseen. She slipped into step among a group, unnoticed, and kept pace as if she belonged with them. No one who saw her with the group questioned why she'd be there.

She knew she would get in without issue, but what then?

She couldn't hope to jump in and rescue him in front of all these people, but perhaps, in the glory of winning and the celebrations of the crowd after the battle, she'd be able to get to him.

He *would* win, she had no doubt, he was a fierce warrior and had already survived so many battles.

A thought occurred to her then that had her hands fisting and her gut tightening.

How would he be rewarded for winning? Would he be given a beautiful young prize to celebrate with? Would he, covered in blood and sweat, high on victory, take the woman?

Her eye stung with emotion at the thought and a betrayal she'd never even felt for something real filled her at the thought of a possible future action that she had no right to be angry about. The reasonable part of her mind tried to remind her that by his own admission he hadn't ever taken a woman they shoved at him, that he had no interest in the cowering fearful females. But jealousy didn't follow reason and fact, it followed fears of future possibilities out of her control.

None of that really mattered though because he wasn't hers; they weren't in a relationship. They'd shared one kiss, it had been a damn good kiss, but that was it. She owed him, and she felt bad for him, but there was nothing beyond that. She couldn't care if he fucked a hundred slaves that were shoved at him as a reward for taking someone's life in the arena. He was an obligation, not a boyfriend.

If that was it though, then why was she even here? Why was she trying to save him rather than taking the thing she knew was within reach that could give her everything she'd ever wanted?

She shook her head and glared forward, the answers to those questions wouldn't help her now, she'd made her decision, she was saving him so that is all that mattered in this moment.

Though if she dragged him out of the arms of a naked conquest it might determine what she did with him after saving.

Prit looked up as she walked under the archway, an image of two gladiators was carved into the stone there. One looked like a Sabitarion though exaggerated in bulk and height, the other was a species she recognized only from images, a native to Stranlion, a sister planet to Sabit. It was a serpent with arms and legs, a head that flared out around a flat face and small beady eyes. In the image the Sabitarion warrior was clearly winning, but in reality, Prit knew that the Stranlion would have wrapped his serpent-like body around the other warrior and squeezed the life right out of him. There was a reason why Stranlion was considered a hostile planet, and its inhabitants were not a part of the SSA.

As the crowd entered the coliseum it split in two, half the group headed around to the right and half to the left. Prit knew that the gladiators were being held to the right where the tunnels led to the cells, so she followed that group. Maybe she could get a look at Saluk before the battle, maybe she could tell him she was there to save him.

She quickly realized it wasn't possible. The crowd wasn't allowed that close to the gladiators, for their own safety Prit assumed, and unless she wanted to get noticed, she had no choice but to follow the flow of the spectators up the stairs without even a glimpse of Saluk or who his opponent might be.

It wasn't until that moment that the reality of Saluk going up against another powerful and dangerous gladiator hit her. It could be any species and it would undoubtedly be someone worthy of his skill level.

He could be injured or worse.

No, she told herself. She knew better, he would win, he had already survived so much more than any one person should have to and he wouldn't lose now. She wouldn't even consider it.

She went up some stairs to a section of the arena seating that seemed to be open to anyone, which meant it didn't move and get closer to the action. Other sections were for the rich and for dignitaries visiting. They could float and move, bringing spectators closer to the action and bloodshed.

It was probably better she wasn't on one of those. If she got close to Saluk in the middle of a fight she'd be all too tempted to jump in and help. It wouldn't benefit either of them to have her cover blown and be stuck back in a cell.

A roar from the crowd had her looking into the arena where a couple of gladiators were entering, it took only a quick glance to know neither was Saluk, they were both Ichites. The screeching sound of their feral start had the crowds excited and Prit scowling. What the hell was wrong with these people that they were so happy to see someone die?

She knew, she didn't have to ask. These were people who had never been in battle themselves, had never held someone who they'd fought beside while they died of a wound that couldn't be healed. They'd never lost friend after friend at the command of men and women who would sit back and watch from a safe distance, then step forward to reap the reward of another planet conquered, another species dominated.

These people cheering for the blood being drawn by the Ichites in the arena didn't see the warriors as people, they saw them as if players on a stage who were there to entertain by any means necessary.

It was disgusting.

Prit avoided looking down at the battle as she made her way to a seat she could take and remain unnoticed. She'd picked one next to what looked like a large group of locals. They gave her a brief glance as she settled, but as expected, went right back to their conversations and watched the battle with bloodthirsty glee.

Prit scanned the crowds all around the arena doing her best to avoid the battling pair, but she couldn't block out the sounds of their screams as they fought for their lives. It was easy to pick out King Lenkin and Princess Treenly with a large group on a floating seating section. They were surrounded by guards and servants and hovered close to the battle. King Lenkin jumped up and spilled his drink on a nearby servant as one Ichite made the killing blow, his long claws slashing through the throat of the other gladiator.

Prit watched as the roars around her reached a new height. The winner stood over the crumpled body unmoving except for the heaving of his shoulders. He didn't celebrate his victory; he didn't play to the crowd and bask in their excitement. When he finally looked up from the body, he'd slain there was a deep sorrow in his eyes that no one in the cheering crowds seemed to notice except her.

Suddenly she knew that she couldn't leave this planet without freeing all of them. She would raze the entire coliseum and King Lenkin's mansion to the ground if she could, this barbaric display was horrendous.

"You didn't bet on the grey one?" the man next to her asked.

"Oh," she said, clearing her throat of emotion. "No."

"Well, maybe you'll have better luck in the next match. Are you going for the Stranlion or the Haladian?"

The blood pounded in Prit's ears so loud she couldn't hear her own voice as she weakly replied, "Haladian."

The man spoke back but she heard none of it as she stared at the arena while the body of the dead was dragged away by a couple of servants. The winner had already walked out.

Winner ... there were no winners here, only survivors.

Saluk hadn't paid any attention to who the guards were setting him up against because he'd already decided he wouldn't fight back. It didn't matter, he would die here today knowing that Prit had come and gone with what she'd needed to make the life she wanted. She was going to be okay, and he could take comfort in that.

He put on the leather kilt and sandals that strapped up his calves. Around his arms he wore leather armguards from wrist to just below the elbow. He had a belt with a sword and a knife hanging from it.

He briefly wondered why he was being given two weapons, they usually only gave him one or none. They didn't ever want the fight to go too fast.

But it didn't really matter because he wouldn't be using either. He refused to give them a show today.

Saluk watched as Glar walked back into the holding area. The gladiator had a blank look to his face that Saluk recognized, he'd seen it over and over on the men who survived the battle. So often pitted against another who they had known from a neighboring cell or the practice and workouts that they were allowed every day to keep in top form. When there wasn't a new prisoner to fight against, Lenkin pit them against each other and that was always the hardest.

It wasn't until the bloody body of Larn was dragged by that Saluk truly understood the horror that had just occurred for Glar. They were brothers forced into the ring together knowing only one could make it out.

"Ready, Haladian?" the guard prompted, and Saluk stepped forward, past the familiar entryway and out into the roaring of a cheerful and bloodthirsty crowd.

A hiss had him turning to face his death and he understood then why he'd been given two weapons.

"When did Lenkin manage to capture a Stranlion?"

"I've been in this horrendous place for a week and I'm sorry, Haladian, but I plan to survive long enough to escape," the man hissed, his forked tongue slipping out and then back into his wide slit of a mouth that held sharp teeth. He was a bright blue, scaled being with a wide, flat face that stretched out to a head that was frilled out and smoothed down without neck to a serpent straight body. His arms were strong and long, his legs short but stout. The real danger was the man's long body and tail which—if it got wrapped around Saluk—would squeeze him until he died.

The Stranlion didn't have any weapons on him, but Saluk knew he didn't need them.

"I have been here too long, and I'm done surviving," Saluk said to the Stranlion as an announcer called out their information and signaled the start to the battle.

The Stranlion looked doubtful and readied to attack. A pod of seats floated close and out of the corner of his eye, Saluk saw Lenkin sneering at him as if he couldn't wait to see his best gladiator perish at the hands of the SSA's most lethal combatant. Beside Lenkin, the princess sat looking bored as usual, unfazed by the violence she'd seen so many times. Saluk felt sorry for the girl, knowing she was forced to watch these battles from a young age. The first time Saluk had seen her seated around the arena she couldn't have been more than ten and she'd been crying while her father frowned at her as if she were a true disappointment. The girl had learned quickly to hide her feelings about her father's gladiators and now she had perfected the blank bored stare no one would question.

"I'd rather kill *him*." The Stranlion jerked his head in Lenkin's direction. "But first, I have to walk out of this arena alive."

"I hope you do," Saluk said and stood his ground as the

predator approached. Saluk didn't move a muscle and he saw suspicion and anger flash in Lenkin's eyes.

There would be no battle here today, only slaughter and that's not what these people came for. Lenkin would be dealing with a disappointed crowd and that was very satisfying to Saluk.

The Stranlion didn't trust the apparent submission of Saluk and lashed out with his tail, knocking Saluk's feet out from under him. He hit the ground hard, a puff of red dust flew up around him and he grunted at the pain.

"Get up you worthless bastard!" Lenkin shouted at him.

Saluk just stared up at the sky, wishing it was a different one, remembering what it had felt like to lie and look up at purple-hued clouds, wet ground beneath him and blood rushing from wounds that he'd earned against a beast.

He should have died that day. His brother never should have interfered. Tuk would have survived the masat's attack, and Saluk would have been honored by his people for his bravery.

"Fight me true, there is no honor in killing," the Stranlion demanded.

"There is no honor in any of this," Saluk said but stood because the Stranlion deserved a solid victory. "I won't fight you. I am done with all of this."

The crowd was screaming for blood and Lenkin's face was purple with irritation. The Stranlion hissed, his forked tongue darting out showing his annoyance. Saluk could appreciate that the man had honor.

The Stranlion circled Saluk a few times, trying to goad him into a fight. He lashed out at Saluk's arm and back with claws, tearing skin, but Saluk didn't react, he'd made his decision. There was nothing to survive for anymore and with his last breath he would be defiant to what his captor wanted from him. He looked at Lenkin again and seeing the man's face twisted with anger, his hands gripping the railing as he sputtered and yelled. Saluk smiled, satisfaction filling him.

Lenkin shouted for his death and the Stranlion was finally ready to oblige. He leaped at Saluk, wrapping his long body and tail around him and began to squeeze. Saluk's arms were pressed to his sides, trapped, and he couldn't have gotten to his weapons even if he'd wanted to now. It would soon be over, and he was ready.

A scream pierced the air, an anguished demand to fight, but Saluk ignored it. He had no fight left, he was tired of fighting and winning just to fight again. There was no true glory in this arena.

He looked up at the sky and prayed that his gods would take him home to his ancestors.

He closed his eyes as the squeeze tightened and the crowd roared with disappointment. They weren't getting what they wanted, what Lenkin had promised, and that was satisfying for Saluk. His mind started to fuzz as the blood flow in his body was being cut off and an image floated up in the darkness of his mind.

Prit, drying her bionic leg at that damn table across from him.

Prit, bent over and pulling on shoes in her tiny ship.

Prit, above him as he woke from wounds he'd received protecting her.

Prit, curled against his body, activating the familial purr of his people.

Prit, standing in front of him on her ship with a sly smile just before she pressed her body to his and they finally kissed.

A scream pierced through the blackness and Saluk opened his eyes, fuzzy and unable to focus but he saw her there as if his last thoughts before death had brought her to life.

Another dream image? A remembered moment?

But no, she was wearing a Sabitarion dress, and a veil was pulled aside to reveal her face. He'd never seen her like that, this was no memory.

"Fight, goddamn you!" She was screaming as a Tradjulian restrained her at the edge of the arena balcony. She looked like she had been about to jump the railing. To save him? Why was she here, she had the necklace, she should be gone, safe and happy. His mind couldn't make sense of what he was seeing, too much time without proper blood and air flow, his senses were dulling and there was a new blackness seeping into his sight.

She is here. His mind screamed at him, making one last plea for life.

"Fight back!" she screamed again and Saluk's mind suddenly cleared. It really was her; she was here for him and if he didn't survive, he couldn't make sure she got off this horrid planet safely. No doubt she was drawing too much attention now, was revealing herself to Lenkin and his guards, she would be captured, she would be harmed.

He roared and pressed his arms out. The Stranlion was caught off guard by the sudden resistance and loosened around Saluk. Saluk was able to grip the small dagger and pull it out of his belt, ripping his arm upward, he slashed through the beast and was instantly freed from the squeezing serpent.

"You fight," the Stranlion said with glee.

"Yes!" Lenkin called from close by and Saluk knew what he had to do. He refused to kill the Stranlion, but he wasn't going to die here either.

"Let's both win," Saluk said just loud enough for the Stranlion to hear. The crowd roaring, now sure they were about to get the bloody fight they'd wanted.

The Stranlion looked at him with confusion, but Saluk didn't have time to explain, he grabbed the Stranlion's tail and swung him. With one great twist he sent the serpent flying toward Lenkin.

The crowd was in an immediate uproar as the serpent gladiator landed on the king. Complete chaos ensued as the Stranlion wrapped around Lenkin immediately and lashed out at the princess with claws. The guards rushed to save their king but were too late. The fat king was bleeding out of his eyeballs almost instantly and the Stranlion was moving on to the closest guard with vengeance on his face.

Saluk turned to where Prit had been moments before, but the crowds were panicking, rushing out now, and he couldn't spot her. The tunnels emptied of gladiators who'd been waiting for their turn in the arena, adding more chaos to the moment. Guards rushed to help as gladiators sprinted for escape.

Saluk didn't know how he was going to find Prit, but he knew he couldn't stay here where the guards might decide to capture or punish him.

CHAPTER TWENTY

Prit had nearly lost her mind as she'd watched Saluk just give up. Seconds from jumping into the ring and taking out the Stranlion herself, she'd been restrained by a guard. Now Saluk was lost to her gaze. She'd been pushed and prodded with the crowd as they fled toward the exit in panic, but she needed to get back to the arena floor. She was near the exit now and knew she definitely didn't want to go past the entrance. She'd never get back in against this crowd before it was too late.

She pushed and fought, breaking to the right and into a space along the wall where a statue of King Lenkin stood. She was able to press her body into a crack and let the crowd flow by without her, but what she needed to do was go against them. She had to head toward the arena but there was no break in the crowd to even hope of getting that way.

She scanned the surroundings and knew her only chance would be going up. She stripped out of the borrowed dress, her veil already lost, and hefted herself up the statue in her sleek black suit. Her legs wrapped around the statue's head and she scanned the panicked crowd for any sign of Saluk. She saw gladiators, nobles, and politicians as well as citizens and guards all running. There was no sense of who should go first as they all fought to live through this disaster.

Saluk was nowhere. She needed to move, needed to search.

She managed to get up to a railing and then she was fighting a smaller crowd to get back around in view of the main arena.

When she once again was able to see the arena floor, it was empty aside from a few dead. A quick glance told her that some were Tradjulian guards, and some were leather-wearing gladiators. Her stomach twisted as she scanned them once and then again but no, Saluk wasn't among the dead, she still had hope.

"If you're looking for the big, scarred Haladian, he went back into the tunnels," the Stranlion hissed, popping up behind her, blood covering his smiling face. "I saw you cheering for him. Your voice saved his life, and mine, too, I think."

"Thank you," she said and leaped off the balcony to the arena floor then rushed toward the tunnels. Why the hell would he have gone back in there?

She slowed when she entered the tunnels, not sure who she might find. She was afraid to call out for him in case she gave away his presence to a guard, so she went as quick and silent as she could back toward the cells that had held the gladiator prisoners.

A new rush of the imprisoned started to flow past her and she knew she was on the right track. Saluk was releasing everyone. He was an honorable man and wouldn't leave anyone behind to suffer the way he had, that must be why he'd come through here instead of heading for freedom, or for her.

She got to the length of cells that had held so many, all now empty and still didn't find Saluk so she continued on, taking the tunnel up to the main house.

She paused at the door, listening, but what she heard sounded like more chaos. She slipped into the hall and saw servants running and screaming as gladiators rushed around looting and destroying. Apparently not all who had been let out had rushed through the coliseum for escape, some were looking for revenge and she didn't blame them.

No longer worried about giving away Saluk's position in this mess, Prit started to call out for him.

"He went that way," the Ichite gladiator who had won a battle today said, pointing toward the stairs.

"Thank you," Prit said and rushed up, calling out for Saluk again.

"Pritalia?" Saluk answered and practically fell out of a doorway.

She jumped into his arms, wrapped her legs around his waist and pressed her lips to his in a desperate kiss then pulled back. "Fuck you!" she snarled and slapped him. "How dare you even think about giving up," she yelled, tears falling down her cheek. "How could you?" she whispered, her voice quivering with emotion. "You were going to die there."

Saluk grabbed her face and pulled her in for a soft kiss. "I thought you were gone. I had nothing more to live for," he admitted. "I don't want to live if it's not with you, Prit, not now that I know what it is to sleep next to you and purr with contentment. I had nothing left in me to fight until I saw you there in the crowd."

"You big, dumb gladiator," she said and released the tight grip of her legs, letting her body slide down until her feet touched the floor. "We need to get off this planet, I think it's about to undergo a massive revolution."

"Do you have the necklace?"

"It's not important. I just need you safe."

"And I need you safe from Barius," he argued. "We need the necklace," he said firmly.

She couldn't help smiling up at his scarred and glaring face, she ran a finger over the marks on his cheek. He was thinking of her, in all this terror and chaos and chance of freedom, he was thinking of her. "Follow me," she said.

She led him to the princess' room and they easily found the necklace under a false floor of a jewelry box. An alarm sounded as they lifted it but they both knew no one was going to rush in to see what was going on.

Saluk grabbed her hand and led the way out of the room and down the hall. There were other gladiators still in the house; their arms full of treasures as they snarled and snapped at anyone who got in the way, but they didn't bother Saluk or Prit. When a Tradjulian guard entered and started making demands as if he were still in charge of the gladiators, Saluk shoved Prit behind him, ready to fight their way out, but it wasn't necessary. Two other gladiators dropped their treasures and leaped on the guard, tearing him apart so fast the guard had only been able to get in one hit with his prod, luckily it hadn't done any damage to the gladiator who was equipped with a hard skin over most of his body, a native of Lixten, a planet near New Earth with a hot, swampy environment.

"Thank you," Saluk said to the men as they gathered up their stolen treasures once again.

"Thank *you*," the Lixtenian said. "You have given all of us a chance at real life and family again."

Saluk grabbed Prit's arm and they were again making their way out of the house. Once outside they encountered more chaos. The locals, many of whom were dressed as servants of the house, were tearing apart the grounds with the help of the freed gladiators. It would seem that the royal family didn't treat anyone well around here.

"Where is your ship?" Saluk asked.

"This way," Prit said and led him in the direction of her camouflaged ship.

She couldn't help laughing at the thought that this was the second time she'd led him away from this very prison, and yet, this time felt completely different. This time felt like she was saving herself too.

Saluk followed her with a lightness in his chest that he couldn't explain.

She'd come for him. She hadn't come for the necklace. She'd come for him.

But he'd gotten the necklace for her. He could finally say he'd paid her back for all the times she'd saved him.

He almost stumbled as another thought occurred to him then. Would she take the necklace and run? Dump him off on Halador and go on with her life the way she'd wanted?

He shook the thought away, it didn't matter, she had saved him, and he had given her what she needed to save herself. Whatever happened next just was.

He couldn't ignore the way that thought hurt.

They made it to the ship with little interference. Everyone exiting the coliseum and mansion were intent on escape before the whole planet imploded with the civil war that had begun.

Saluk practically shoved her up the staircase and into the ship. "Get us out of here," he snapped. He smiled when he saw the canister that held his brother strapped into the seat, he quickly traded places with it as she jumped to the pilot's seat and the staircase closed up.

"You aren't going to complain about my driving?" she asked as she flipped switches.

"Not right now, far and fast sounds perfect."

"I can do that," she said, throwing a smile over her shoulder at him as the engines roared to life.

And she did. They shot straight up and she dodged dangerously around a few other fleeing ships before jetting forward. He lost hold of the canister and it rolled and banged around a bit, but eventually it made its way back to him and he was able to trap it between his feet.

"Hold on, babe," she said as she made a few quick movements.

Twenty minutes later they were flying smooth and steady. She set autopilot coordinates then stood up and stretched. Saluk's gaze drank in every line and curve of her body, starving for the sight of her after their time apart.

When she turned to him with flushed cheeks and a wide smile, he unstrapped and crossed to her, pulling her into his arms. He crushed his lips to hers and when she responded by running her hands up into his hair and pressing her body against his, he groaned.

"If we get attacked this time I'm not stopping," he warned as he kissed along her neck.

"Good, because I would rather go down with a burning ship and have your body writhing naked over mine than lose this moment."

Saluk groaned again and nipped at her neck, making her shudder against him. He did it again and gloried in the reactions that her body gave to his touch. She was perfect. Her hands moved along his bare back and when she hit a new open wound he couldn't hold back a slight hiss.

"Oh fuck, I forgot you're hurt," she said and pulled away.

"I'm fine," he said and grabbed her arms, pulling her roughly back against him.

"If you hiss when I touch you, you're not fine. I want nothing but sounds of pleasure coming from your mouth when we have sex."

Just hearing the word come out of her mouth was enough to

make his body tighten even more, which he hadn't thought was possible. He was ready to burst like an untried youth and embarrass himself in front of her.

She reached up and touched his face gently. "Saluk, let me care for you," she whispered.

The words tore through him and he nearly crumpled with the feelings it brought up. Not sex, but care. She wanted to care for him and that was something he desperately craved, something more intimate, something deeper. He was almost afraid to speak, his throat so full with emotion.

"Okay," he finally said, his voice gruff. "But I'm barely wounded, you just surprised me with the touch," he added, not wanting to look weak in front of her.

"Bleeding isn't nothing, and it should be cleaned at the very least to avoid infection."

He couldn't argue with that, it wouldn't be the first time he ended up with an infected wound after a battle.

She pushed him gently to sit backward in the chair and pulled out a first aid kit. She cleaned the couple of minor wounds on his back where his opponent had scratched him, then dabbed on some cream.

"I will cover it to keep the cream on, but it's not bleeding anymore so I think you'll be okay."

"I know I will," he said. When she straightened, he turned around and pulled her onto his lap. "I am with you, there is nothing that could make me not okay in this moment."

"Saluk," she whispered and cradled his face in her palms, then pressed her lips gently to his. She shifted her body until she was straddling him. He gripped her ass and pulled her tight against his body. She kissed along the scars that lined his face, following them down his neck. "You are the strongest person I've ever met." She punctuated each word with a kiss. "You have been through things that no one should have to endure." She nipped at his earlobe. "In your moment of escape you thought of me," she said and sat back to look into his eyes. She pulled the necklace out of her pocket and eyed it with triumph. "You thought of me and my needs at that moment and I want to repay you for that kindness."

Saluk froze as she bent to kiss him again. She wanted to repay him. She wanted to thank him for getting her the means to live her life.

It was like a blast of cold water on his desire.

He stopped her, grabbed her upper arms and pulled her back. "I think I should rest," he said gruffly.

"Oh," she said, her cheeks heating, "Oh yeah, of course. See, I told you that you were more hurt than you thought. Now that the adrenaline is worn off, you're tired." She jumped off his lap and hit the button to release the bunk. "Rest, I'll take us safely on for a few more hours."

"I'll sleep easy knowing you're in charge," he assured her and laid down on the cot, giving her his back.

He stared at the wall and listened as she pulled Jet out of his cupboard and fed him, then settled into the pilot's seat. No doubt confused by his rejection, but if he slept with her when she was only feeling thankful and not the deep aching need that he felt for her, it would be a hollow experience. He wanted more than her gratitude, even if he didn't deserve it.

When she left him on Halador and went on with her life, he didn't want to know what she tasted like, what she felt like under him. He didn't want to know what she sounded like when she came undone around him. It would be impossible to forget, or to move on from and no female would ever be able to compare, he knew it.

His body reacted to the thoughts of her, hardening even more than before and it took all of his control to just lie there and feign sleep until eventually his body relaxed.

Hours later when she crawled quietly and gently in beside him to sleep as well with her back pressed against his and her breathing even, his purring started up and he finally started to fall asleep.

He never wanted to fall asleep without her again and knowing he would have to was like an open wound he couldn't stop from seeping painfully.

CHAPTER TWENTY-ONE

The next few days were uncomfortable. There was no teasing, no kissing, and every time Prit accidentally brushed up against Saluk, he pulled away like she'd burned him. After the first morning of torturous silence, Prit suggested she take him to Halador straight away, but he'd again insisted on paying her back by standing behind her when she negotiated with Barius. She was confused, and more than a little hurt by his silence. Was he offended that she'd kissed him? Had he stopped her because she'd thrown herself at him like a floozy again and he saw it as a bad thing? Maybe she'd misinterpreted every little touch and look from him this entire time and he'd never been attracted to her. He talked about duty so often, was that all every action of his had been. Just his duty to her for saving him the first time?

She didn't know, and every day that passed made her more and more frustrated, angry, but most of all, sad, disappointed, and hurt. She knew how to keep it all in though and just get the job done, that was something she'd learned in the military. You don't get emotional about a mission.

And so, three days later they were barely talking to each other when they asked permission to dock with Barius' ship.

"You don't have to do this," he said for the thousandth time. "You can just sell it yourself, can't you?"

"That's not the point. I want to squeeze Barius for every cent possible and show him that I can steal anything. And besides, I have a reputation to keep. I am a thief that is always successful and never double crosses. I am The Shadow. It's why I am paid so well for jobs."

He just grunted and strapped on another weapon.

"Permission to dock granted," came the response over the radio and Prit took a steadying breath as she eased the small ship into the opening docking portal. She guided the ship in with such skill she swore she heard Saluk grumble about her purposefully bad driving and for just a second she remembered how things with him had been before she'd thrown herself at him so completely.

It would never be like that again; she'd ruined the fun friendship they'd had.

She had to realize and accept that she wasn't what he wanted. He wanted his family and his planet, perhaps the mate he'd hoped to have before he was captured. The best thing she could do for him was to get him to Halador as soon as she finished this run, because she owed him, and she cared about his happiness, maybe more than she should.

The doors closed behind her ship with a jarring thud and Prit gritted her teeth as Barius' men poured out of an interior door as soon as the airlock was activated and oxygen rushed into the docking room.

Apparently Barius wasn't going to be the trusting type today; the men were armed.

Prit wasn't strapping on any weapons, a show of confidence

and peace. She was wearing tight black shorts so she'd have access to her leg, but she was pretty sure Barius wasn't aware of what she hid there. She wasn't stupid and she wouldn't let anyone harm Saluk.

She hooked the necklace around her neck and its bright pink stone shone brilliantly against her black high neck tank top. She wasn't usually one for jewelry, but she liked the feel of the heavy stone today, like a badge of honor, it had been one hell of a trip getting the damn thing.

The Bularian race was ugly; short and wide with bright orange flesh covered in scales. They had black teeth behind plump lips and tended to drool a lot due to their rather large tongues that also lent itself to a slurred sort of speech that took some getting used to. The warriors like Barius and his men shaved their heads and wore metal adornments on their skulls that also served as a sort of protective layer in a fight. The only real difference in their women were the enormous breasts they all seemed to have, and they usually kept long hair, braided down their backs and encased in metal that sometimes even sported spikes to deter anyone from grabbing it in hand-to-hand combat.

It wasn't a species that anyone wanted to mess with, and Prit had desperately taken a job from their warlord. Now she was coming in, flaunting success, ready to demand more than they'd agreed upon. It could be the biggest mistake she'd ever made, or it could be the most successful job she'd ever done.

Prit turned to Saluk who was standing and ready. He had a fierce set to his face, his hair braided to the side, and he'd shaved the side of his head just that morning, making his scars more prominent there, which added to his dangerous appearance.

He was beautifully frightening, and she couldn't stop the smile from breaking out on her face as she looked at him. "You look good, stud," she said but he only grunted and frowned at her, reminding her that they weren't being friendly now. She dropped the smile and hardened her tone. "Ready to do this?"

"I'm ready to get this over with," he grunted.

Hurt squeezed her stomach. "Right, and then you'll be on your way home finally," she said with what she hoped was only cheerfulness in her voice. But there was something else in her throat, something else in her chest at the thought of dropping him off on Halador.

His face was unreadable as usual, so she had no idea if he'd heard the strangled tone. She hit the button to let down the stairs and moved to descend first.

He was right behind her, and as he reached the platform, five Bularians stepped forward. Two went right and two left, leaving one glaring at her from the middle, obviously in charge.

"Barius is waiting to receive you, Shadow, but he didn't say to expect anyone else," the man said, gesturing with his chin to Saluk.

"Well, if he wants to see me and this," she said sweeping a hand over the bright jewel on her chest, "then he'll welcome my bodyguard as well."

The man just rolled his big grey eyes and snorted. "I'm sure he'll be thrilled, follow me." The man turned and walked through the door but the others stood waiting for her and Saluk to follow.

Prit went through the door with head held high, not letting any hint of unease show, Saluk right behind her. They passed into a hallway and the other guards followed. When the door to the docking bay closed behind them all, Prit barely held back a shudder. They weren't helpless, but that didn't mean they weren't walking into the belly of the beast right now. She felt Saluk move closer behind her, and she drew strength from him. She wasn't alone, she reminded herself.

"Got anything to drink?" she asked with her false confidence.

"I'm not here to serve you, female," the man sneered.

"I come here after a successful mission, I think I deserve a celebratory drink," she scoffed back.

"Successful would have been weeks ago."

Prit glared at the man's back. Thankfully they'd arrived at a door and a need for response was lost. They walked into a large room, bare except for a black throne at the back wall. The entire space was smooth black and gave a cold stark impression that matched what she knew of Barius' personality.

The man himself was seated on his throne in a robe of gold that clashed garishly with his skin tone, and an ugly smile on his face.

"The Shadow has returned," Barius said with a slight rise to his wet lips, his big tongue flashed out and added more drool to his chin.

"Successfully," Prit agreed, touching the necklace for emphasis.

"My necklace has finally arrived."

"Not yours," she said, stepping forward quickly, knowing any hesitation would be seen as weakness and any weakness he spotted would be used against her.

His eyes flashed with anger.

"You sent me for this, yes, and I failed, no harm there, you hadn't paid me yet."

"And yet here you stand, with the necklace, and in my chamber," Barius said, pointing at her, his voice dangerously low.

"Because *after* your men tried to shoot me out of the sky, I went back for it on my own, not under your orders. So this thing is mine, and I know you want it, so, the question is, Barius," she paused and smiled sweetly. "What are you willing to pay for it?"

"Your confidence is unfounded, thief. We had a deal and if you're backing out, you're far outnumbered even with that Haladian warrior behind you."

Prit fingered her leg where a sharp spike hid, she could have it in hand and thrown at his neck or chest before he knew to be afraid. But then the five guards in the room would be on her and she knew that getting out alive at that point would be very risky. She hadn't come here to kill anyway; she'd come to get paid.

Barius' eyes flicked to her fingers. She quickly switched her movement and stuck the hand at her hip, cocking it out and with her other hand she stroked the necklace.

"We are both negotiators at heart, Barius. I have what you want, our original deal was void the moment your ships came after me. I went back and was successful, lucky me. Now, what are you willing to pay for this pretty piece? I'm even willing to forgive the whole trying to kill me thing, for the right price."

"You know what, Pritalia, you're right," Barius said with a smile that immediately put Prit on edge especially paired with her real name, she didn't usually use it when dealing in these situations, she wasn't even certain he'd known her real name.

Something was wrong, she stiffened and behind her she heard Saluk give a low growl.

"As usual," she said carefully and turned her bionic eye on. She'd left it off so she wouldn't be inundated with how dangerous the beings she was surrounded by were but now she worried she'd missed something.

It immediately started telling her she was in grave danger, but nothing she didn't expect.

"We did have a deal, and due to circumstances, that deal is void. You were unsuccessful, as you said. Unfortunate for your reputation, I didn't expect such a lack of preparedness from The Shadow."

"So let's make a new one," she said, hoping to hurry things

along. She wanted back on her ship, back out in space. She didn't like what was happening here, not at all. She'd take anything he offered at this point just to get away safely with Saluk.

"Well, you see love, I already made a new deal, just not with you."

Doors opened around the room and suddenly she was surrounded by Mindal and her father's men.

She heard Saluk pull a sword, but she held up a hand to stop him, he'd never win against this many and she knew that Mindal wasn't here to kill her, it was so much worse. He was here to possess her.

"Did my father approve of this plan?" she sneered at Mindal. No longer worried about Barius, he wasn't the biggest threat to her future in this room anymore.

"Your father agreed that getting you home by any means necessary was in everyone's best interest. Now come along and we won't have reason to harm your guard." He narrowed his eyes at Saluk. "I hear you're fond of him, so I expect you'll do as necessary to keep him in one piece."

Prit looked behind her at Saluk who was waiting for her instructions, sword still halfcocked. She shook her head again and he sheathed it, but he frowned at her as he did.

"I'll go back to Elude. I'll talk to my father," Prit said with a heavy sigh. "This is ridiculous, he could have sent a message, I would have gotten it eventually." She tried to keep her tone light, exasperated but playful to diffuse the tension between Saluk and Mindal.

"It's too late for that, my dear, you're coming on my ship. I'm delivering my bride personally." Mindal had crossed to her while he spoke and he smiled down at her with malice, making her wonder if he was hoping she'd resist so he'd have a reason to manhandle her a bit.

She heard Saluk growl behind her again and knew he'd gotten closer to her as well, but she didn't dare look at him now. Not knowing what she was going to have to do to save him.

"Fine," she gritted. "But I still have some business with Barius to attend to."

Mindal reached up and touched her chin. "Good girl," he whispered, making her cringe, then he trailed his hand down her neck to the necklace. "This is no longer your business," he snarled and grabbed the stone, yanking hard enough to break the clasp and leave a scratch on the back of her neck.

Prit gasped and pressed a hand to the scratch, feeling it sticky with blood. She heard the slide of Saluk's weapon and then the sound of others around them. He couldn't defend her, not here, not now.

"Leave it," Prit hissed at him over her shoulder. "I'm fine, just leave it," she said, a tear threatening her eye knowing he had a dozen weapons pointed at him and if he made one more move toward harming Mindal, he'd be dead before she could scream no.

Mindal laughed and tossed the necklace to Barius who cackled with delight and walked out of the room, apparently done with the situation. His men followed him out and it was just her and Saluk with Mindal and his loyal men.

Saluk hadn't put his sword away, but it was pointed at the floor now and Mindal's men stood with their own weapons half ready. The tension in the room was explosive and as much as she wanted to scream and yell at Mindal for giving away her hard-earned freedom like that to Barius, she knew she couldn't. Not with Saluk's life in danger. Mindal and his men wouldn't kill her, but they looked like they were thirsting for an excuse to take Saluk's blood.

"I can't just leave Saluk here, or my ship," she insisted, hoping to find a bit of reason in Mindal if she didn't argue. If he really wanted her to marry him, maybe he'd be a bit reasonable.

"Let him take your ship, you won't need it anymore. I won't be allowing my wife to traipse around the galaxy like a feral pirate. It's a piece of old junk anyway, should have been decommissioned years ago."

Prit fisted her hands, wanting to defend her ship but knew it was useless, Mindal had made up his mind and she couldn't fight it here, not in enemy territory while he thought he had complete backing of her father. She just had to hope maybe he didn't.

She looked at Saluk, but his face was unreadable. Did he have any idea how to drive a ship? Could he get himself home? He'd been watching her carefully, he seemed to be a fast learner, did he pick up enough? Why hadn't she taught him how to fly when she had the chance?

She knew why, she never let anyone touch her ship, and he hadn't ever asked. But he had watched, she had to hope it would be enough because she didn't have any other option. Not with weapons trained on Saluk. If it was just her, she'd have fought and she'd have run, but she wouldn't put Saluk in that kind of danger.

"I need Jet," she insisted.

"Fetch her pet and bring it to the ship," Mindal ordered one of his men, then grabbed her arm in a bruising grip and pulled her out of the room.

Saluk just watched her go with an ever-darkening gaze and she prayed he wouldn't fight for her, that he would just let her go.

"Thanks for all the help, get home safe," she whispered as she passed him. She knew she'd survive what Mindal and her father had planned, she knew she'd get away, unmarried. But she didn't know how long it would take and she didn't want

Saluk to have to be involved in it anymore. She met his gaze for a second and gave a wry smile, this wasn't exactly how she wanted things to end between them. She hoped he understood that too.

She walked on with Mindal, out of the room and down a hallway to a different docking bay than her ship was in. This one held a large ship she recognized as one of her father's. It was his signature blue and had plenty of weaponry.

"You had to know you wouldn't get away with that little stunt, right?" Mindal whispered in her ear, his hand squeezing her arm tighter.

"I didn't want to lose out on the profit of that take," she scoffed, "And not to mention my reputation for never failing a job."

"And the Haladian?" he challenged.

"Makes a great bodyguard, I don't trust Barius," she said with a shrug.

Mindal snorted, disbelieving, but didn't argue with her as they reached the ramp and she hurried ahead as if eager to get on his ship. He let go of her arm and as soon as she was through the doorway she demanded the closest guard show her to a private room where she could shower and rest.

One thing she didn't have to worry about was Mindal's affections before they arrived on Elude. Her father had strict rules, no one touched his daughter and if Mindal thought he'd already won, he wouldn't push those boundaries.

She was taken to a room that was spacious considering what she was used to. A bed and dresser, a private bathroom that held a shower, sink, and toilet. Not that it was much comfort when she knew she wasn't free to control where this ship was taking her.

She paced the small space until someone arrived with Jet. She wanted to ask if Saluk had made it back to the ship, if he had taken off yet, if he was okay. But she had to let them think she didn't care too much, so she just took Jet and kissed him fiercely. She may never know what would become of Saluk, and that hurt.

Saluk waited until they'd taken Jet from Prit's ship before stepping into it. As soon as he closed the hatch of the ship, the doors to the docking bay opened and he knew he was being kicked out. It was good, he reasoned. Being stuck here with the Bularians would likely prove deadly.

But what the hell was he supposed to do? He'd watched Prit close enough to know a bit about how this ship worked and after a couple moments of second guessing himself he started to throw switches and push buttons. The ship lurched forward, damaging something with a crunch, but no alarms went off on the ship, so he knew it wasn't Prit's ship that had been damaged. He smiled, happy to leave Barius with a bit of hurt. He pushed a different button, and the ship flew backward out the door barely missing the ceiling as he went.

When he was a little distance away, he stopped the ship's movement and watched Barius' ship until another door opened and a large blue ship that he recognized as the one that had taken him from Elint to Sabit emerged. Prit was on that ship now and he wanted to rage, wanted to attack, wanted to save her like she'd saved him so many times.

But he didn't know how, and her words stuck in his mind. He knew what she'd meant, she'd been telling him to just leave her, to just get home and forget about her. But how could he?

An honorable warrior would never, and he had never wanted to be anything but honorable. He looked at the canister that held his brother's ashes.

"What would you do?"

Saluk nodded as if his brother were speaking.

"Yes, I agree," he said softly and then set a course like he'd seen her do so many times. There was one place he thought he could go to get help, because a warrior always knew when to call in reinforcements.

CHAPTER TWENTY-TWO

A week later Mindal's ship was pulling into the atmosphere of Elude. Prit stood at the window and watched as the bright planet rushed towards them. She was dressed in a traditional Eludian tunic and pants to please her father and because she hadn't thought to grab her clothes off her own ship, only Jet in those final moments. Mindal was all too happy to see her dressed like this, which was annoying, but she knew it would gain her a few points with her father, which she was going to need.

Elude was a planet of oceans and mountains, nothing in-between. Its cities were built in the air, stilted high above the ground where the small plots of usable land were farmed. The buildings were beautiful and blended well with the surrounding waters. They looked like ice sculptures with sharp peaks and unwelcoming angles that spoke of power. The ship landed on a pad surrounded by workers ready to do whatever was needed of them and welcome Mindal and his men back home.

The workers wore sleeveless vests and flowing pants, showing enough bare skin to make their muscles obvious. All in shades of blue, the royal color. Their tails lashed out behind them, and more than one held a weapon that Prit knew could blast a hole through anything. Even when a recognizable ship came in, they were on alert.

They were barbarians with weapons. Their technology advanced so fast that their culture wasn't able to keep up and they had the mentality of cave dwellers fighting for resources still in many ways. It had served them well, because they were a force to be reckoned with, even the SSA stepped carefully around them.

Once the ship was settled, Prit grabbed Jet and made her way off, not waiting for Mindal or anyone he might send to escort her anywhere. This was her home, sort of, and she would act like it when it benefited her. Thankfully Mindal would be busy ordering people around for a while so hopefully she'd have a chance to speak with her father before he got the impression that she was a willing bride.

As soon as her feet hit the glass walkway beneath the ship she was met by her father who had a frown on his face and his arms crossed over his chest. "Pritalia," he said with a shake of his head. His grey hair was in a long braid thrown over his shoulder, his eyes bright and sharp. He was getting older, but he was still in charge. His thin lips were pursed in disappointment, and he had his arms crossed over his chest. She felt like a naughty child come home with mud on her clothes and she hated that he could make her feel that way so easily.

She owed him nothing, hadn't been raised by him, didn't want his money or influence.

She'd take his love and support though and she admittedly used his name for clout here and there, but she didn't think he'd earned a right to parent her. Not like this.

"Father," she said with as much brightness as she could muster, not allowing him to know how his disappointment made her feel small. She embraced him briefly and he gave her an awkward pat on the back.

"I hear you've been causing trouble out there."

"Oh, just making a name for myself among the seedier parts of the universe," she said with a wink because she knew he would appreciate the sentiment, he wasn't known, himself, for being an upstanding member of discovered space.

"Yes, but from what I hear, you've been galivanting around with some male."

"Bodyguard," she hissed between clenched teeth. As if it mattered, she was no virgin and didn't pretend to be.

"You're just lucky Mindal hasn't taken offense to the close quarters you've shared with the *bodyguard*; he is still willing to marry you."

"Lucky me," she groaned and rolled her eye. "You want to know how I feel about Mindal?" she asked with clenched teeth.

Her father gave her a hard look. "Off you go, I need to talk to my men, lunch is in an hour," he said, dismissing her. Frustrated that her father wasn't willing to talk about the situation, but knowing better than to push him, especially in such a public place, she hurried into a hallway. It was completely made of glass, nothing more than a tunnel really, leading from the landing pad to the main building. Underneath was a bustling city all encased in glass as well. It was unnerving still, no matter how many times she'd been here. She didn't look down or around, just hurried forward. When she reached a door at the end of the walkway she was relieved to step into a solid room. No glass floor here, but it was bright white and blue with gold accents and plenty of windows. This was a common area for anyone coming and going from the space docks. To get to the main house she had to go through another glass walkway and into a part of the building that felt a little more personal, this was a place that people outside of the royal family were not allowed. Guards were stationed here and there, all greeting Prit as she passed.

She went up some stairs and down a hallway then sighed with relief when she entered her familiar rooms. She didn't spend much time here, but one thing her father had done well, was provide her a space to call her own within his home. She appreciated the gesture, he wasn't an emotional man, wasn't very fatherly to any of his children that she'd seen, but he cared, she knew he cared that she was his.

It just didn't transfer to how she felt about marrying Mindal, that was all about what he wanted.

The room was decorated in the royal colors of white and blue, but there was something more her here. Colors popped in the room, a chair in green, a painting of abstract shapes in bright colors. Even a rug in bright yellow. She'd managed to make it a little bit her own. Remnants from her life on New Earth were scattered about as well. A few childhood memories that were too precious to leave behind. She'd never felt completely comfortable leaving everything she valued on her ship, just in case she ever had to abandon it.

Her thoughts drifted to her ship and Saluk, as they tended to do at least a hundred times a day. She hoped he was home by now, she hoped he'd been welcomed into his family's warm arms. She hoped they'd celebrated his return with a feast and perhaps some heavy drinking.

How long before he found the girl he'd hoped to mate with, how long before he started that family she knew he craved. Would he even remember her after a year or two? Would she be just a blip on his long adventurous life but not really that important in the end?

It hurt, more than she wanted to examine, to think of him forgetting her. Especially when she was certain she'd never stop thinking about him and their brief time together.

She took a shaky breath and set Jet into his own little habitat that the room held. It was a large cage near a window that had a bed, a food bowl and a large flat stone cupped just enough to catch a bit of running water for his bath. He happily went to the water first and rolled around with sounds of pleasure.

"I need to freshen up, too, before lunch," she said, patting his head and walked to the bathroom.

She needed to prepare herself for some convincing conversation. She didn't want to leave any room for her father to doubt her desire to never marry Mindal.

Thirty minutes later Prit was following Mindal down the hallway. She hadn't activated her eye since she'd arrived on Mindal's ship, no reason to assess danger when she was so heavily guarded, and she didn't activate it now in her father's home.

"Your siblings are almost all in house today as well," Mindal said brightly.

"Great," Prit answered dryly. It was just another sign that the man didn't know her at all if he thought it should please her to know people she barely knew and who certainly didn't care for her deeply were here to witness whatever argument was about to happen.

They entered a dining room set up for a midday meal. It was a large, starkly white room with a glass ceiling that let in the bright sun making it almost blinding.

"Shit, can we at least set the shades?" she grumbled, shielding her eyes.

"Sensitive human eye," Mindal said with a sigh as if it were a cute little quirk of hers. But he did hit a button and the glass ceiling shaded.

Once she was able to see clearly, she looked around the

room and assessed the people present. Nothing surprising, just family and servants, all Eludian, all dangerous, she didn't need the bionic eye to tell her that. A long table was set with food she couldn't wait to eat, but her stomach clenched at the faces surrounding it. Her father at the head of course. At his right was her oldest brother, Alinas, and next to him was her oldest sister, Calta who was only a year younger than herself. On her father's other side sat her younger brother, Dradas and next to him was Binta, his twin sister. All full Eludian and all feeling like they were better than her and deserved to be treated that way. None of them thought her father should recognize her even a little, especially since she didn't present with any visible Eludian traits.

But her father didn't care. He'd decided she was as much his as any of them and so deserved his idea of fatherly attention, not that she wanted it most of the time. Though a lot of that could have most to do with her connection with New Earth, it looked good for him to have a New Earth daughter when he had to deal with them for any kind of treaties or skirmishes. It made him seem less like a purist out only for the interest of Elude, though that's exactly what he was.

"Father," she greeted with as bright a smile as she could and then nodded to each sibling, not bothering with individual hellos, they didn't care. This wasn't a happy family. She took a seat next to Binta.

"Welcome, Pritalia, so good to have you here, it's been too long. You travel too far," her father chastised.

Mindal took the seat across from Prit looking pleased with himself. "I agree, King Dofsh. It's great to have her back in the house," Mindal said. "I am so glad I could deliver her home."

She glared at his choice of words.

"Yes, it is wonderful," her father said.

"I don't live here," she mumbled.

"Then where do you think you live, Princess Pritalia?" Mindal asked. "You can't go to New Earth it seems, the military has you marked as a deserter and traitor. I hear they wish for your head on a platter because of some kind of misunderstanding and stealing of a ship."

All four of her siblings turned a glare to her.

"Home is nowhere," she answered and stuffed her mouth with some bread from the table. *Somewhere that no one is trying to kill me maybe.* She wanted to say but held back. "But since Barius has what he wanted from me, at least *he* doesn't want to kill me anymore. I'm pretty safe out in space with the circles I tend to run in. I just need a ship," she added with a glare at Mindal.

"You will marry Mindal, and you will stay here," her father declared.

Across the table Mindal gave her a bright smile.

Her siblings all pouted and Prit choked on her lunch. "No, still no," she said and Mindal's face fell into an angry glower.

"He will make a good husband; he will take care of you when I'm gone."

"I can take care of myself," Prit snapped.

"You need to be here to take care of Father," Alinas hissed.

Prit glared at Alinas then Mindal across the table who were both giving her a firm look, as if they were shaming a disrespectful child.

"You don't need taking care of," Prit pointed out to her father, knowing she'd never get Mindal or Alinas on her side.

"Not right now, that's true, but you need to marry and have your children before the time comes that I need all your attention."

"I don't like Mindal," she said simply. "And besides, I don't even know if I want children, so no reason to rush."

"That doesn't matter," her father scoffed. "Marriage and

having children are about political moves and power over those around you. You need children so that Mindal can be in good standing with his own family and carry on their name, he is the only son. It is his duty to provide named grandchildren."

"Oh, how could I forget," she grumbled. "I need to make sure you and Mindal have your archaic traditions satisfied."

"Sir, your guest has arrived." A servant said from the doorway.

Her father nodded and the man disappeared. Prit turned on her eye as she watched to see who her father was expecting and in walked New Earth commander, Charles Paul.

Species: New Earther
  Sex: Male
  Age: Sixty-five
  Danger: Minimal, no weapons detected but possible hand to hand combat ability.

His brown gaze locked on her, and his lip lifted in a sneer.

"Pritalia Dofsh, I have been looking for you," he said darkly.

"Commander Paul," her father said, standing in welcome. "I am so glad you could accept my invitation on such short notice. I know there's been some trouble between you and my daughter, and I want to resolve this. I don't want anything between Elude and New Earth as we navigate that new territory this side of the Ice Stretch. I know New Earth has been curious about what treasures might be found just outside of my galaxy."

Prit perked up at that news, what the hell was her father saying, was he going to allow New Earth to get a hold of a piece of the Blue Galaxy beyond their little station on Zenzi? That seemed completely out of character for him. It had to be a trick, but it didn't make her less nervous because this deal could include where Halador was, and she definitely didn't want anyone to snoop around and destroy Saluk's home. She definitely didn't want the New Earthers to get their grubby hands on it. They'd strip the resources so fast it would even surprise her father. One thing she'd always thought her father was good at, was taking what was needed carefully. They didn't need anything from Halador, it had been deemed an unnecessary and primitive planet, like many small planets throughout the discovered galaxies.

"I am happy to be here as an official of New Earth, and see some kind of justice done," he added darkly, his eyes narrowing on Prit. "It's important that the two greatest powers in the SSA have a good working relationship."

"Working relationship, yes. But you know that New Earth laws aren't in place here," her father said with amusement. "Sit, eat," he ordered. "We will talk."

Commander Paul took a seat next to Mindal, his eyes locked on Prit. Clearly, he wasn't here to negotiate anything other than her head for treason, well, for sleeping with his wife really, but he'd call it treason by way of stealing an old ship they didn't want anyway.

Prit ate when the food was served. She wasn't worried, not here. Her father would never let her be arrested, he needed her for his own plans. But she was uneasy about the Commander being here, unsure of what was about to happen. Surely he wasn't going to just walk away without her either.

Around her there was mundane conversation, none of it held her attention. They didn't mention anything important, no doubt not wanting the Commander to overhear anything. Meanwhile he stared daggers at her as he ate and engaged in very little conversation.

When dessert was served and it didn't seem likely that she was going to get any answers about what the hell was the plan in bringing the Commander here, she finally asked. "Why did you bring him here?"

Her father gave her a look that indicated he thought it a rude question to ask before the meal was finished. "I assumed you would deny Mindal because you do not know that he can provide and protect as a husband should. So he must prove himself."

Confusion filled her and no doubt her face showed it at that answer. Then Mindal jumped from his seat, positioned himself behind the Commander and ran his steak knife across the man's throat and it all made sense in a horribly gruesome way.

It was all done so fast, too, that the Commander had no time to react. His blood poured out in a wave and his wide eyes were still locked onto her as life left him.

His head fell to the table with a clunk, splatters of his blood reaching across the table and ruining her pie.

Mindal smiled at her with pride.

"See. Not only can I negotiate better than you with scum like Barius, but I will take down your enemies, Princess Pritalia, I can take care of you," Mindal declared happily, setting the knife down on his empty dessert plate.

Prit shook her head, unable to respond to what she'd just witnessed and the reasoning behind it.

"You're going to start a war," she whispered, looking back at her father. "Do you really think the New Earth president will just overlook this crime?"

Her father just shrugged. "This is the way of our world, Pritalia. New Earth needs a reminder, I think. They shouldn't be giving us pushback over the area we want to claim, and you couldn't accept Mindal because he'd never proven himself worthy. Now he has, two problems solved," he said simply. "We will have a celebration tomorrow night to announce the engagement."

Her father stood then, followed quickly by all her siblings except for Alinas, and they all filed out the door, leaving behind a dead body as if it were nothing at all. A guard hurried forward to remove the Commander's body and Mindal wiped his hands off on a napkin with a satisfied smirk.

"See you later, Pritalia, perhaps we can take a stroll this evening after dinner?" Mindal said and walked out. The rest of the room cleared quickly until it was just her and Alinas left.

"Pritalia," Alinas sneered at her. "You should know that Calta is quite upset with your little engagement. She'd set her sights on Mindal a while ago."

Pritalia rolled her eye. "Let her have him," she grumped.

"Father says he's to marry the oldest sister and take on the duties of being his eldest son in law. It is a coveted position, and important to Father."

"Lucky me." Prit glared at her brother. He looked so much like her father, just a touch shorter. His hair was dark, much like their father's had been in his youth. He had the same hardness in his eyes and the same determination to take what he wanted by whatever means necessary. He was going to inherit everything here when their father passed, and she wondered if he resented the fact that he'd have to share that with her and Mindal if she married the man and became what her father wanted her to.

"You were always an ungrateful thing," Alinas spat. "You're being honored, no matter that you're a fucking halfling, and you try to run away," he accused.

She gave him a look of mock shock. "Why would I run from all this," she said, sweeping a hand toward the bloodstained table.

Alinas stepped closer. "Give me a reason to remove you

from Calta's way," he hissed. "She'll be a better eldest sister in every way."

"Help me get out of here," she challenged back. "Let them think me dead and Calta can have whatever the hell she wants."

"Ha, you know as well as I do that if I did that, Father would have my head and Jattin would take the throne. No, you will wed Mindal and I will deal with you when I am made King of Elude."

"I am so glad to hear my future marriage has the blessing of my oldest brother," she hissed with a wicked grin. "It isn't going to happen; nothing will get me down an aisle and saying *I do* to that man."

"There are other ways to solve this problem, ways that wouldn't raise Father's suspicions," he threatened and spun on his heel then went out the door. His words hung in the air.

CHAPTER TWENTY-THREE

Prit hurried back to her room, head spinning. Whatever was about to come as a consequence of Mindal's actions here, she didn't want to be on the planet to see it. She also didn't want to give her father or brother a chance to succeed with any plans for her. She needed to find a way off Elude sooner rather than later.

There was only one solution she could think of in that moment. If she could get to the town docks, she could steal a ship. They wouldn't all be locked up as tight as the ones here, and they were meant to be flown with a small crew that was going to nearby space ports to buy and sell goods. It could work, but she'd have to wait until the middle of the night so she'd have shadows to blend with. Which meant she'd have to get through another meal with those people and try to get out of any kind of romantic stroll with Mindal. Maybe she could fake an illness, she certainly didn't feel great at the moment so it would be an easy lie to say she had space flu.

A knock brought her out of her pacing and planning. She opened the door to find Mindal standing there with a huge smile and a flower in his hand.

"I would like you to match this for dinner tonight so that we will be complimentary," he said and handed her a gold petaled flower.

"Sure," she said and took it. She started to close the door and he stuck out a hand to stop its movement.

"Is there something else?" Prit demanded.

"Would you invite your fiancé in? Give us a private moment?" he asked, his voice low with meaning.

She barely held back a gag at the thought of spending intimate time with him. "No, I need to wash my hair," Prit said, annoyed at his sudden presumptuousness. He'd been a gentleman on the entire flight, apparently killing her enemy made him horny.

Mindal laughed and stepped back, allowing her to close the door without intrusion this time.

She threw the flower on a nearby table and groaned. "He's such an ass," she said and flopped onto the couch.

She stared at the ceiling and her thoughts turned quickly to a man who wasn't an ass. What was Saluk doing now, she wondered. Was he home, lying on a bed of his own or perhaps on the ground and staring up at a sky he'd missed? Her heart ached; would she ever not miss him? Thoughts of him turned to thoughts of his planet and then wondering what her father's plans for keeping New Earth off of Halador were.

She needed to find out without making him suspicious of her curiosity.

She decided indirect was going to be the best approach. She stood and gathered Jet with a plan.

Making her way out to a garden she knew Binta frequented, she acted surprised to see her sister when she walked out onto the grassy space and set Jet down to get some fresh air.

"Binta, how have you been?" she asked.

Binta looked surprised by Prit's question, and she cursed herself a bit, maybe any conversation with this sibling she'd barely said two sentences to in her entire life was not going to come off as impromptu and unimportant.

"I am well," Binta said, standing from a bench where she'd been sitting in the shade of a fruit tree.

"Don't get up, I'll join you. Jet just needs a little fresh Eludian air, he does love it here."

"He's fat," Binta pointed out.

Prit clenched her teeth, Jet was not fat he was just ... well-loved is all, and it was damn hard to get exercise on a ship her size.

"Father never should have gifted him to you, he probably didn't think you'd take him off planet."

Prit thought Binta was probably right about half that at least, her father had given her the thing as a birthday present when she'd come to Elude for safety after initially leaving the New Earth military.

"I wish he had more room to run on my ship. I suppose when I get a new one I can try for a bigger space for him."

"You aren't staying?" Binta asked, shocked.

"I—" Prit knew she needed to proceed carefully. "I am just sure I'll still want to do some flying on my own no matter what."

Binta nodded. "Father will probably allow it; he has so many interests so far away now. Mindal is in charge of expansion so maybe you'll get to fly with him, his ship is very big," she said, clearly impressed with the man's ship size.

"Mindal is into expansion, huh, I thought he was just doing stuff around here to help out."

"Oh no, he's being sent out. He checks in with Jattin of course since he's stationed out in the middle of nowhere, but Mindal's made runs as far as Rentin regularly."

Rentin, Prit knew that planet, a small one in the Red Galaxy, that was comforting. He wasn't making trips in the direction that would bring him close to Halador. "Oh, is that another place they're looking at expanding, out past Rentin?"

Binta shrugged, "No one tells me a damn thing. I'm just extra."

Prit felt sorry for the girl. She wanted to tell her she didn't need to be just extra, that she could leave. She could do whatever she wanted, wherever she wanted. But Prit held herself back. What could she really offer as advice, she was running from the law, she was a thief by trade, and she didn't even have a goddamn ship of her own.

It wasn't as if she had her life together.

"Well, I'm sure you'll find your place soon," Prit said, wishing she felt better about those words. She stood and grabbed Jet from where he was munching on some flowers and headed back inside.

If they were expanding toward Rentin, Halador was safe ... for now. Maybe if she married Mindal she could keep a close eye on it all, make sure they stayed far from Halador. Make sure they saw the value of expanding on the opposite side of the Ice Stretch to keep others as far from Elude as possible. She didn't think it would be hard to convince her father of that, she just had to make sure he didn't suspect her real reasons.

Could she sacrifice herself in marriage like that though? She wasn't very good at doing something she didn't want to do.

Maybe she could just warn Halador. She could get off Elude and stop by the planet. Not to see Saluk, but just to warn them that the known universe is coming their way, and they might want to be prepared.

It would be the decent thing to do, and Saluk, well he was probably already back in his old life and not thinking about her at all. She'd just stop by, give a warning to whoever she met up with and leave, no big deal.

Satisfied with her decision, Prit entered her room and looked at the flower Mindal had dropped off.

Yeah, there was no way she'd be able to fake a marriage to that man. Even if she could get Saluk and his kiss out of her head, she'd never be satisfied with someone like Mindal.

Prit stared at the clothes in her closet. It was all dresses and crap she hated to wear. But it was what they all expected here, and she'd always done what she could to play the part when she was here. She'd spent a lot of time hoping that her father would accept her as she was if she tried to blend in with what he expected.

But he hadn't ever seen her as anything more than he wanted her to be, and that was proven when he'd given her to Mindal without a thought to what she actually wanted. He just expected her to do what he said, to follow along like an Eludian Princess should.

She wouldn't, but tonight she'd play the right part.

She pulled a gold dress out and threw it on the bed. She was a good thief and a good thief blended in until it was time to strike. She had to make it through the next few hours without tipping anyone off that she planned to run, and so she'd wear the dress and she would entertain Mindal's attention, to a point. If he got handsy she couldn't be blamed for cutting off whatever touched her.

One thing was bugging her though. Why hadn't there been a backlash for the commander's death yet? He wouldn't have arrived on Elude alone, which meant either there were a bunch of New Earth military personnel being held captive here, or there was a ship nearby that was about to start questioning his disappearance.

She was going to find out which as soon as dinner was over. She needed to make sure she wasn't blamed in any way for his death.

She slipped into the dress. It was all gold from its high neckline down to where it brushed the top of her feet. It was a bit on the dressy side for dinner with the family, but it was all she had in gold as Mindal had requested. It was tight all over as well, which she usually avoided over her bionic leg. Hard to access weapons when she couldn't wiggle free of the material.

She walked to a cabinet and pulled a sharp knife out of a drawer; she had weapons hidden all over this place. She reached down to the bottom of her dress and with one quick movement she slit the material up the entirety of her bionic leg, stopping just as she touched skin. "That's better," she said with a grin.

Prit strode out into the hall with her head high. Her mind already on to what she'd need to do after dinner.

Check for prisoners.

Sneak out with Jet.

Steal a ship.

Maybe never return ... She didn't love that, as much as she hated what her father was trying to make her do. She didn't want to lose all contact with the only family she had left. Maybe she could return in a few years, after everyone's anger settled and they figured out a new plan for their future.

The dining room looked much the same as it had earlier, devoid of blood of course and everyone had dressed up a little more for the occasion. Mindal looked irritatingly bright in a gold vest and light blue billowy pants. His face lit up when she entered and he walked over to her, reaching for her hand. She allowed it.

"You look ravishing, I knew gold would be our color. I'm

thinking our wedding will be all gold." He looked at her hair with a frown. "I think perhaps you'll have to lose the blue, it won't match."

"Mindal," she said, holding back a cringe as he brought her fingers to his mouth and pressed his dry lips to her skin.

He led her to a seat and took the one beside her.

Her fingers danced over the dull knife next to her plate, contemplating the consequences of ending this insanity right here with a quick stab to his jugular. Surely her father would understand, even respect her for the decision to remove an obstacle to her happiness.

Prit cleared her throat and let go of the would-be weapon. It was a risky move, and she had others available at the moment. She'd leave murder as a last resort.

"How is the New Earth military taking the death of their commander?" she asked to hopefully get an answer without searching.

"Politics," her father huffed. "Not talk for the dinner table."

That answer told her enough. Her father was still working out the details of dealing with possible backlash. But he also wasn't worried about it, her father felt untouchable. The New Earth government needed him as an ally, and her father didn't need them for shit. New Earth wasn't powerful enough to take out a species without backlash from others, so they had to play nice. They had to pretend that they valued every species, that they weren't hoping to force everyone into an alliance that centered around themselves.

Besides the risk of war with a powerful army, Elude was also the number one provider of some essential minerals New Earth needed. Mined from their deep oceans, the minerals were used in everything from ship fuel to weaponry. Things that most species had come to rely on as space was settled and species were brought technologically forward. New Earth wanted to keep the peace with Elude, but they also might take an opportunity to come in for a hostile takeover of the place if they thought they could be successful.

The New Earth military had made it clear they'd expected her to be present to negotiate with her father when she was a part of their ranks. It was why she'd moved up so quickly and had access to so many top people and their families, all trying to ingratiate themselves to her and gain her loyalty.

She had played into it for a long time, really she'd never questioned it until they'd turned on her. So fast she'd gone from one of the most important people, at least in her small section of the military ruled by Commander Paul, to enemy number one. That's when she'd seen what she really was to them. Just a pawn.

Her father had made it clear from the beginning that she was to side with him or be punished accordingly. Keep the New Earthers in line and keep him updated on what they planned. She hadn't done much of that during her time with the military, she'd been loyal, she'd pledged her life to New Earth. She had fed her father various pieces of unimportant information to keep him satisfied however. It was rather easy for him to imagine she wasn't important enough to know much thankfully.

At least he'd been honest in what he wanted from her and what he expected her to be able to do. There had been no subterfuge from her father, and she could appreciate that.

She didn't want to be anyone's pawn though. Hadn't then and didn't now. But she was older and wiser now and knew when to play along and when to run. So she smiled and ate and ignored Mindal as best she could.

She grunted here and there to Mindal's prattling on and on about things she didn't care about. Futures they would never have. Her siblings glared at what they saw as her complete betrayal of the family, and her father smiled, unwilling to believe he hadn't won in this situation.

When dinner was over, she declined Mindal's offer of a walk but couldn't stop him from insisting on seeing her back to her room. He tried to grab her hand as they left the dining room but she tucked her arms around herself and walked at a fast clip.

Mindal's face showed raw anger for a second before he washed it away with a look that indicated he thought she was stupid or perhaps playing coy.

Prit stopped in the doorway of her room and blocked Mindal from entering. He stopped so close to her she knew he'd expected to follow all the way. He was absolutely clueless if he thought she was ever going to invite him into her personal space.

"Goodnight," she said firmly.

He smiled and reached up to run a finger over her cheek. His tail was swishing behind him eagerly. "Why don't you invite me in, we can share a drink?"

"No thanks."

Mindal's eyes flared angrily again, and his jaw clenched. His tail slapped the floor. "As you wish, Princess. I will see you tomorrow," he gritted out then turned and stormed away.

Prit hurried into the room and sighed in relief when the door shut.

"What an asshole," she snapped toward Jet, then went to change into something better for sneaking around in.

Prit's nerves calmed after tearing off the dress and throwing it in a corner then she pulled out a soft, black, long-sleeved shirt and matching leggings that were made specially to go around her bionic leg, leaving it bare. She slipped her feet into soft black leather shoes that would make no noise as she walked. Wearing this made her feel in control, this was where she was powerful. She could sneak, she could listen and see, she could figure out what her father was doing and how to get off of this planet before she was forced to kill Mindal, because that was definitely going to happen rather than a marriage of any kind.

It was easy to sneak around the place alone, she'd done it plenty of times. She headed first down to the bottom levels where prisoners were held. It would make the most sense to find the Commander's crew locked up, if they weren't already dead.

She seamlessly avoided servants as she went, and a couple of siblings. She got to the door to the underground prison and listened. If there was a guard behind it, the likelihood of prisoners was high. She didn't hear anything and risked a slow peek.

Empty hallway, lights off. She was almost positive now that the place was empty.

To be sure, she snuck in and past the cells: all empty. It wasn't common for her father to have a prisoner since the death penalty was a high price for most simple crimes and that kept the locals in order pretty well. But she doubted he'd have killed off an entire crew just yet. Even for him that seemed a bit drastic. Which meant they must still be in the atmosphere waiting to hear from their commander. They must not have been allowed to depart their ship with him. What a stupid move on Commander Paul's part, why the hell would he trust her father enough to come alone and unarmed?

But it had saved his crew, lucky them.

She made her way back up to her room before she headed out in hopes of finding a ship she could steal. She couldn't leave without Jet. But when she reached her bedroom Alinas was there with her pet in his arms.

"Sneaking around?" he asked with a disapproving look at her outfit.

"Just stretching my legs after that meal, something didn't sit right with me," she answered, grabbing Jet out of his arms.

"You won't be leaving. I know father trusts you, but I don't, not even a little. Mindal sent guards out to the docks so there won't be a ship for you to steal."

Fuck, how did he know?

"Why do you care?" she snarled.

"You will marry Mindal and care for father, it is your duty and you've been allowed too much freedom for too long. That ends now."

Alinas left with those final words and Prit was seething. What the hell was she going to do now?

CHAPTER TWENTY-FOUR

The next night Prit was dressed in a gown of royal colors. A dark blue that matched her hair nicely. It was a sleeveless gown that hugged her hips then flowed down in strips about three inches wide allowing for a lot of leg to poke through as she walked. It was cut perfectly to hide her private bits but didn't leave much to the imagination. She wasn't ashamed of her body and held her head confidently high as she walked out of her bedroom. Maybe she could seduce someone into flying her off this damn planet. She had risked a walk toward the docks earlier in the day and confirmed that they were still being heavily guarded as Alinas had indicated.

But they were underestimating her abilities and she wasn't worried, yet. She just needed to wait and watch, there would be an opportunity.

She swung her hips a little extra as she made her way down a hallway to the ballroom where her father was hosting an engagement party. She didn't want to go in there and pretend that she had any interest in marrying Mindal. She didn't want to parade around in front of the entire city as if she was about to claim her place beside her father with a husband on her arm. But she knew she had to. She had to act like she was going to accept, though unhappily, the plans they had made for her.

"Welcome, Princess," one of the servants said as he opened the ballroom doors for her.

The scent of sweets assaulted her immediately, the tendency for the Eludian people to eat sugary food had always turned her stomach. She preferred the savory flavors common on New Earth. The room was large and her eye immediately went to work assessing the people in it.

Five species present
  Eludian
  Sabitarion
  Ionite
  New Earth
  Dravian

"Shit," she mumbled. Why the hell would her father invite more New Earthers here after killing the Commander? Dravians were a common species in the galaxies, a quiet and small in stature species, they were usually in positions of servitude and likely here as servants to the Ionite who, if they were traveling here as guests, were likely of the Five Families and therefore rich. They also weren't fans of her, she'd have to steer clear. Sabitarions here, that was interesting, they couldn't be of the royal family that had just been overthrown, unless they hadn't been on planet, perhaps they were here seeking some sort of assistance in reclaiming what King Lenkin had just lost. They also wouldn't be fans of hers if they had any idea what had occurred there. Shit, she wasn't going to find a friendly face among these people and that would make sleeping her way to an escape route impossible.

She strutted farther into the room of enemies, most of whom were milling about and trying to not make it obvious how much they were staring or glaring at her.

"Pritalia!" Mindal called out, spotting her and hurrying forward. "My bride has arrived, break out the champagne!"

Prit took a deep breath, reasoning that her only option was going to be killing him. A true smile lifted her lips at the thought, she could enjoy this party knowing it was his going to hell celebration, even if he didn't realize it.

"Why can't we go now?" Saluk snarled at Josh. They were currently in orbit around Elude and he knew Prit was down there, possibly suffering the unwanted attention of Mindal.

"When you came to me for help, Saluk, you admitted that you had no idea how to go about saving her. Trust me now, we have to time things right. Those ships over there are New Earth ships and if the chatter I heard over the radio is correct, they are about to wage an all-out war if King Dofsh doesn't produce the Commander immediately."

"Which is exactly why we need to get in there and get her before things start exploding!" Saluk jabbed a finger in the direction of the planet.

"If we wait until the attack starts, we can go in with the other invading ships. This one is still marked as New Earth military, I never bothered to change it. They won't suspect us beside them. I promise I don't want Prit hurt any more than you do, she's my family, man. But we have to be smart here and we have to trust that she's doing everything she can down there to take care of herself. She isn't helpless, you've spent enough time with her to know that."

Saluk hated that this New Earther was right. Which is why he'd gone to him instead of straight to Elude when he'd figured out how to make the ship do what he wanted it to. He hated to leave Prit alone with Mindal any longer than necessary, but he had to trust that not only was she capable of taking care of herself, but her father would not be okay with harm befalling his daughter. He wanted her married to the man, not imprisoned by him.

Stealth, which he knew she was good at but had never been his strong suit, was what this mission called for. But he was determined to save her because he was her bodyguard, and he had failed her.

Chatter started up over the radio again and Saluk leaned in to listen.

King Dofsh still refuses to answer for the whereabouts of the Commander. On planet team says he is celebrating an engagement with dignitaries from both Ione and Sabit but no sign of the Commander. Ready the invasion and extraction team. Battle ships on standby.

"What does that mean?" Saluk asked, panic over every part of that message filled him.

"That means they are going in to try and find the Commander and if they don't, they are going to start shooting. And that means it's our time to go in too," Josh said with an eager smile.

Josh maneuvered the ship from where it was hiding in the shadow of the main command vessel to slide right in behind a group of smaller ships much like the one they were on, only looking newer.

It was the perfect cover, and as the other ships stealthily made their way under cover of darkness into the atmosphere to land seaside around the castle, Josh slipped his own ship to a spot he must have known already existed. A small garden atop a portion of the impressive building.

"You've been here before," Saluk said when it was obvious no one was about to come rushing out to stop them.

"Yeah, Prit and I have known each other a long time, obviously. I visited with her a few times before she left the military. This garden is only used by her youngest sister and if there's a party, it's definitely empty."

They left the ship and crept through the dark garden. Luck had them through a hallway and down two flights of stairs before they had to hide from the first Eludian servant. The woman passed them without notice and they continued on. As they neared the main part of the house the sounds of cheerful celebrations was cut off by screams.

"Sounds like the military just found out their commander isn't enjoying a vacation here," Josh said. "Stay out of sight, or the New Earthers might think you're one of the bad guys here too."

Saluk ignored the warning and rushed forward. If Prit was in that room and the military was invading, he needed to get to her. He couldn't get this close only to lose her to another enemy.

"Shit," Josh hissed behind him, running to catch up.

At least he'd have someone at his back. He didn't pull any weapons, knowing that would make him an instant target, but he had them strapped on and would use them if necessary. No one was going to stand between him and Prit, not this time.

When he entered the main dining room it was utter chaos. The Eludian guards were engaging the New Earth military in hand-to-hand combat and well-dressed others were sprinting from the room in all directions. From one quick sweep with his gaze he didn't think any of the Eludian royal family was still in the room.

"Where did they go?" Saluk demanded.

"There are escape tunnels and servant passageways all over," Josh said. "She's probably on her way to an unplanned escape."

"Where is her room? She would go for her pet first."

Josh gave him a wide smile, "You know her well." Josh turned but they came up against two New Earth military members blocking the exit.

"Josh, what the hell are you doing here?" the younger of the two asked.

"Oh you know, a little vacation, mind if we get back out?"

"You know, I never thought what happened to Pritalia was fair," the older guard said. "Get on out, we found the Commander's body and our orders are to destroy the family."

"Thank you," Josh said and rushed past the two.

Saluk followed close behind him and when Josh stopped outside of a door to listen, Saluk pressed his ear close as well.

"You have no idea who you've messed with," Prit was saying to someone. "They are going to destroy this entire planet; they don't give a shit."

"Ha! No one is capable of taking out the Eludians," a male voice answered. "Even now our ships are surrounding theirs. The men downstairs will be killed and all will be restored with us as the rightful rulers of our corner, and you dear, will be my blushing bride. Don't worry, I won't let a little thing like this stand in our way."

"Fuck you," she snapped.

Saluk had heard enough, he pushed the door open and saw Prit standing, looking absolutely stunning in a blue gown with Jet in her arms. Mindal was in the room looking cocky and when he realized who had entered his eyes took on an angry heat.

"You," Mindal growled.

"Saluk," Prit gasped, her eyes wide with a surprise that he wished wasn't there. She should have expected that he'd come for her, that he would never leave her behind in enemy hands.

It wasn't what a bodyguard did.

"I should have killed you, Haladian. I didn't think you were this stupid."

"Likewise," Saluk said and stepped forward. He didn't draw a weapon, he wanted to kill this man with his bare hands.

They circled each other. Saluk knew there was no time to waste, they needed off this planet but he wasn't leaving this loose end alive again. He jumped forward and grabbed Mindal by the throat, squeezing. Mindal made a quick movement with his arm and Saluk felt a knife hit his side, but Mindal wasn't used to combat, he was used to ordering people around, and although there was a sharp pain that made Saluk drop his hold on the man's throat, he could tell it didn't go deep enough for any real damage. Mindal wasn't strong enough to take down a gladiator.

Saluk wasn't thrown off his attack for long, he pulled back his fist and punched Mindal in the face as hard as he could. The spray of blood and crunch of his nose was satisfying. Mindal's eyes rolled back into his head and he crumpled.

"Saluk?" Prit rushed forward, her hands going to the minor wound in his side and completely ignored her crumpled fiancé at their feet. When she seemed satisfied that it wasn't life threatening, she straightened and looked into his eyes. Her eye was deep and glistened with emotions that Saluk was afraid to guess at. "Why are you here? How are you here?" she whispered.

"We need to get off this planet," he said, instead of

answering her questions. He grabbed her arm and started toward the door.

"Josh," she said in surprise when she saw her friend standing there as lookout.

"Hey, got what you need?"

"All I need is Jet," she said and kissed the thing's head.

And all Saluk needed was her.

CHAPTER TWENTY-FIVE

Prit didn't understand why Saluk was here, why the hell he was with Josh? He was supposed to be safe on Halador by now, but as she strapped into the copilot's seat on Josh's ship, she was thankful. And as they blasted out of the atmosphere she sighed heavily in relief. She was safe from Mindal and her father's plans.

"Do you think you killed him with that punch?" she asked.

"No, unfortunately," Saluk said. "But killing a passed-out man has no honor, so he lives another day."

"Are you worried about your family?" Josh asked as he flipped switches and set the course.

"No, I'm just hoping this is the end of the military's vendetta against me. With the Commander dead, maybe they'll let it go."

Josh nodded. "Who killed him?"

"Mindal did it as a sort of engagement gift," she grumbled. "I would have appreciated the gesture if it hadn't come from such an idiot."

"Oh?" Josh said slyly. "Is there another hulking man you'd like to be engaged to? One who perhaps has a bit of honor in who he kills?" he whispered, his eyebrows darting up and his chin twitching toward the back of the ship where Saluk sat strapped in with Jet in his arms.

"I just want to get away from all this shit and be left alone," Prit said without as much force as the statement should have had. She stared out at the blackness of space and contemplated the confusing feelings she had.

Saluk had come for her. He'd had the opportunity to get home safely, and he'd come for her. He could have escaped on Sabit, but he'd gone in for the necklace for her. He risked his freedom for her. Twice.

Well, that's what a bodyguard was supposed to do. She reminded herself. It didn't mean anything else. He was obviously an honorable man; he'd proved that in not killing Mindal when he was passed out.

An explosion behind them had Josh flipping switches to change the image on the screen and they all watched as Elude's battle ships attacked the New Earth command ship that was hovering just out of the atmosphere.

Eludians were vicious in everything they did. There was a reason they weren't already part of the SSA, and the New Earth military was seeing it now. Without mercy, the ships attacked until the command ship was ripped apart. There would be no survivors. No one to bring back the story of what happened.

"I'll never be welcome on New Earth, even if they drop the charges," she said with a laugh. "Not after this. All Eludians will be marked as highly dangerous and unwelcome in the most loyal to New Earth parts of the SSA." She shrugged, New Earth had never been her plan. It had never felt like home.

"Ah well, it's a pirate's life for you then, huh?" Josh said with a laugh.

"As always," she agreed. "I just need my ship and I can survive." But why did that not feel true anymore?

"As always," Josh said, "I am eternally grateful that you are so hard to kill."

Saluk was silent through the entire exchange and Prit glanced back at him. He was stroking Jet and staring blankly at the wall. She'd give her left leg to know what he was thinking.

"I'll get you home soon, don't worry," she called to him, and he grunted.

It was an easy flight back to Zenzi and when Prit saw her ship sitting there half crashed, she felt a tear prick the back of her eye. How the hell had Saluk managed to get here at all?

"We can fix it, Frankie's already been working on it, I think. It's not as bad as it looks, the big guy just doesn't know how to land."

"Thanks," she said, clearing her throat of emotion. "Maybe I'll give you some flying lessons," she said over her shoulder to Saluk.

He shrugged. "I can fly, it was the landing that got tricky, and I won't need the skill again ever I expect."

Prit supposed that was true, he wouldn't be leaving Halador again once she left him there. He'd be a hunter or a farmer and a family man. A simple life with a family.

"The ship really does do all the work flying once you put in the coordinates," Josh said, lucky for the big guy you had my location saved.

"Very lucky," Prit agreed.

They descended from Josh's ship and Prit took a deep breath of the familiar hot air.

Frankie rushed out of the building to embrace his dad. She didn't miss the relief there in the young man's face. She hoped to never have to see that again, she never wanted to be the reason he looked like he wasn't sure his father would ever return.

She had to stop putting people in danger.

Frankie moved to her, and she embraced him, whispering her apology in his ear so Josh wouldn't hear it.

He just pulled away and shook his head. They both knew that Josh would risk everything for family and in his mind, Prit was family.

"Let's investigate the damage the big guy did," Prit said, putting an arm around the young man's shoulder. "Your dad said you started repairs already, how bad is it?"

"Bad," Frankie said, looking back at Saluk. "That guy has no idea how to treat a machine like this."

"He's a gladiator, not a space fighter," she agreed with a laugh.

"I won't apologize for that," Saluk said.

And she wouldn't want him to, she liked what he was, maybe a little too much.

She quickly changed into her own clothes on her ship then investigated the damage, which was mostly just cosmetic, but one engine was damaged enough to need to be replaced. It was not a one-man job and although Frankie had dragged a newish engine out to the ship, he hadn't been able to attempt the swap until they returned.

"I'll cook, you guys fix," Josh offered, and they agreed.

Prit was exhausted, she'd taken a short nap earlier on Josh's ship, but exhaustion was definitely creeping in on her now.

Saluk must have noticed, no matter how well she thought she was hiding it, because he basically pushed her back and moved beside Frankie to help heft the damaged engine off the ship and lift the working one up.

She stepped in to help with the bolts just as Josh came out to tell them food was ready.

"We can finish it all up in the morning," Frankie said with a satisfied smile. "Though it's never going to look pretty again."

"You are amazing, kid, you know that, right?" Prit said.

Frankie blushed under her praise. "Where will you be off to next?"

"Halador," she said firmly. "I have to finish my deal with Saluk. He's done more than enough to deserve a ride home." She didn't look at Saluk as she spoke, afraid to see the relief in his eyes. She just slung an arm around Frankie and walked into the building where Josh had set a table with steaks and vegetables he'd grilled, and beer of course. Thank the gods for cold beer.

"New Earth really knows how to do it with this stuff," Prit said, grabbing a can and opening it. No other planet seemed to get it quite right. There was something about a metal can that just hit the spot like nothing else when she was hot and hungry. She chugged one, then ate and sipped a second.

She watched Saluk eat twice the amount of anyone else as they talked about what had happened on Elude. She wasn't traumatized, she wasn't angry, she was just tired. She didn't want to fight with her father about Mindal. She didn't want to watch her back for the New Earth Commander, although that one was resolved at least, and Josh said he'd do all he could to speak with the right people about closing the case on her, seeing as the worst she'd done was steal the unused vehicle.

"I think that's it for me," Prit said as she stood and started to gather up plates and empty cans.

"I got this, head to bed, you wear yourself to the bone, you know you don't have to do that," Frankie said, quickly standing to take the mess from her. "You look like you're dead on your feet already."

"Just what every lady wants to hear," she teased, then turned with a pink tinge to her cheeks to Saluk. "You coming to bed, big guy? Or you want to sleep on that couch?" she asked, pointing to the one in the lobby that would have been too small for her.

"Thanks for the food," Saluk said to Josh and they exchanged a fist bump that surprised Prit. She supposed an adventure like the two men had undergone to save her had bonded them. She liked that, but then she realized their friendship would end the next day and she was sad again.

Saluk and Prit didn't talk as they walked to her ship. Didn't say a thing to each other as she stripped down to a tank top and underwear then slid into bed with Jet cuddled to her front. Saluk laid down beside her without a word and when his body began its comforting vibration she felt a tear slip out of her eye.

She hadn't felt this kind of homecoming since before her mother died and she knew her days with it were severely limited.

Saluk did something he'd never done before, as if sensing her need, he turned and spooned her, his hand resting on her hip. She waited a breath to see if he would do anything else, but he just laid there, offering his silent comfort which made her heart ache even more.

It was best this way, she knew that. But it didn't dampen the desire to take everything from him while she could, to drown herself in him just so she could stop this feeling of loss. She took a deep breath to steady herself and relaxed into his warmth, knowing she would dream of this moment for the rest of her life.

Saluk laid awake for a long time after he heard her breath steady into sleep. She twitched her body against him every now and again, her round ass hitting him so sweetly. Thankfully she was asleep because otherwise it would be embarrassing at how his body was reacting, which is why he usually only gave her his back. Tonight though, he embraced the ache, knowing that these moments were limited. In the morning they'd finish fixing the ship and they would be on their way to Halador.

And she would leave him there to pursue her own life. Would she even think of him again after that? He knew he would never forget her, doubted he would ever find another female that he wanted as much as he wanted her. But he didn't want just her body, which he knew was willing. He wanted her soul, her life, her motherhood. If he couldn't have it all, he wouldn't take any of it because leaving her was going to be hard enough without knowing what she felt like underneath him, and what sounds of pleasure she made. And although they'd been through some shit since that kiss that he'd stopped, the reality hadn't changed. It was better not to know; it would make the hurt of loss easier to bear.

When he finally drifted to sleep, he dreamed of Halador and her. He dreamed of introducing her to his family and seeing the delight on their faces to know he'd come back a proven warrior, and worthy of a mate.

Then he dreamed of watching her ship leave the atmosphere above his homeland. He dreamed of screaming out in rage as she left him behind. He dreamed of cutting his hair and shaving his brow in the tradition of a warrior who had lost his mate. Because even though he'd never claimed her as a mate would, she was everything a mate could be to his soul.

He woke up with wet eyes and a heavy heart. His future was written in her small warm body sleeping soundly beside him. So close and yet, already gone.

It was still early, but he needed to get some fresh air, so he slipped out of the bed and left the ship. He was surprised to find Josh standing at the entrance to the office. He was leaned up against the frame with a steaming cup in his hands.

"Can't sleep, big guy?" Josh asked as Saluk approached.

Saluk sighed as he got closer to the man who he would have

never predicted being important to him. But somehow, after what they'd gone through to get Prit, Saluk would say Josh was his friend, although perhaps he'd never tell the man that. Which was fine, he'd probably never see him again after today. They'd had some time to talk and get to know each other before arriving at Elude, and Josh had told Saluk all about Prit as a young and fierce woman, about her sister who sounded like the exact opposite, sweet and timid. He felt like he knew Josh and Prit better than ever. "I guess not."

Josh nodded and looked at the ship. "She's something, isn't she? So fierce and independent, so capable," Josh said, sipping his coffee and eyeing Saluk.

"Yeah, it's too bad she lost out on the necklace. She could have gotten everything she wants."

"She doesn't know what she wants," Josh said with a snort. "She never has. Ever since her mother died, she's been searching for a place to belong. It's why she liked the military, forced unity. But then that was betrayed. She felt betrayed by her sister's death too. She just wants a place to call home and the closest she's been able to get is Jet and that damn ship that's falling apart."

Saluk nodded agreement, she did seem lost.

"She is crazy to think there's anything out there she can steal to make herself happy. The life she's chosen is not really what will make her happy, it's not really what she wants, she just can't admit it to herself because she's been chasing it for so long. She's convinced herself that she can't trust anyone, that she can't rely on anyone because they will all betray her or die. You know, I think she might have thought herself in love with Eileen, too bad the woman was married to the Commander and when caught, started to blame Prit for seducing her. I think that hurt more than the military turning against her."

Saluk wasn't sure if Josh was right or not, but he did know

that there was no way Prit was going to listen to anyone telling her what she should be seeking out for herself. She was too strong-willed, too determined to be independent. She had to figure out what she wanted on her own. He just wished what she wanted was a quiet life on a small planet.

"Want some coffee?" Josh asked.

Saluk nodded and followed the man inside.

CHAPTER TWENTY-SIX

Prit woke up alone and she sighed heavily. "Just you and me, Jet. Like always."

Jet chuffled sleepily and nudged her hand demanding pets. Prit obliged, picking up her pet and sitting up to look around the ship. It was a small space, comfortable for her and Jet, tight with Saluk but also somehow, when he was in it, more comfortable. She missed him and wondered where he was now. Why he'd left her asleep like that.

He was probably anxious to get moving so he could get home. He probably just couldn't sleep for the excitement.

"I suppose we should finish fixing the ship and get out," Prit said to Jet and set about getting ready for just that. She fed Jet and pulled on some clothes, then headed in search of coffee. She was shocked to walk into the office and find Saluk seated at the table across from Frankie playing some kind of card game with a smile on his face.

That smile really did something to his fierce look. It was crooked due to the scars, but it filled his whole face with a joy she wasn't sure she'd ever felt herself.

"Ha! I win!" Saluk declared and Frankie laughed, throwing his cards down in defeat.

Prit smiled, watching them and changed her mind. She had felt that kind of joy before, here with these men she'd felt it, with Josh and Frankie, and with her sister once upon a time too. More recently she'd felt it with Saluk, more than once on their journey she'd felt that joy of camaraderie and play.

"Coffee?" Josh asked, handing her a cup.

"Thanks, I am going to need it if I'm going to finish up the repairs this morning. It's a bit chill out there."

"Yeah, a storm is moving in," Josh agreed. "You know there's no rush to leave, right? I heard the chatter on the radio, no one is looking for you. I'll still go talk with command when you leave the planet and make sure the right people know the right story, but they aren't worried about you without the Commander's input."

"I know, but I made Saluk a promise and I am finally going to keep it."

"Are you sure he still wants that?" Josh challenged quietly.

Prit gave Josh a surprised look, but he just walked away leaving her confused.

"Time to work, who's helping?" Prit called out.

Saluk and Frankie both turned to her. Saluk's face instantly shifted to unreadable with a touch of annoyed, his usual look.

"I'll help," Frankie said quickly, jumping up. "I'm tired of losing to him anyway. I taught him the game; you'd think he'd have the decency to lose at least half the time."

"Life isn't kind to those who lose on purpose," Saluk said wisely. "I'll help too, just tell me what to do."

Prit turned and walked out to the ship. She gave orders and worked alongside them for a few hours until there was nothing left to do but take off. Which is when the first drops of rain started to fall.

Prit lifted her face to the rain and let the drops try to cleanse her soul.

It didn't work, she still felt deeply confused and angry. "I am going to shower in a proper bathroom while I have the chance, we can head out after we get one last good meal from Josh, too," Prit said.

"I'll let Dad know to start up the grill for lunch," Frankie said.

Saluk stared at the ship with a furrowed brow.

"It won't take more than another hour, then we'll be on the way," she assured him and walked away. If he was that anxious to leave, he'd just have to suck it up. She did want a shower after that work, and a hot meal before the long trip, too.

Prit took her time in the shower and when she emerged clean and fresh, the men were already deep into the burgers.

"Don't worry, we saved you some," Frankie said with a mouthful.

"I should hope so, what ever happened to ladies first?" she mock-scoffed and grabbed a burger off the plate.

"Ladies that take thirty-minute showers lose that privilege," Josh said with a wink.

Saluk didn't comment, just seemed to be eagerly devouring another burger and beer. Prit took the empty seat and ate contemplatively. "Any news from the military?"

"Just that Elude is officially a hostile planet and any talks of treaties with them will be held with extreme caution."

"I wonder how Eileen is feeling now that she's a widow."

"I think she'd welcome your company now more than ever but we both know she's no grieving widow. She just inherited a whole lot of wealth plus his death benefits. She'll be queen bee of her social circle till she croaks," Josh pointed out.

Prit was happy for the woman. The commander was an asshole and although his wife was more than a little bit of a bitch for using her and turning on her, Prit hoped she'd find happiness now. She'd legitimately cared for the woman at one time.

"You know you could come back here and live with us," Frankie pointed out. "Since you're no longer the military's number one enemy."

"Yeah, but with the Elude tension I don't think I'd find myself welcome at the base bar. Where would I find eligibles to bed if I couldn't leave this office?" she teased.

"So you think you'll just go back to thieving anyway? Or will you try and find legitimate employment?" Josh asked.

"I think it's all I have as far as options. I'm not really qualified for much that I'd want to spend my time doing. Same old problem as before but with one less species trying to kill me. Or maybe not, I might be Sabitarion enemy number one, if the royal family managed to stay in control after the uproar Saluk and I caused." She tried to sound jovial, but it was depressing. Her chosen path in this life seemed dimmer than ever. Probably she just needed to get back in the groove, have a couple successful takes and then she'd be reenergized in the game.

No matter how she tried to convince herself, she kept coming back to the same question. What the hell was she doing with her life?

She did not want to examine that question though, so she stood and grabbed another burger. When in doubt, move out.

"Let's hit it, Sal. Get you home."

Saluk grunted and stood as well. Josh and Frankie rose to give her hugs and wish her luck.

"See you soon, I hope," Frankie said.

"Think about what you want your future to be," Josh whispered in her ear as he embraced her. "You have more choices than you think you do."

She gave him a dramatic eye roll then left, Saluk following behind.

What the hell did Josh mean? Was he reading her mind now? Or was she exuding an air of uncertainty? That wouldn't be helpful in negotiations. Confidence had always been one of her biggest assets.

She needed to get her shit together, and that started with getting Saluk out of her life, she decided. After that she could refocus on herself.

They flew for a day and half before they had to make a pit stop for fuel and food, enough to make it to the distant planet that Saluk called home. On for another three days of strained companionship that Prit hated. She wanted the easy camaraderie they'd shared before, but maybe this was better because it would certainly make it easier to say goodbye.

Saluk watched Halador come up on the screen. A green and blue paradise that he'd been wanting to set foot on since he'd left it, but suddenly he wished it wasn't right there. He wanted more time with her, he regretted the silence they'd shared the last few days, wanted to go back and do it differently, to make more happy memories he could hold on to when she was gone.

Now it was too late.

"You should let my clan honor you for getting me back, it will be important for them. They will want to celebrate my return and your part in that should not be left out," Saluk said, one last desperate attempt to put off their separation.

"I suppose a little time off the ship to stretch my legs before heading out to find something valuable to steal would be good,"

Prit said. "I know Jet would appreciate the fresh air. Where should I try and land? Where is your village?"

Saluk hoped nothing had changed so they wouldn't be setting down in hostile territory, not that much changed quickly on Halador. "There is a clearing near my village, inland from the largest lake, follow the river toward the large snowy mountain. My people reside at the base of the mountain but before the village there is a grassy area where we often hunt small meats." Saluk was able to identify and direct pretty well once they were through the atmosphere. His heart hammered in his chest as the familiar sights came up on the screen, things grown but not different. His stomach twisted when he pointed to the clearing and he thought he might puke when she gently landed in the middle of it.

Fuck, he was home.

He grabbed the canister that held his brother and stared out at the only slightly changed area, a little more overgrown in spots, cleared out in others as if his village had come for wood to build new housing.

How had his people grown and changed since he was taken? Would he even have any family left to celebrate his return? He hadn't let himself seriously consider the passing of his mother and father, but he knew they would be very old if they were still alive at all. His mind hadn't allowed him to imagine the clan aging, it had been too painful, better to imagine them stuck in time while he was away.

Prit turned to him and smiled softly. "It's okay if you're nervous."

"I have been gone a long time," he whispered. "It's been twenty years."

"Well, this is where you want to be, right? You want to see them; you want to be with them?"

She eyed him expectantly and he wondered if she was

seeing more than he intended with that eye of hers. Could she tell how scared he was, how vulnerable?

"We've been spotted," he said instead of answering that question. There was movement outside, someone had noticed their landing and was investigating. He needed to get out there and assure them that this was a friendly visit before anyone got too worked up.

"Well, let's go meet the fam," Prit said, grabbing Jet and hitting the button to release the stairs.

Saluk rushed to leave before her, if anyone had the idea to shoot first, he didn't want her to be in the line. He was hoping as soon as they saw he was a Haladian they would come out friendly, if a bit wary.

The scent of home hit him hard. It was warm and damp, fresh like it had rained just that morning, which was likely, it rained a lot, and the sun shone a lot. This was paradise as far as he was concerned. There were so many scents carried on the slight breeze that he couldn't identify them all, but he knew them all, they were as familiar to him as his own hand and he sucked in deep lungfuls of air to try and get more of it, more proof that he really was here.

He was on Halador. He stepped to the ground and scanned the surroundings.

"Three in the nearby brush according to my bionics," Prit offered.

Motion had him turning right and he waited as a form stood from the long grass and moved forward. The sun shone brightly on the figure and Saluk couldn't tell anything about the person coming forward at first, but as they moved he realized it was a large hulking male figure, dressed for hunting small game with traps hanging from a leather belt and a bag slung over one shoulder. Saluk stiffened, ready to defend Prit from this man.

"I am Saluk of Halador, I have returned home with a

friend." Saluk spoke in his native language, and it felt foreign to his ears and tongue.

"Saluk?" the man said in a deeply timbered voice.

"What language is that?" Prit asked beside him.

"Haladian, we don't speak the international language here. I learned after capture."

"Just you and your woman?" the man said.

Saluk knew he should correct the assumption but didn't, what would it matter, Prit didn't understand anyway. "Yes, just me and Pritalia, she has a pet as well, what is your name?"

"I am Benduk," he said proudly. "Is my father not with you?"

Saluk gasped and Prit touched his arm, looking at him questioningly as if she were ready to either attack this newcomer or run, whatever Saluk wanted.

"It's okay," he assured her, "He is my nephew." Then to Benduk. "Your father didn't survive after we were taken, but I have brought him home to finally rest." Saluk lifted the canister.

Benduk kneeled and the two others who had been hiding nearby rushed forward to kneel with him. Saluk could see they were both young males and he wondered if they were Benduk's children, had he been gone so long that his little nephew was now a father of growing young men? He didn't want to believe it, but the proof was in their matching expressions of grief and curiosity. They all three eyed Prit with a bit of fear, not understanding her mechanical parts.

"We want to go to the village. I want to know who is still alive," Saluk said.

Benduk stood and the others followed. "Your mother still lives, but your father passed a few seasons ago. He was buried near the river and will welcome his son being laid to rest beside him," Benduk said sadly.

"I thought they were eaten by the mountain beast," one of the young men whispered to the other.

"We almost were. We were attacked, and I will gladly tell the story around the fire tonight," Saluk said. "What are your names?"

"These are my sons, Saluk and Tuk."

"Honorable names," Saluk said with a smile.

"It was agreed that when you two didn't return, it was the loss of a great battle and two true warriors. We honored your spirits even though we didn't know what had passed."

"I am grateful, and I know your father is as well," Saluk said.

Benduk nodded. "Come, your mother will skin me alive if she thinks I dallied in bringing you and your mate to her."

Saluk turned to Prit and explained most of the conversation that had passed, she made a surprisingly soft noise when he told her the names of the two young men.

"I am so glad you have family here," Prit said with a smile he wasn't sure was genuine. "Maybe Jet and I should head out. I was going to make sure I wasn't leaving you stranded but it sounds like you've got everything you could want right here." Her voice was uncharacteristically high and strained.

Saluk wanted to tell her how wrong that statement was, but he knew he shouldn't. He also knew he couldn't let her leave. "No, you have to celebrate, and you deserve a rest as you said. Jet needs the fresh air. Stay and see my village, meet my mother. She will want to thank you for saving her baby boy."

"How could I deny her that pleasure," Prit said with a laugh. "As long as you don't mind playing interpreter anyway. I hate to be a burden."

"Not at all," he assured her, then turned to Benduk. "We are ready."

They followed Benduk although Saluk could have found the village in his sleep. The area had hardly changed. The path was well worn outside the village and as the small wooden houses came into view and the sound of children playing reached his ears. He knew he was barely holding back tears as he clung to the canister.

Sensing his upset, Prit grabbed his arm. Her touch steadied him as the village buzzed with the news of their arrival and people rushed to greet them. He was smothered with hugs and kisses and chatter from people he thought he recognized and a lot he didn't. They all seemed to know who he was though, even those too young to have known him seemed just as excited by his arrival.

Prit was brushed from his side at some point and when he realized it and searched the crowd, a bit desperately for her, he saw she was standing to the side with young Saluk, watching him with a sad sort of smile on her face.

He was about to push his way to her, but the crowd grew silent and parted in front of him as an elderly woman was led forward on the arm of a woman he thought he recognized but couldn't name.

"Mother," he said on a breath as his gaze landed on the still bright blue eyes of the woman who'd raised him, fed him, and loved him. The woman who had kissed him goodnight and cared for him when he was sick. "Mother!" he said louder and rushed to embrace the frail version of the strong woman he remembered. "I have returned to you. I have brought Tuk home for a proper burial."

"My sons have returned," she said with a quiet voice, rough with age. Tears streamed down her face as she pulled away and held her palms against his cheeks, staring into his face she touched his scars and frowned and cried some more. "My son."

"Mother," he whispered and smiled at her.

"You will tell me everything," she demanded, not having lost any of her ferocity with her age.

"I swear it, let us feast in celebration and I will tell my story around the fire."

"Like a warrior returned from the mountain," she said with a raised eyebrow. "No animal to feast upon but perhaps a wife claimed?"

Saluk glanced behind him to where his mother was now focusing her gaze. Prit stood there watching him with a genuine smile now.

"That is Pritalia, she saved me and brought me here. She is not my mate, just a friend." He could never lie to his mother.

"Oh," his mother said suspiciously.

"Well, then I guess it's a good thing I waited all these years for you, isn't it?" The woman who had been helping his mother pushed herself forward and Saluk realized why he knew that face, though it was a bit older, the blush of youth all gone, and a plumpness derived from a life more sedentary than he'd have expected, had taken over her frame.

"Shaknu?" he asked.

She laughed loud and deep, a familiar sound that brought back so many youthful memories he couldn't help smiling and embracing her just for making him feel like he'd traveled back in time.

"Of course," she said, returning the embrace with enthusiasm. The crowd around them cheered and soon they were all heading toward the center of the village where a large fire would be lit, and food would be brought to share and celebrate the return of one of their warriors.

CHAPTER TWENTY-SEVEN

Prit stayed where she was as the crowd moved with Saluk. The look of pure joy on his face as he'd embraced that woman could have indicated a relative he'd been happy to see, but the way she'd blushed and kissed his cheek told a different story and Prit was getting former girlfriend vibes.

Was this the woman who he'd planned to marry after proving himself a warrior on the mountain?

Prit was changing her mind about this whole thing, was about to turn and slink back to her ship, make a quiet exit and leave Saluk to his celebrations. But he paused in the middle of the moving crowd and turned, his gaze seeking her out.

"Pritalia?" he called, and the entire crowd turned to look at her. Then his two young nephews were at her sides and urging her forward. She didn't want to make a scene so she went along, figuring she'd duck out when everyone was distracted.

Her eye assessed the crowd, inundating her with information so she shut it off. They were a long living species, many of the members here well into their eighties and still moving well. They were also a dangerous group; her eye had told her they were highly dangerous. But she wasn't worried, she knew Saluk wouldn't let anyone harm her.

They were a warrior people, much like her father's and she respected that. The buildings they passed on the way to the center of the village were all wood stuck together with mud and roofs made of reeds. Smoke billowed from some, but it was a warm planet and even here at the base of a tall mountain that had snow at its tip, she was warm and a bit sticky from the moist air. She didn't hate it.

The people seemed happy, although they could just be wrapped up in the excitement of Saluk's return. She wondered how happy they were in their daily lives. There weren't that many of them in reality. It felt like a lot, all gathered around one person, but it couldn't be more than a hundred people here. She'd have to ask Saluk how many other villages were close by. There was likely a bit of marriage between villages to keep the bloodlines varied enough.

Not that it mattered, she wasn't staying, she probably wouldn't even have a chance to ask Saluk about it. She'd be snuck off before having another word with him.

She felt her heart squeeze with the thought. Would she really never speak to the man again?

No, she needed to say goodbye at least, she'd stay that long. Just to say goodbye then off to find her next job. She'd gotten low on supplies to get here and she wasn't going to make it much farther without some more gold.

That thought usually excited her, but right now it felt like a daunting chore. With so much time alone.

The center of the village was a large, cleared circle with a big open firepit in the middle, likely used for a lot of cooking when it was too hot to do it in the houses. She imagined there was a strong sense of community here. She thought of the way they were built to vibrate comfortingly next to their mates and children, they were a family-oriented group for sure. So much different than New Earthers or Eludians.

Prit was glad that Saluk's mother was still alive, and his nephew and two great-nephews. He had family to embrace him and Saluk was still young enough to take a wife of his own and have a child or two. The woman who'd kissed him, the woman who had obviously been taking care of his mother, looked a little on the older side, but she could likely still produce at least one child for him.

Prit tried to stop her mind from telling her that her own young body could produce multiple strong children for the big guy.

She wasn't interested in that.

She looked around at the gathered people all chatting in a language she didn't understand. A few tried to talk to her but quickly gave up when she couldn't respond. They did eye her curiously, interested in her bionics and probably wondering why the hell she was even here. She didn't mind the looks, just sat and listened to their conversational tones. It was a weird experience to be surrounded by people who didn't speak her language. The musical cadence to their speech was easy on the ears and she tried to pick out any sense of it, but she was at a loss. Too bad she didn't have a bionic ear that could translate.

There were tears of joy and old friends embracing and children running around in excitement over someone they'd obviously never met. Food was being brought out and loaded onto a table nearby and a few women started throwing things in a large pot over the fire.

She watched as Saluk talked with his mother and suddenly motioned at her. His mother let out a scream of joy and motioned her forward.

Prit wanted to stay back and just observe, it was uncomfortable for her to be a part of whatever this was about to be, but when Saluk gave her a hopeful look and the woman beckoned her forward again, she moved toward them.

The woman spoke in a rush that Prit couldn't understand and grabbed her face.

"My mother wants to thank you for saving me, multiple times," Saluk said.

"It was my pleasure," Prit said and Saluk reiterated to his mother.

The ex-girlfriend hovered nearby giving Prit a sour look. She spat out some words and Saluk shook his head.

"What did she say?" Prit asked.

"Nothing important. Shaknu just wanted to know if you plan to stay."

And he'd shaken his head. He was already letting her go.

Prit's throat tightened and she was horrified by the sting in her eye indicating tears begging to come out. She cleared her throat and stepped back.

"Yeah, I should get out of here," she said.

Saluk's mother looked at him and started talking fast again. Saluk answered her and she talked back, then he turned to Prit. "My mother wants you to stay, enjoy a feast with us and the night." He cleared his throat. "If you want."

"Oh ..." Prit did want, but she also wasn't sure it was a good idea. But when the woman pulled her forward and cried on her shoulder, she didn't feel like she could say no to that.

"What is your mother's name?" Prit asked as she awkwardly patted the large woman on the back.

"Leituk, she was born Leinu, a female takes the last part of the male's name upon mating, the 'nu' means unwed. Like if we were mated you would be Prituk," he said then looked almost shocked at himself for uttering such a thing. Beside him Shaknu, who wouldn't have understood anything but didn't miss *Prituk* glared at Prit.

"Prituk, wow, that's really pretty," Prit couldn't help saying with a bright smile knowing she was making the other woman jealous.

"Well, it's tradition," Saluk said uncomfortably.

Shaknu pressed herself closer to Saluk and talked quietly in his ear making Prit want to reach out and scratch her face.

Leituk pulled back and wiped her face, so Prit schooled her features and smiled at the woman.

Almost out of spite, Prit kept a smile on her face, and stuck close to Saluk for the rest of the celebration, which wasn't difficult, he wasn't trying to get away from her.

He sat at the table next to his mother and she sat on his other side, seconds before Shaknu tried to slip into the spot. Leituk called Shaknu over to her other side though and she gave Prit a triumphant glare as if to say she had the more important spot next to the matriarch. A language barrier didn't impede that message, which only made Prit want to play harder.

"Saluk, wow, this all looks so great, tell me about everything," she said sweetly and touched his arm.

He turned to her with a confused expression then started to tell her what each dish was. Mostly fruits and roots. Meat was in the stew and there was water or a fermented fruit juice to drink.

Shaknu said something from the other side and gained Saluk's attention back, whatever it was made him laugh and Prit clenched her teeth.

The meal proceeded with everyone trying to talk with Saluk, and him regaling them all with the journey he'd been on. When he spoke of her he looked at her with pride and she blushed as everyone oohed and ahhed and cheered for whatever it was he was saying about her. Well, everyone except Shaknu, that is.

By the time the story was done and the meal was eaten, Prit had drank a little too much of the fermented juice. So when she stood, she found herself wobbling and clutching Jet to her chest. She never would have been able to stop herself from landing on her face if it wasn't for Saluk right there wrapping an arm around her back and frowning.

"What's wrong?"

"I think I drank too much juice," she said.

Saluk laughed. "Yeah, strong stuff. I guess I should have warned you. Let me get you settled. My mother has a room we can use."

"We?" she said in alarm, not sure she hated the idea.

"Yeah, there aren't a lot of places for guests in the village so we will have to share tonight, not like we haven't been sharing on the ship though, right? No different."

"Yeah, no different," she agreed. But the looks that were being thrown their way told her that the entire village thought it was very different. The glare she was getting from Shaknu made her sway her hips a little extra and lean in a little tighter to Saluk as they headed away from the main fire.

Leituk's home wasn't far from the center of the village and she was already there, settling the canister that held her eldest son's remains on a table.

The place was cozy. One large room with a table and a couple of comfortable looking chairs made of some sort of woven reeds and leather. Much like the clothing she'd seen everyone wearing. A small cooking fire and a few knickknacks were scattered about. It was a clean and tidy space despite the stone and dirt floor. There was a kitchen area with some sort of contraption she assumed gave them running water and a door she hoped led to a bathroom. There were doors on either side of the main room, she assumed for each bedroom. Saluk kissed and hugged his mother, and she grabbed Prit's face, planting a kiss on her cheek as well before saying what Prit assumed was goodnight and heading to one door.

Saluk led her to the other.

This room had a window with a breeze fluttering a thin leather curtain and a large bed that was really just a pile of furs and she wasn't complaining. It looked extremely comfortable in her drunken state.

"Lay down," Saluk instructed her, and she did. Falling right down into the softness with Jet and giving a little groan of delight.

"Why don't I have a bed like this on the ship?" she said.

"Because you have a much more modern setup, this is practically archaic by your standards," he said with a huff.

"Modern isn't always better," she said and rolled to her side.

When she felt him lie beside her she scooted back until her back was pressed against his side. There may be room for them to sleep without touching here, but that didn't mean she wanted to. And when he began to vibrate, she smiled.

"I bet Shaknu is standing outside the window waiting to hear if you vibrate for me and if we make mad, loud, passionate love."

Saluk snorted. "I bet she's at home, sleeping."

Prit turned and rested her head on her hand. Saluk was laying on his back and staring up at the ceiling.

"You could marry her and have kids," she said.

"I could," he agreed.

She waited, but he didn't say anything else. "Will you?" she prodded.

"No," he said.

"Why?"

"Because I don't love her."

Prit felt a knot of tension ease out of her belly. "Did you once?" she asked quietly.

"I think so, in the way of young people. But what I've been through," he shook his head, "I could never commit myself to someone who would never be able to understand my scars."

Prit reached out and ran a finger along the scars on his face. "You got these on this planet, she'd understand."

"Yes, those she would understand, they are the mark of a warrior. She understands warriors, fighting animals for food and clothing. She would never understand the blood I spilled killing other men and women in battle for the entertainment of others."

"You had no choice," Prit whispered, her voice rough with emotion, appalled that anyone would judge him for such a thing.

"It is not something my people know," he insisted.

"So you'll just die alone and childless over it?" Prit scoffed.

"If I must."

"It's not what you want, you are built for family, it's in your blood."

"Yes, but I know that a mate without love is not one I want."

"You'll find love here, there were a lot of women at the party."

"No, there is no mate for me among these people. Now go to sleep, Prituk," he said and rolled to give her his back.

Prit sunk down and stared at the ceiling. He'd called her Prituk, and it had made her heart sing.

He vibrated beside her, and she cuddled close to his back, falling asleep quickly thanks to the drink.

Saluk laid awake, staring at the window and wondered if Prit was right. Would Shaknu stand there and try to discern their relationship? He'd told everyone they were not mates, but that didn't stop the knowing glances that were thrown their way, especially when he'd walked her to his mother's home for the night. There were other options, despite what he'd told her. Many people had an extra room, or would offer their own for a guest, but he couldn't stand the thought of sleeping without her.

Prit wanted to know if he'd marry a woman here and he hadn't lied. He couldn't imagine taking a wife among these people who knew nothing of what he'd endured. He didn't feel like one of them, didn't think he ever would again. He'd wanted nothing more than to set foot on Halador again since he was taken, and now that he was here, he wasn't sure he belonged anymore.

The only place he'd felt like he belonged in the last twenty years has been with Prit, on her ship, on Zenzi with her friends, on Ione drinking and eating and watching her steal from vacationers.

She was his home, he realized.

The realization thrilled and terrified him. He knew sleep wasn't going to come and Prit was snoring away beside him, so he rolled off the bed and snuck out into the main room.

"Can't sleep?" His mother said from beside the fire. "I'm making tea, sit."

Saluk knew better than to argue with his mother, so he sat at the table. It was the same one that they'd had when he and Tuk were kids, their father had built it. It was sturdy and worn down with loving meals made by his mother.

"It's weird being back here," he said when she handed him a steaming cup.

"I can imagine. If I was gone for so long and experiencing life in ways never imagined, I think I would feel strange returning to my childhood as well."

"I won't marry Shaknu," he said.

"I would expect not. She isn't for you now, even I can see that. She'll get over it. She's been a godsend to me since your father passed, but only because her own parents passed and she's alone too."

"Why didn't she ever marry?"

Leituk shrugged. "Who's to say? Perhaps she waited for you too long and when it became clear you weren't going to emerge from the woods it was too late and all the men who would have married her were taken. The younger men were interested in younger girls, so she missed her chance. Perhaps she'll find a widower to marry, and give him one last child. She has options if she wants them."

Saluk felt guilt and anger for the way not only his life had been stolen that day but Shaknu's too, an unforeseen victim in his kidnapping.

"No one expects you to take her to wife now, Saluk. Not unless you want to." Leituk looked at her son with a raised eyebrow. "Prit is a very pretty girl, strong too, I can see that clearly. You two spent a lot of time alone together?"

Saluk sipped his tea so he wouldn't have to say anything just yet. He knew what his mother was implying, even though he'd told her that Prit wasn't his mate. Could she tell that there was something there, that Saluk wished for Prit to be his mate?

"She is a special woman, but she would never be satisfied here and I … I have wanted to get back here since the moment my feet left the planet."

"And now you're here, how do you feel?"

Saluk looked down into his cup and frowned. "Honestly, mother. It's not what I expected at all. Perhaps I am not the same man I was when I left."

"Of course you're not," she scoffed. "You have spent twenty years being tortured and used. You escaped and were taken back and escaped again. You have seen more than anyone else on this planet ever will and you cannot expect to be the same man you once were."

Saluk smiled at his mother, she'd always been wise.

"I'm not sure I belong here," he admitted.

"This is where you are from, it will always be. But you belong wherever you are happy and if that is with Prit on some other planet or on a spaceship, then that is where you should be. Don't let your past dictate your future." She shrugged. "Perhaps Halador is your past as is your time on Sabit. Things you have to let go of so you can embrace your future."

Saluk didn't know how to respond so he kissed his mother's head and went back to bed. When he slipped in beside Prit and she curled against him, mumbling in her sleep he felt at peace. Jet moved to cuddle by his feet as his body began to vibrate for her.

If she left him, he would never feel this again, he was certain.

The next morning Saluk was up early, he left a still sleeping Prit, kissed his mother, and headed up the mountain. No matter what was to come next for him, he had to make peace with one last part of his past.

CHAPTER TWENTY-EIGHT

Prit woke up with a massive headache. She groaned and rolled over, getting a face full of fur that confused her at first, but she recognized Saluk's scent immediately and remembered where she was. In his mother's house, alone. She could tell he wasn't in bed with her, his warmth was missing and there were no comforting vibrations. But his scent lingered and if she didn't feel like her head was about to split open, she might smile.

Jet snuffled beside her, likely ready for breakfast.

Prit swung her legs around and slowly lifted her upper body to a sitting position. She groaned as the whole room spun and her stomach threatened to expel everything in it.

The door opened and Prit expected to see Saluk walking in with a less than sympathetic look for her plight, but it was his mother, surprisingly, and she had a very sympathetic look on her face as well as a cup of something steaming in her hand.

The woman didn't try to speak, which Prit appreciated, just held out the cup to her. When Prit took it with a half-smile the woman picked up Jet and walked out of the room. Prit assumed the woman wasn't about to roast her pet for dinner, so she didn't move, just sipped the strong tea. It was bitter and the first taste made her gag, but she took another and immediately felt her body accept its medicinal intentions.

She managed to drink half of it then laid back down. She closed her eyes until Leituk came in again, this time with a tray of food.

"Thank you," Prit said with a smile and the woman just nodded and walked out. She wondered where Saluk was as she nibbled at the meat and fruit on the tray. It was better than a lot of meals she had on her ship, which reminded her that she was going to be back on that ship soon, should be today, and alone, just her and Jet and crappy food.

She decided she'd better get on with it since she was dreading it so much. She got up and brought the tray and cup out of the room. She wasn't surprised to see Shaknu there helping Leituk. The woman glared at Prit from behind Leituk's back. Jet was curled up on a chair looking content.

Leituk came forward and took the tray from Prit and turned to the small kitchen.

"Saluk?" Prit asked Leituk.

The woman spoke and gestured but all Prit could get was that he wasn't in the house.

"Okay, great," Prit said with a smile and grabbed Jet. She'd find her way to her ship and at least clean herself up, maybe leave ... maybe it was better if she just left and didn't try to say goodbye to Saluk.

As she walked through the village there were people moving all around doing different daily tasks and they all smiled and waved, a few even called out what she assumed were greetings. A few children came close to gape at her leg, give Jet a quick pet and then run away giggling, but she didn't mind. They hadn't seen anything outside this planet before, she envied them a bit and hoped they would live a quiet, happy life here. Which reminded her that she needed to warn Saluk about the possibilities of expansion in this area. She'd almost forgotten that. She supposed it meant she wasn't leaving, just yet anyway, but clean clothes were still a must. So she continued on to her ship.

She found her way with little trouble and when she stepped into its quiet metal interior she frowned. It didn't feel like her safe place anymore, it felt like it was missing something.

A big, scarred warrior.

She shook away the feeling and concentrated on what she'd come to do, shower and change, then she'd find Saluk, deliver a warning and final goodbye.

"We have each other, Jet. That's always been enough," she reminded him as she set him into his cage.

Saluk was exhausted, bloody, and victorious. It had taken a good part of the day, but he was returning the way he should have all those years ago. With the body of a mountain beast in tow to prove his worthiness to claim a mate. Tradition stated he'd prepare the beast before returning but he didn't have time for that and this was about more than tradition, this was about proving to himself that he was worthy of what he wanted.

As he approached the village, he was surrounded by children excited to see the huge animal and all the blood. Adults started to come around to the noise and cheered for his good fortune and bravery. As he reached the center of the village Shaknu ran towards him with a smile, but the look on his face stopped her in her tracks and she dropped her outstretched arms.

"This is for her isn't it," she accused. "You want to mate with that alien, that half metal female?" she accused.

"I never expected you to wait for me, and I never expected

to fall in love with someone else," he said as answer and she turned from him, walking away with head high as the villagers avoided looking at her. Saluk wished he hadn't had to make such a public denouncement of her, but she had left him with no other choice with her assumptions. "Where is Prit?" he asked his mother who was slowly moving through the crowd.

"She took off this afternoon after some food and tea. She was looking pretty rough; the kids say they followed her to her ship."

Panic filled him; what if she left? He dropped his kill and ran. The crowd parted for him, and all exhaustion left his body as he imagined the worst. A life stuck on this planet, or any other for that matter, without her. When he broke through the trees and saw her ship still there the relief was overwhelming, he didn't stop running until he reached the stairs and climbed inside.

She was standing there, looking the same as always in a pair of short shorts and a tank top, hair wet from a shower and eye wide as she took in his bloody appearance.

"Dear lord, Saluk are you okay?" she gasped and rushed forward, her hands searching for wounds under the blood.

"It's mostly not mine," he said and wrapped his arms around her, pulling her body against his and crushing his lips against hers. He kissed her with everything in him. Pushing every feeling of desire and need, every thought of forever into it until her body melted against him and then he pulled back and stared into her eyes.

"I thought you'd left me," he said a little breathless.

"I wasn't sure what I was going to do, honestly," Prit admitted.

"Why?" he demanded.

"What do you mean why?" she asked, trying to wiggle out of his grasp but he only held tighter.

"Why weren't you sure, aren't you going to leave, go back to search for riches? Isn't that what you want?"

"I—yeah, I guess, maybe ... fuck! I don't know Saluk, why do you care?" she snapped and finally managed to free herself. She turned around and grasped the back of the pilot's seat, her shoulders stiff and her breathing heavy. "What does it matter what I'm going to do?" she whispered.

"Because you are my home, Pritalia, you are where *I* want to be."

Prit straightened and turned slowly. "What are you saying, Saluk?"

"I am saying that I want you to be my mate, my partner, my everything. I want to live with you on Halador or on this fucking tiny spaceship if it makes you happy, because nowhere will I be happy if it's not with you. I know that with a certainty now that I cannot deny."

Prit gasped and jumped into his arms, wrapping her legs around his waist, her arms around his neck and pressed her lips to his. She put everything into that kiss. This was her chance, she knew it. She had to show him that he was everything she wanted, too. He occupied far too much of her brain now and she couldn't imagine leaving him on this planet. She swept her tongue over the crease in his lips and he parted them on a groan. She pushed her tongue inside, and he met it with eager strokes of his own. She fisted his hair and he growled, his hands on her ass pulled her body even closer until she could almost painfully feel his hardness press against her clit.

"I need you now, Saluk. Don't stop, please," she begged, so afraid he'd leave her wanting again, so afraid something was going to stop this from happening and she thought she might just explode if it didn't happen, just burst into a frightening spray of unmet desire.

He grunted and slammed her back against a wall, then he was ripping at her shorts, the stretchy fabric giving way to his strength, and she bit at his lip in approval.

Once she was bare he made a quick move, pushing his pants down then his cock was free and there was no hesitation before he slammed it into her wet and willing body. She clenched around him, desperate to not let him back out once she had him there. He was big, she had known he would be, so big, and he filled her to perfection without an ounce of pain, just completeness. They stayed like that for a time, both gasping, hearts pounding and a feeling of destiny blossoming where they were joined.

"Are you okay?" Saluk finally asked, his lips against her ear making her shiver.

"I have never felt so okay in my entire life," she said with honesty and laughed then rolled her hips as best she could in this position, encouraging him to start moving. He took the hint and started to slide out then back in.

Prit could only hold on as he expertly worked her body, one hand on her ass to hold her up and the other snaked up her belly and grasped at her breast, both squeezing and massaging and adding to the sensations as he stroked against her most sensitive parts until she was writhing between him and the wall.

When she wasn't sure she could take another second, he switched it up. She found herself suddenly on her back on the floor and his head was between her legs.

"Come apart for me," he said, then his tongue was replacing his cock, and she was helpless to do anything but obey that command. Her body spasmed, her back arched and her scream echoed in the small ship as she came for him.

He lapped it up and kissed her thigh, then rose up and

grinned in that smug way men get when they know they've just given you an orgasm worth gossiping about. "Good girl," he growled and crawled up her body. She strained her neck to meet his mouth, kissing him deeply and feeling the head of his cock at her entrance, but he wasn't entering her, and she mewed in frustration. When she pulled back to ask what was wrong he flipped her to her stomach and she knew exactly what he wanted, she hopped up to her hands and knees, arched her back and waited as his hands slid along her sides. He smacked her ass hard then gripped her hips and once again entered her with ease.

After a few quick strokes his hand wrapped around her front and started to stroke her clit, still sensitive from her orgasm, she was moaning and shivering in no time. This time when she came, her cunt clenching his cock, she felt him shudder behind her and he lifted her body so she was seated in his lap as he pounded up into her a few more strokes before he bellowed his own release, one hand on her breast, one still pressed between her thighs.

Saluk collapsed onto his back with her clasped to him and they lay there, connected, sweaty, and satisfied.

"I love you, Prituk," Saluk whispered.

Prit rolled until they were face to face. She rested her hands on either side of his head and looked down into his eyes, seeing so much vulnerability there it made her ache.

"Saluk," she said, kissing his nose, then his lips softly. "I love you too and that scares the shit out of me. I don't know what I will do if I lose you."

His arms locked around her, crushing her against him. "Love doesn't have to be scary; I promise not to try and change you or make you do anything you don't want to do, I just want to be with you, always," he said.

"I want you with me always."

"I have killed a beast and come back to the village a man. I am ready to claim my mate and start a family."

"Family ..." Prit said carefully, pushing back so she could look into his face. "Like now? Or like someday down the road?"

He frowned. "I think it's too late to change your mind. I already planted my seed in you."

She rolled her eyes, "You know that's not all it takes. I'm not some young dumb virgin. I am not unprotected."

He narrowed his eyes at her and she slipped off of him and smiled.

"You don't know about birth control? How do your people not get pregnant?"

"If you aren't trying to make a family you don't plant the seed," Saluk said with a duh in his voice.

"You were trying to knock me up!" Prit accused, now his confusion had gone from cute to aggravating. "You were trying to trap me?"

"You said you wanted to be with me," he growled, sitting up now.

"I do, but that doesn't mean I want to get pregnant in this moment, are you insane? Where will we even live?"

"Here."

"Here? Like here on my ship or here on Halador?"

He shrugged and reached out, gripping her chin lightly. "Here," he said again, motioning between them. "You and me together, we will live wherever you desire. On this ship, in space, here on Halador with my people, on Zenzi with Josh and Frankie. It doesn't matter, *you* are my home, Prituk."

"Don't call me that, I never said I'd marry you," she snapped but there wasn't much anger left in her.

"You are my mate, you are Prituk." He leaned forward and kissed her lips. "If you never want children, we will never have children. Don't you understand, I just want you."

She kissed him back and sighed. "I want to be with you too, Saluk, I meant it when I said I love you. I just don't know if children are ever going to be in the future for me." That wasn't as true as she wanted it to be, she had been thinking about Saluk's children since they arrived here, and she'd seen him embrace his ex-girlfriend. For the first time in her life she thought children were a definite possibility for her future, but she didn't want to raise them on this ship. Children needed people, community, and family. It was one reason that Josh had never taken Frankie away from the New Earth community on Zenzi though they stayed apart from it. Frankie had friends there. Friends were important too.

"When we have a family," Prit said carefully seeing Saluk's eyes light up, but he pressed his lips together obviously keeping his thoughts to himself. "We should raise them here, among your people so they know where they come from."

"That would be wonderful, I am certain," Saluk agreed.

"And you'll teach me to speak Haladian so I know when your ex-girlfriend is trying to talk shit about me."

He laughed but nodded.

"And until we decide that we are ready to settle down, we will explore a bit of space together, take on some jobs and make enough money to get us to the next one."

Saluk frowned. "I don't want you risking yourself."

"I'm far too good a thief to get caught," she scoffed. "I'm a fucking shadow out there among the stars, especially with my hunky bodyguard lurking close by."

"You are a good thief," he agreed. "You stole me twice and I think that means you have to keep me for yourself."

"Are those the rules of space thievery?" she asked.

"Definitely," he said and pulled her to him for a deep kiss.

CHAPTER TWENTY-NINE

"Are you sure you're ready for this?" Prit asked Saluk as she set their newer and slightly larger ship down on Elude. She was covering her own indecision by pressing him for constant reassurance. They'd spent the last two years since leaving Halador continuing much the same as she always had. That is until she'd decided that she was ready to settle down, then they'd switched to only taking on jobs that were retrievals of goods stolen, no straight thieving anymore. She felt it was more honorable a way to make a living while still using her skill set and it gave her the adventure she craved.

Saluk had become a great sidekick, and at times bodyguard. He wasn't as stealthy as her, but when the job didn't call for so much stealth he went along. When she left him behind on the ship he complained and growled and didn't relax until he set eyes on her again, which made her feel incredibly loved.

Much of that adventurousness had taken a back seat recently, however.

Prit stood and picked up the squirming bundle from Saluk's arms.

"Rytuk needs to meet his grandpa and this little guy will be just the thing to smooth things over." She hadn't returned to Elude since escaping the night the New Earth military attacked. She'd had some communication with her father, but she hadn't wanted to risk face to face contact.

"You really think he won't harm the boy?" Saluk asked for the thousandth time and Prit reassured him again.

"My father values family and this little guy is definitely family." She pulled the blanket from the tiny body revealing a short tail, an Eludian trait her father would appreciate.

Prit held the boy so that his tail would be immediately noticed as they exited the ship. Not surprisingly her father met them on the dock. He looked exactly the same as he had two years earlier and she was thankful his health was holding, she wasn't sure Alinas would be as welcoming if he were already in charge of Elude.

"Father, I have come to introduce your grandson, Rytuk."

"A grandson," he whispered and held his hands out for the child. "Haladian?" he grunted, eyes flicking to Saluk.

"Yep, and a quarter human, but look at that strong tail," Prit pointed out.

Dofsh held the child with surprising care and smiled down at the boy who gurgled and babbled up at his grandfather as if telling him a story.

"Perfection all the same," Dofsh declared, and a tight knot loosened in her chest.

"He is," Saluk agreed, putting his hands on Prit's shoulders. She smiled up at him and he leaned down to kiss her lips. This had been a hard decision, but she was thankful they'd made it. Family was the most important thing, even if that family was a little bit barbaric and controlling.

"You know, this means you're related to the Haladians, you need to protect them, keep their planet off the radar of New

Earth," Prit said, sticking in one of the main reasons they had made this trip.

No one had moved to take over or settle Halador yet but she heard rumors, it was one of a few planets that New Earth wanted to expand their empire to.

"Halador will stay as it is," Dofsh said as he smiled down at Rytuk. "Someday this little prince will rule that planet for his grandfather."

Prit looked up at Saluk and rolled her eye, at least it would keep Halador safe from New Earth. Being an outpost for Elude was a better option for those who lived there.

They stayed on Elude for a week, all of her siblings seemed to adore the baby, the first grandchild but not for long. Calta had married Mindal and was pregnant with their first. The happiness on Calta's face made Prit thankful that they hadn't killed Mindal when they'd had the chance. It helped that Mindal seemed devoted to Calta and indifferent to Prit.

Leaving Elude and her father was harder than Prit had expected but knowing she'd be welcomed back any time made it easier. She wanted her son to know this part of his family, so they'd visit often.

"Where to?" Saluk asked, sitting in the pilot's seat. He'd come a long way in his flying, though she didn't let him have control if they were doing any dangerous or tight maneuvers.

"Zenzi, Josh should have a job for us, he said something about a missing girl."

"Saving people seems to be your specialty," Saluk agreed and set the course for Zenzi.

It had been five years since they'd left Halador. They'd visited of course, but this time, they planned to return for a good long while. Prit was pregnant with their second child and Rytuk was three. He was toddling around and needed more room than a spaceship could offer.

She wasn't sure how the Haladians were going to react to the children, the last time they'd been here she'd been pregnant with Rytuk and she was worried. "No one is going to make fun of Rytuk," Saluk assured her again as she fussed over the child.

"If they do, I am going to stab them in the eye," she snapped. Her hormones had her acting like a crazy woman, so protective of her family she was ready to battle anyone who even thought her son odd with his tail.

"It will be fine," Saluk said again.

They landed in the same spot they'd landed on their first trip and were greeted by the same three men, only slightly older this time. The welcome was just as warm and when Prit greeted them in their language, though a little slow and stunted, they cheered and embraced her. They welcomed Rytuk, the new member of the family, with joy which had Prit crying against Saluk's shoulder.

His mother had unfortunately passed, which neither of them was surprised to hear, but it still hurt, knowing she'd never been able to meet her grandchildren.

"She had hoped you'd return someday with your family," the young Saluk said. "She wanted the house saved for you."

"It will be an honor to raise a family there," Prit said, hugging Saluk.

"It will," he agreed.

They walked to the village where everyone hurried to greet them and meet Rytuk. Many exclaimed over his tail but no judgment as far as Prit could see, only curiosity. These people didn't even know what an Eludian was.

There was a mumble in the gathered crowd as Saluk's ex-girlfriend walked up to them, a toddler on her hip.

"You return, Saluk and Prituk," she said with a grin. "Meet my Leiknu, I am Shakar now, mated and complete," she said with a sigh, brushing a lock of blonde hair out of her daughter's face.

"She is beautiful," Prit said then lifted Rytuk into her arms. "This is our son, Rytuk."

"A handsome boy, just like his father," Shakar said. "Perhaps they will mate one day," Shakar said to Prit as the two toddlers stared at each other.

"Or perhaps Rytuk will travel among the stars and be a thief like his mother," Prit said with a laugh.

Shakar didn't laugh just cocked her head. Prit didn't expect the woman to understand but she would never expect her children to stay here, not unless they really wanted to. Exploration is what had made her and Saluk understand and appreciate the peace of Halador. In fact she would encourage their children to explore, to see new things and how other people live.

MEET THE AUTHOR

Courtney Davis is a mother, teacher and author crafting tales in urban fantasy, paranormal, and supernatural fiction. Living in North Idaho with her family, she balances a life between family, teaching, and writing. She enjoys soaking up the blissful summer sun or wrapping up next to warm winter fires. A true enthusiast of the written word, she's transforming her love for reading and writing into a blooming career. She loves nothing more than to transport readers into the captivating realm of her narratives, far away from the mundane!